ADVANCE PRAISE ⏐ ⏐ ⏐ ⏐
UNCAGED SUMMER

"A heartfelt novel about life's uncertainties, the mystery of relationships, and the journey of self-discovery. Colet created a poignant story layered with humor and vulnerability about one woman's quest to find the true meaning of happiness and to fall in love...with herself."

—GIULIANA RANCIC, *New York Times* Bestselling Author and Journalist

"Who says pain, tragedy, heartbreak and not knowing if you'll ever fall in love again can't be slap-your-knees funny? Colet will have you dancing between laughter, tears, and the warm embrace of a delicious journey toward self-actualization. Her book is a beautiful reminder that family is who you love and who loves you. And, at the end of the day, isn't that all that matters?"

—ANNALYNNE MCCORD, Actress

"Colet Abedi is known for weaving intricate storytelling along with bringing in her Persian roots in a way that's masterful. Colet never ceases to amaze me with her poignant words and plot. I devour her stories from the first page. You won't want to miss this."

—RACHEL VAN DYKEN, #1 *New York Times* Bestselling Author

UN CAGED SUM MER

A NOVEL

COLET ABEDI

POST HILL
PRESS

A POST HILL PRESS BOOK
ISBN: 979-8-88845-172-4
ISBN (eBook): 979-8-88845-173-1

Uncaged Summer
© 2024 by Colet Abedi
All Rights Reserved

Cover design by Jim Villaflores

Post Hill Press
New York • Nashville
posthillpress.com

Published in the United States of America
1 2 3 4 5 6 7 8 9 10

—❧—

For my grandparents, Touron and Ali Tavassoli...

For your strength, wisdom, and unconditional love.

We couldn't have asked for better teachers.

—❧—

Dots

"You can't connect the dots looking forward; *you can only connect them looking backwards.* So you have to trust that the dots will somehow connect in your future. You have to trust in something—your gut, destiny, life, karma, whatever." [Emphasis added]

—Steve Jobs

94957
MARIN COUNTY
"Bye Bye Birdie"

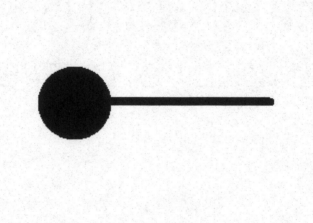

CHAPTER 1

"THE ROAD LESS TRAVELED"

"YOU HAVE TO FIND HUSBAND before it's too late!"

My mom's thick, Persian accent echoes through my SUV like an ancient call for war, booming through the Bluetooth speakers.

"Or you vill reach a point vhere nobody vill marry you! *Nobody*!"

This is her raison d'être—my future marriage. Even though I am just finalizing a hellish divorce.

In my mother's mind she has an aging, *divorced* daughter she needs to find a man for, and the clock is ticking. And even though my ex *has been lying and cheating for years,* can arguably be called the spawn of Satan, and any normal mother would give their daughter a minute to process...it's not happening in this Persian family.

To make matters worse, I'm about to embark on an unexpected journey she highly disapproves of for the summer. To be fair, I'd probably feel the same way if I was in her shoes. But my whole world is in shambles, and I need to find answers. I need to know who I am, what I want in this next half of my life, and where I'm going. The brutal reality is that I've come to realize I never had these answers before. But since I can't go back in time, all I can do is try to put the broken pieces back together.

And there are more than I can count.

"Avalie?!" My mom sounds worried when I take so long to answer.

Avalie means "strength" in Farsi. I wonder if she regrets giving me this name. At this moment in time, I'm leaning toward a strong yes.

"I hate to break the news, but the last thing I want—or *need*—is a husband. I'm still trying to get rid of my last one," I remind her. "Give me a break and let me get to Pegah's and decompress—"

"You vant to decompress on other people's couches?!"

She's referring to my plan of bouncing around and staying with my best friends and some family, with the hope that I'll have figured my life out by the end of the summer. Wishful thinking on my part? Who knows. But I'm going to give it a fighting chance. And it's not like my mother has to worry that I'll be suffering at my friends' homes—most of them live in places others only dream about.

"Mom, I just left my whole life behind," I remind her, hoping for sympathy. "It's *all* gone—"

"It vas a shitty life," she interrupts so fast I fight not to laugh.

Hey, she's not wrong. But there are some things I'm grateful for.

Like the three suitcases in my trunk filled with all the belongings I have to show for my thirteen-year marriage to my high school sweetheart (barf), Darian Monfared (extra barf). I have my car, even though it's leased, *and* I have to turn it in at the end of the summer....

And I have my health.

My mental health is another issue altogether, but I'm hoping this little journey of mine will straighten me out and help me realize where I went wrong in my life.

Am I having an existential crisis at thirty-eight?

Fine. Thirty-nine...

Maybe. To both.

She quickly changes the topic to an important one for every Persian parent. "Did you eat food?"

"Not yet."

She tells me in Farsi that if I eat, my breasts will grow back.

"I never had big boobs," I remind her.

"You vere size C," Mom says, like it's true. "You tink I don't know my daughter's body?"

I've been a small B cup my entire adult life.

"You concentrate now on driving. Call me vhen you get to your cousin's," she commands without missing a beat.

"Okay, Mom," I say with a sigh. It's absolutely useless to argue. "I love you."

"I love you too, Avalie-Joon." Joon means "dear" in Farsi. "I promise everything vill be okay."

Even though I'm middle-aged, receiving reassurance from my mom is like the best kind of hug. It still works the same magic it did when I was a kid. I hope she's right.

I stare at the road ahead. "One day, this will *all* make sense, Mom."

Mom takes a second before responding.

"Maybe it vill. Maybe it von't.... It's okay, either vay. That's just life."

CHAPTER 2

"LOVE BITE"

I MAKE IT TO MY cousin's house in Marin County in good time.

I pull into her driveway and take in the woodsy vibe. It's an incredible property, with over two acres of breathtaking greenery. The trees on her land include towering, majestic redwoods. Her place reminds me of a magical forest getaway. It's no wonder we can never get her to leave.

As soon as I open my car door, my cousin pops out of her house and runs over to me. I collapse in her arms. Memories of our childhood bombard me—playing with Barbies, making forts, getting excited over a pizza party or a Baskin-Robbins ice-cream cake... life was so easy then. Why did we have to grow up?

"I'm so proud of you," Pegah whispers as she rubs my back. "Leaving Darian and choosing yourself was so brave. I promise it only hurts like this in the beginning."

She pulls away from me and I stare at her. There's something about family that is so comforting. You can drop all pretenses and just be you—the good, the bad, and the ugly parts. They get to see your bare soul, raw and unguarded. And if you're lucky enough to have a good family, they love you regardless of the shadows that are lurking there.

"I'm so happy I get to take care of you for the next few weeks. My mom and dad can't wait to see you. You should see all the food they bought."

"You guys don't have to do anything." I'm embarrassed, but not surprised.

"Ava," she says, "you spent your whole life making sure everyone was okay. Your home was a halfway house. Anyone could come and go...cousins, family, friends. It's time for you to get a taste of that kind of love. So, accept this! And be excited. It's a whole new world."

While Pegah helps grab some of my stuff from the car, I give her a once-over.

"You look good." I take in the whole boho vibe she has going on. My cousin is an incredibly beautiful woman, with almond-shaped brown eyes and straight, jet-black hair. She's always been the center of attention with men.

"Thanks," she says, then gives me a funny look. "So, I have something to tell you."

"You're dating someone?" I guess, as I wheel my luggage to her front door.

"Not quite." She laughs, amused by the suggestion. "But almost the same amount of work."

I look over at her, trying to decipher her sheepish expression.

"I guess I'll just let you see for yourself. Don't be nervous," she says.

Of course now I'm immediately nervous. She gives me an awkward laugh, then opens the door to her foyer.

The inside of the house feels like a home you'd find in Bali, refreshingly open with plenty of wood detail and plants that fill up the space. I can't wait to lounge around and relax, especially after that seven-hour drive from LA.

That's when I hear the call of the wild.

This is not a normal shriek from a bird. This is an angry one. Like something you'd hear in a remote area in the jungles of the Amazon right before you're about to be ravaged to death.

It happens so fast, I'm unprepared for what I know is a carefully planned attack. I see a glimpse of bright orange, yellow, and red feathers before the exotic bird attacks my hair—claws first, beak open, looking ready to throw down.

"Zelda!" Pegah screams out. "No! *Bad girl!*"

Zelda, my cousin's surprise *new friend* couldn't care less, and she bites the back of my neck before Pegah is able to swat her away.

The tears. The pain. The shock.

My reaction is immediate. I feel like I'm Tippi Hedren from Hitchcock's classic, *The Birds*, and I drop and cover. I want to cry, to wail like a baby. But I'm too shocked by the attack to even move. I can hear my cousin cackling at my pose.

"No," she tells me. "That was just a love bite."

WTF.

"What *is* that thing?" I demand to know as I hide from what I'm convinced is a descendant of a Pterodactyl.

"She's my sweet baby." Pegah sounds like she's in love.

"Sweet baby?" That was no Gerber baby. That was the love child of Captain Hook's parrot and Freddy Krueger.

"Her name is Zelda."

GodZelda, more like.

The bird takes that moment to fly right onto Pegah's shoulder. My cousin grabs hold of her and kisses the hell out her, smothering her feathered head with love. Zelda looks like she's blissed-out and so does my cousin. I stare at the two in shock.

Am I having a nightmare? What is going on?

"I love you," Zelda chirps out to Pegah, who mushes her feather face and gives her even more kisses. I don't even know what to say.

"Who's my favorite girl?" Pegah talks to the bird like she's an infant.

"I'm so confused." I finally voice my thoughts while still hiding in my position on the ground.

"I've adopted a few birds that needed homes," she admits.

In that moment I hear the faint sound of what can only be described as being dropped in the middle of a tropical rainforest. I can hear birds everywhere. And when I say everywhere, I mean *everywhere.*

"How many birds?" I wonder how many other Zeldas I'm going to have to look out for. Am I going to need to invest in protective gear while I'm here? I stare at the bright orange bird and give her the stink eye. I swear Zelda gives me the look right back and even squawks. Loud. I'm guessing it's her version of the middle finger.

I still feel the pain in the back of my neck. I do not appreciate her "love bite" one bit.

"I built an aviary out back," my cousin explains. "That's been my secret project for the past six months. My dad's team is helping out."

My uncle owns a successful construction business and Pegah is his accountant.

"How many birds?" I ask again.

"You'll see." If she's avoiding the answer, as well as eye contact, I know it must be excessive.

"Is that where Zelda stays?" I know I sound a little too hopeful.

"No." Pegah dashes the sentiment in less than a second. "She lives in the house with me. And I like to bring some of the other ones inside too. I have a little guy whose name is Jasper; he's so cute. He also lives in the main house with me."

"Is his personality like Zelda's?"

Zelda lets out another blood curdling cry and I feel as if my ear drums might explode from the sound.

"No. Jasper's super sweet and fragile." I'm in awe. My cousin is completely immune to the noise. "He's got a lot of health issues, but you'll meet him later. You'll just have to watch out for him because he can't fly. He walks around on the ground."

"Why doesn't he fly?" I picture being chased around the house by the Road Runner.

"He was dropped on his head as a baby," she explains. "He has neurological issues but is a total lovebug."

It's a lot to process. A bird of prey. A handicapped bird... I wonder what other kinds await in the aviary.

"So, no other bird is going to fly at me to attack?" I ask, finally gathering the courage to stand. I can't help but look around in fear. I watch as Zelda suddenly stretches out her wings like she's trying to flex.

"I feel like she wants to attack me again," I say, with growing trepidation.

"That's just her being friendly," Pegah says, but she grabs hold of Zelda. "She likes to bite sometimes and doesn't realize how much it can hurt.... Kind of like us, huh?"

CHAPTER 3

"QUICKSAND"

"WHY HAVEN'T YOU TALKED ABOUT your bird sanctuary before?" I ask Pegah as we settle into the booth at a local bar. I had barely dropped my bags off in my room before running back out of the house and calling us an Uber.

Now we're both sipping margaritas and eating a huge plate of vegan nachos.

"Because people think it's weird."

"It *is* weird," I reprove. "Especially considering you've never even shown an affinity for birds before in your life, and you're almost forty years old."

"I had an epiphany." Pegah sounds surprised by her own declaration.

"What? When? How?" It occurs to me that I'm asking questions that apply to my own life's journey. "More importantly, *why*?"

"My breakup with Jason changed everything," she says. I remember it well; we were all so worried about her. "You saw how I was during that time, Ava. I was so unhappy."

Like me. Except I kept silent. For years.

"I was going to marry him, even though I was miserable," she says, wide-eyed. "I was almost *resigned* to it—like this is what you do when you've been with someone for so long. You swallow your unhappiness and all the uncertainty and just do it, even though you know something is missing inside. But I guess that happens sometimes. We get stuck and don't realize it's quicksand and that it can quickly suffocate and consume us."

"That's a great analogy. I guess my marriage to Darian was like being stuck in quicksand."

"But you got out," she says, taking a bite of the nachos. "And you went in thinking the ground was solid."

"I was too young to think," I reason. "We were high-school sweethearts. He was Persian, my first boyfriend, the family liked him at first.... At the time, it just made sense."

"And then it didn't. You should have known when you had that crazy chemistry with New York City." The moment the words leave her mouth, my heart begins to pound.

That's a code name I haven't heard in a while. *New York City*. The man I met sixteen years ago when I went to said city for a conference on wellness. He approached me in a bar, and we had a few drinks together. Our chemistry was off the charts, and we ended up talking for hours. But I was engaged to Darian. Those days we were off and on, but that was just the way our tumultuous relationship was designed. Too bad we didn't remain permanently *off*.

I fantasized about New York City for quite a while after our meeting, but because of my relationship, I let it go. The best way I can describe him is this—gorgeous. Nordic looking, manly and hot. I was wildly attracted to him. He also happened to be brilliant—probably a card-carrying member of Mensa—and of course, that quality is also quite attractive. Even more, he was witty and charming and was a true gentleman.... I just felt like I had known him forever. He was so familiar to me. Safe, even. At the time, I wanted to make out with him in the bar in front of the world. But I didn't. And to this day, it's one of my biggest regrets.

"I don't even know when the last time was we messaged. It's been at least a couple of years." We had stayed in touch over the years here and there on Facebook, but nothing more than general pleasantries.

"Reach out to him," Pegah encourages me.

"Are you crazy?"

"No! Why is that crazy? You totally should."

"What would I even say?" My head is spinning. "*Hey, I'm single now, are you?* For all I know he could be married with children."

"He's not." Pegah takes a chip and dips it in the guacamole.

"How do you know?"

"I did some investigation—"

"You mean stalking," I correct her.

"Call it what you like," she waves me off, unconcerned. "I know everything about him. In succinct detail."

"That sounds crazy."

"I'm trying to help you out," Pegah says innocently. "And...I always liked him."

"You've never even met him."

"I liked the conversation you had with him." She smiles. "I loved what he said about destiny."

I remember his words. He told me that whatever was meant for you, whatever your destiny was meant to be, was an inevitable fate that neither time nor distance could withstand. His words remained with me over the years. They made me always wonder about him.

"And he seems great," my cousin continues. "He's philanthropic, he travels the world, and the cherry on top? He's sexy."

I feel my heart rate pick up when she says that last part.

"Then *you* can date him." I hate how Pegah has piqued my interest in a man I hadn't thought about in a long while, a man I regretted never pursuing.

"Just reach out to him. What's the worst thing that can happen?" Pegah asks. "I think you're well aware that you've officially hit rock bottom...and speaking of rock bottom, have you seen your ex?"

"Not in four months," I admit as we lock eyes. Pegah looks surprised and I can't blame her. "It's crazy—this guy has been in my life since I was sixteen years old. I've seen him almost every single day since, and now, even though he's tried and wants to talk and smooth it out between us.... I can't. I'm not ready to face him, or..."

Myself.

I let my cousin come to her own conclusion.

"You will when you're ready," she says softly. "All you have to think about is the smooth sea in front of you. No clouds, storms, or quicksand in sight..."

We clink glasses.

"So, what's the story with Zelda?" I change the topic back to the bird version of a T-Rex.

"She's such a little cutie!" Her eyes light up. "How sweet is she?"

"Pegah..." I choose honesty. "Her name should be *GodZelda* and I'm not convinced that was a 'love bite' she gave me."

At least my cousin laughs at the reference. I don't think she realizes I'm dead serious.

"I promise it was!"

"I don't know...."

"I know Zelda's a lot," she admits. "She's spicy. But I love her so much. She makes me happy. I rescued her and all the others. I saw all these poor birds in cages, and something came over me. I wanted to help them. They'd all been either neglected or abused, and then made to live the rest of their lives cooped up in some cage, staring out at the world.... How unfair is that?"

"It's very sad and unfair." My heart softens a smidge toward my new nemesis.

"Can you imagine, Ava?" Her eyes glisten. "Living in a cage your whole life?"

Yes, I guess I can. Except mine was the kind I built on my own and willingly locked myself up and stayed in.

"You had to free them."

"Yes," she replies, and looks down at her drink.

I wonder if rescuing all these birds is some type of metaphor about her own life, and I see it clearly now. "You finally have a purpose."

She nods and smiles. "I've always been searching for one...I think we all are. Some of us get lucky and just find it faster. That part of me is now fulfilled."

"You're so lucky."

"But you have your travel blog." She's talking about my part-time dream job that now feels like an anchor around my neck.

"*Couples* travel and *romance*... I haven't posted anything in over six months," I remind her. "And it's not like it was some super successful blog. It wasn't generating any real money—nothing significant enough to bring me out of the debt Darian surprised me with."

I'm waiting for the moment when I don't have a complete panic attack when I think about losing everything I've worked for. Any and all safety I built for myself—gone with the wind.

Or down the hole of the dark web and whoever else's hole he paid for.

"But you love your travel blog," Pegah says.

"I did," I concede with a shrug. "In full transparency, I lied over ninety percent of the time about my perfect husband and perfect marriage, and all of our fun travel experiences together. The journeys alone were definitely a lot more enjoyable."

"Then come clean and tell your readers the truth about your life. Tell your audience about this travel expedition you're doing now," she says with excitement, then winks. "The different couches at friends' homes... That's kind of romantic. And it's real."

I laugh when she says it like that. And then my mind starts working. *Maybe...*

"At least think about it, Ava. Could be fun."

The waitress comes over and takes our order.

"Am I going to have to worry about GodZelda planning another attack?" I can't help but ask. "I feel like that was a totally strategic swoop in."

"Honestly?"

"Yes."

"You'll have to be more on guard." I'm surprised she's admitting Zelda might want to take another *love bite* from me again. "Just keep your eyes wide open. I don't know why, but I sense that Zelda is triggered by you."

I trigger a bird? *WTF?* I take this as a bad sign then excuse myself to use the lady's room. I leave my cousin and meander down the long, darkly lit corridor and into the bathroom. Since I have a good buzz, I take longer, lingering on my lip gloss and then staring into my blue eyes. I give my long, curly black hair a good shake and am ready for the world when I leave. Birdzillas and all.

CHAPTER 4

"LONDON BRIDGE"

As we know in life, timing is everything.

It is, at this moment, London enters my world.

In every which way.

When I leave the ladies room at the restaurant to head back to our table I literally fall into his arms. Not on purpose, of course, but because I am so mesmerized by the emerald green in his eyes that I forget how to walk. But as I'm cradled in his arms and look up into his handsome face, I am smitten. At that moment, feeling his strong arms around my body is all that matters.

No other man has touched me in over fifteen years. The only time I ever had any other experience with the opposite sex was during the six months Darian and I took a break.

And God, that was fun.

That was when I met Mr. New York City. The only man I've ever fantasized about *and* would have been tempted to cheat on Darian with.

"Are you all right?" he asks me in a sexy, posh, English accent.

I die.

"Yes," I choke, helplessly.

"Can you stand?" He looks concerned.

He is seriously gorgeous, equal bits of rugged and handsome.

"Yes, of course." I try and push away from him, but he doesn't let go of my body.

"Don't rush off." His accent is as divine as Belgian hot chocolate.

"Pardon me?" I ask as my heart accelerates.

"I meant, until I know you're okay to walk." He says this part with a flirty smile that makes my heart go into overdrive.

"I promise I'm okay." If he only knew the reason I tripped was because I was busy staring at his hotness.

He puts his hands on my hips and gently moves away. I'm sad to lose his touch.

"What's your name?" He folds his arms over his chest and cocks his head to the side as he stares at me. The intensity in his gaze makes my toes curl.

"Ava."

"Nice to meet you, Ava." He smiles sexily. "I'm—"

"London." The name comes out of me before he can even finish his sentence.

I die again.

Where the hell did that come from? Am I possessed? I cover my mouth with my hand and try not to hyperventilate. How embarrassing! It's like I've been locked up for years and just reintegrated into society.

Kind of true, Ava.

Thankfully he laughs, and it's music to my ears.

"I like that. You can call me London."

I can feel the shame heat my cheeks, burning me to a crisp, and I don't even know how to form words. Instead, I manage a smile.

"So, Ava..." he drawls out after a moment and it's sexy AF. "Are you here alone?"

"I'm here with my cousin."

"That's good." He looks pleased and my heart races. "You're beautiful, you know."

When London says this my knees nearly give out from under me.

"Thank you."

"Thank your parents."

I can feel my blush intensify.

"So, Ava..." London gives me another flirty smile.

"Yes?"

"Can I buy you and your cousin a drink?"

A thousand times, YES!

"Yes," I manage evenly, "thank you."

He makes a polite motion for me to start walking to our table and he follows behind. Pegah is busy on her phone looking at her nanny/bird cam. I'm pretty sure she's watching Pterodactyl—Zelda. She looks up when I reach our table and her eyes widen as she takes in London standing next to me.

"Pegah, this is—"

"London." He finishes for me, and reaches out to shake my cousin's hand.

"Nice to meet you, London." Pegah gives him a big, amused grin.

"Pleasure is mine." He is without a doubt charming. He looks down at our drinks. "If you'll excuse me, I'll be back with another round for us all."

London walks over to the bar while I sit down and place my hands on my burning cheeks.

"Did you just pick up a man?" Pegah asks in complete and utter shock.

"No," I say. "I fell on him."

"What?"

"I tripped and fell into his arms!" I whisper as I look over to the bar and check out the gorgeous London.

"Right...." Pegah elongates the word dramatically, then smirks.

"I'm serious!" I exclaim. "But how hot is he?"

"Gorgeous," she acknowledges. "The accent is definitely yummy."

"Oh my God...he's coming back over with a hot friend," I whisper to Pegah as I watch London walk toward us with a handsome stranger. Pegah's back is to the bar so she can't see, but he has dark black hair and arresting, amber eyes.

"A friend?" My cousin looks like she's been hit by a bus.

"Yes." I'm alarmed at how pale and uncomfortable she suddenly seems. "You do still like men, don't you?"

"Yes!" Pegah hisses at me. "I'm just feeling unprepar—"

"Hello ladies," London says as they come up to the table.

"Hey." I'm trying to sound as cool as possible.

"I was here with a friend and couldn't leave him all alone," he says. "I hope you don't mind, I invited him to the table with us."

"Not at all." I hope I don't sound overly eager.

London gives me a sweet smile. "Then allow me to introduce you to my mate. His name is Dublin." At first there's an awkward silence, but once he begins speaking we all start to laugh.

"It's a pleasure to meet you, ladies." Dublin is indeed from Dublin with an Irish accent that sounds like the best kind of rough sex. My cousin looks intrigued.

"It's nice to meet you, Dublin. My name is Ava."

Dublin gives me a roguish smile.

"I'm Pegah." As Pegah smiles at Dublin, I watch his eyes sparkle in fascination.

"Thank you for allowing us to join your party," he says.

The bartender brings out the drinks London ordered and more chips and guacamole. We clink glasses, then Dublin turns to Pegah. The two quickly engage in a more private conversation. I watch them for a bit—happy my cousin looks like she's having fun. And then a feeling of dread washes over me—is she going to talk about her bird sanctuary to Dublin? I feel like that's more of a second or maybe even third date kind of reveal.

London leans into me and whispers, "Ava. I think we might have just made a love match."

I turn to face him and we're uncomfortably close. His gaze rests on my lips. And this is definitely an in-your-face, you-are-now-single-Ava, moment. *Oh my gosh.* He can lean in and kiss me, and I can let it happen. And it *won't* be cheating. I lose my stomach just thinking about what a kiss from London would feel like.

"We'll see," I whisper back. "Seems too early to tell."

I lean away from him and fold my arms across my chest, praying I look cooler than I feel.

"Where's your sense of romance?" He openly flirts with me.

"My divorce might have beat it out of me," I say, deciding to throw out that little piece of information.

London's eyes narrow in fascination.

"Recent?" He cocks a brow.

"Slightly."

"Are you ready?" he asks.

"For what?"

"To start over." The way he says it makes the blood in my veins pump.

"I'm open to all possibilities."

CHAPTER 5

"LA CAGE A FOIS"
THE BIRD CAGE

As I stand inside Pegah's aviary, I have only one thought moving through my mind—

How did this *ever* happen?

I am standing in a geriatric bird sanctuary. Some are missing claws. I just watched one land on its stomach. Murray, the bird, looks like a flying squirrel. Sampson, who I had the pleasure of meeting earlier, walks backward on the ground. Not only that, he likes to roll up newspaper pieces and stick them in his back.

And guess what? Her aviary is fancier than her main house. It's a giant jungle paradise screaming with bird chirps, blood curling shrieks and songs. And some cries that sound suspiciously like Zelda.

"So?" Pegah smiles at me in excitement as we look around at her new passion.

"I'm in awe," I say, speaking the truth.

"What kind of awe?" Her voice sounds suspicious.

"All kinds," I confess.

Pegah laughs.

"But what you've done is unbelievable," I rush to tell her, because it's also the truth. "How many birds have you rescued?"

"Probably fifty," she says nonchalantly.

All I have to do is look around to know that's a big lie. "Seems like double to me."

She gives in with a sigh. "Maybe. I can't help it!"

"Look, if the tables were turned here, I think you'd be pretty surprised by all this as well. So, forgive me if it's taking me a moment to digest. But I will say, what you're doing is selfless. I mean it. This is some serious love and devotion."

She walks over for a hug. "That's the best compliment."

"You deserve it."

As we pull apart, Pegah's phone pings. When she glances down and her cheeks get all flushed, I know exactly who it is.

"Dublin calling?" I cock a knowing brow.

"Maybe." She has a silly smile. "How cute is he and that accent?"

"To die for."

"I think I'm going to go out with him," she admits. "But I want to get to know him over text some more before I commit to that."

"That's a big move for you," I say.

"Going out yesterday made me remember how nice it can be. I was thinking about that in bed last night. I've just been at home with my babies for so long now."

"You had your reasons," I tell her. "But it's been a while now. It's time to fulfill the next bucket. The birds are great, but you need human companionship too."

"I think so."

"I *know* so," I encourage. "You've got so much to offer someone. If it's Dublin, Los Angeles, Abu Dhabi or Singapore, he'll be lucky to have you."

"Same goes for you. London is pretty damn handsome and super smart. I'm glad you found him, even if it's only while you're here. He'll bring some spice into your life and to your blog."

"Maybe." I am slightly winded by the idea.

The thought of the mystery British hunk does brighten my mood. We exchanged numbers at the restaurant after our drink, and he's been showering me with attention since. The sweetest kind, the kind that's almost too good to be true. In twenty-four hours, he's told me I'm beautiful more times than my husband did the entire duration of our marriage. I guess I hadn't realized how starved I was for that kind of attention.

"Peh-lease," Pegah says, throwing in the Persian accent for good measure.

"I know!" I exclaim in embarrassment. "I don't know, he made me feel alive again. I guess he kind of lit my fire."

"Ava! This is so exciting!" Pegah's eyes look like they're welling up with tears. "Think of all the first moments you get to have all over again."

My mind races.

"The first time he reaches out to hold your hand," she says, sighing dreamily. "The first time he looks at you like he wants to kiss you."

She closes her eyes.

"The first time he leans in to capture your lips..."

I get butterflies at the thought.

"The first I love you..."

The moment is poignant.

And then...

GodZelda makes her grand entrance.

I thought we were safe. I even watched Pegah lock the connecting door—but I guess that feather head figured out how to unlock it. She makes a beeline straight for me. I don't know where to run or hide because there's nowhere to go, so I just squat, lower my head, cover my face, and hope for the best. I decide I'll endure the pain of the bite, then run like hell out of my cousin's home to my aunt and uncle's house, which is only five minutes away. Screw it. I'll just have to stay with them for the next few weeks.

Zelda lands directly on the back of my head. Her claws are immediately entangled in my curls and she just sits there for a moment.

"Don't move, Ava," Pegah says, like I would ever do something so foolish. Is she nuts? Move? I'm not even going to speak.

And then the unthinkable happens—

Zelda begins to move her rear around and around, then starts to kind of grind it into my hair. It feels like she's really working it.

"She likes you!" Pegah says, thrilled. "I *knew* that was a love bite. She's imprinting on you! And maybe nesting because your hair looks like one."

"Oh my God. Stop talking," I command. "There is a bird *humping* my head!"

"How cute is she?" Pegah says this like I should appreciate the attention, but all I'm trying to figure out is how I'm going to move. If I stand, is Zelda going to rip my scalp off?

It feels possible.

"You have to help me," I say in desperation.

"Zelda, Auntie Ava doesn't want you to nest on her head anymore." She says this in such a gentle voice I want to scream.

Zelda talks back to her. My guess is, she's not budging.

"Please fly off, you little sweetie." Her tone is one you'd use with an infant.

Zelda squawks again and plants her beak on my scalp. I can feel the hives come on. She could bite at any time. I silently pray, but I don't think she's planning on going anywhere.

"Pegah!" I'm on the verge of screaming and making a run for it.

"Fine." She sighs and moves to pick her up, but it takes a moment to disentangle Zelda's claws from my hair. Once she's done, I give my cousin the stink eye then head right out of the aviary. She follows behind me and cackles.

"I think you should be flattered," she says, to my utter disbelief.

I stop in my tracks.

"Is this what my life has come to?" I am horrified. "You want me to be flattered because a bird wants to nest in my hair?"

"Yes!" she exclaims like I'm an idiot. "And London was attracted to you too!"

The fact that she's comparing London to Zelda is just astronomical. I pick up my phone once I'm safely back in the family room, and sure enough, he's texted.

London: I would love to take you out to dinner tonight.

I'm excited by the thought of seeing him again, but I don't want to seem too eager.

Me: That sounds nice, but I'm having dinner with my aunt and uncle. Raincheck?

He wastes no time responding.

London: Tomorrow.

I like his confidence. There is nothing sexier in a man.

Me: That sounds good.

London: Give me a moment and I'll text you a location. Looking forward to seeing you again, Ava.

CHAPTER 6

"1-800-PSYCHIC"

"Hi *Khanoom!*"

My Aunt Nedda says "hello lady" the moment she sets eyes on me. I'm quickly pulled into her loving embrace.

"I missed you, Khaleh Nedda," I say to her. My auntie is the best.

In Persian culture you have more than one set of parents. Khaleh Nedda and Uncle M are those for my sister, Layla, and I. The second parents lecture us with life advice but are way cooler than they'd ever be with their own children. Kind of like the ideal parents who aren't your real parents.

"I made you lots of food," my aunt says as she checks me out. "Your *mah-der* (mother) told me I have to feed you."

"Can't wait." I know she can hear my sarcasm.

"Vhere is Pegah?" Khaleh Nedda looks over my shoulder. "Vhy you guys drive separate?"

"She'll be right here. She said she had to take care of something at the house," I explain.

"Vit dhose birds?" My auntie flares her nose, and it's not a good sign. The nose flare is a significant move in our family—it usually means someone is about to get their ass handed to them.

Poor Pegah.

"They're so cute." I feel like it's my duty to defend my cousin's special needs bird farm.

"Von hundred five birds are cute?" Apparently, Auntie Nedda has counted *all* of them. That must have been quite a discovery.

"She's happy." I try my best to diffuse the flare.

"She's *happy*?" Unfortunately, it expands even more. "Vith dhose birds? I don't know how she still has hearing."

At that moment, Pegah walks into the house. I'm not surprised to see her holding two birds in a small travel cage. One is the severely disabled Jasper, and the other is a blue one I don't recognize—I guess he or she must have been hiding in the aviary.

I look over at my auntie. Uh oh. The nose flare is next level.

"You can't come von day vith-out bird?" She puts her hands on her hips and demands to know.

Pegah rolls her eyes. "Jasper's been alone all day, so I couldn't leave him. And I brought you and Dad a surprise."

"No—" My aunt waves her hands from side to side as if she knows what is about to happen. She starts to curse up a storm to my uncle in Farsi. (The short version is that she's pretty pissed and thinks their daughter will end up marrying a bird. And she wants my uncle to be prepared for a bird marriage.)

"Mom..." My cousin has obviously been in this rodeo before. "It's just for a few weeks until I can find little Horus a home."

"Vat you say?" My auntie looks horrified. "You name de bird, 'whore'?"

I start to giggle.

"Mom, it's a rescue!" Pegah looks annoyed as hell. "His name is Ho-rus."

"Vhat?"

"An Egyptian God," I explain to my aunt. "People like to be clever."

I look at the light blue bird, and honestly, he doesn't look like much of a Horus. But what do I know?

"He needs love like Jasper, and I don't have the time now," Pegah pleads.

"Vhy you no have time?" my auntie wonders rhetorically. "You alvays vit bird."

"Ava and I went out last night for drinks and dinner," my cousin reveals with a big smile. "And we plan on going out even more while she's here."

I decide to throw down.

"Pegah met a guy." I feel like telling my aunt this will somehow mollify her rising ire.

"She did?" Khaleh Nedda's eyes light up, but then she looks at me in disbelief. "Really?"

"Yes!" I exclaim. "And he's super cute. And Irish."

"Dhey drink too much," is my aunt's first comment.

I lock eyes with Pegah. We are both doing our best not to laugh.

"So do Persians," I remind her. "The only difference is that we do it in secret."

"That's right," my uncle joins our conversation, amused. "We do a lot of things in private. No judging allowed, Nedda Khanoom. Speaking of drinking, I'll go get us a bottle of wine to go with our kabobs."

Thirty minutes later the four of us are seated at the dining table with enough food for ten people. It's all delicious: basmati rice drizzled with touches of saffron; beef and chicken kabob; a green celery stew that I happen to love; and an entire plate of potato tadig, which becomes crispy on the bottom of the pot once the rice is done cooking. My aunt even put out a platter of sangak bread and feta with mint and walnuts.

With the half-eaten dinner still on the table, my aunt brings out dessert and tea. As if we have any room. She also carries the book of Hafiz—another ritual I absolutely love. I'm immediately excited. All of the girls in our family are obsessed with the great Persian poet. Growing up, my auntie would always read fortunes for us from Hafiz. The legend goes that you can ask the wise Hafiz a question and then you close your eyes and pick a page from his book of poetry. Within his masterful poem, you find your answer, but it's no easy task to interpret what he's trying to tell you. Luckily, my aunt happens to be an expert at it.

"I knew you vould vant dhis." She wears a happy smile as she sits down and places the book in front of me.

"What about me?" Pegah sounds annoyed.

"You only have bird to ask about," my auntie retorts without batting an eye.

"Touché," Pegah says, and giggles.

"Ask eh question," Khaleh Nedda urges me.

I close my eyes and place my hands over the book, thinking about the most important question I have for Hafiz that he might be able to help answer.

Is London a good guy? No! Stupid. You just met the man.

Is New York City a good guy? Gah! What is wrong with me? Why am I only thinking about the opposite sex? There are so many more pressing issues in my life right now!

But the answer is obvious—I want to make out with someone so, *so* bad.

Okay, what's another question I can ask?

Am I going to figure out my whole job situation? No. Way too boring.

When is my life going to feel normal again? Nah. Kind of blah. And really? Can Hafiz answer that? Think, Ava. Think. My question should be about my life. My future. Stability and internal happiness. The who, what, when, where, why, and how. Finding my Zen.

"Vell?" My auntie prods.

Is true love in the cards for me? Will I see New York City again?

Luckily my auntie doesn't know what's happening internally and begins to read the poem to me in Farsi.

I try to decode the words and I'm so confused. I hear a lot about sins and a tent. What sins is Hafiz referring to? Mine? New York City's? This doesn't sound too good.

"Who has the tent?" Pegah looks as baffled as I feel.

"Hafiz could be referring to me and my lack of home," I wonder out loud, trying to figure out the cryptic message. "I could very well be living in a tent."

Alone. Forever.

My cousin's eyes light up and she puts her finger on her nose. "That's good! That's definitely it!"

"No, dhat is not it." My auntie shakes her head with a grimace. She looks over at me and narrows her eyes. "Did you ask about eh man?"

"No." I can feel my face flush. I can't make eye contact with either one of them.

"I asked about love."

Khaleh Nedda smiles in pleasure and points at the book. "Dhere is a man who is tinking about you."

"Really?" I dare to dream and listen to an ancient sage's prediction.

"But he has issue." When my auntie says this my heart sinks.

"What kind of issue?" I ask in dread. "Does he live in a tent?"

"No. Hafiz says, he is drunk on love and has a tent, or someting like an altar, set up for you," she says with a knowing smile.

Huh.

"London?" Pegah narrows her eyes in confusion. I'm too embarrassed to admit my question.

"I don't know if I believe that." I shake my head.

"And it sounds a bit serial killer-ish," Pegah says.

My auntie gives us both a dirty look. "Eh! It's a poem about love! It's about dreams! It's about destiny! Vhy you guys so negative?"

I do my best not to roll my eyes. I might have believed this fantasy land fun stuff twenty-years ago, but now I know what real-life looks like. And trust me, it would be hard to find any guy sitting in a tent praying for love. And as for destiny...I said no to that at the Bowery Hotel thirteen years ago.

"Hafiz says, be patient," my auntie says knowingly.

"I don't think I have any other choice."

☙

There is never one moment.

There are a series of them, over time, that drive you crazy. That drove you crazy before you were married. Ones that make you mad during and after. Mad because each of those moments chipped away at the real you a little more. Mad because you don't know why you stayed so long—so much time wasted, and for what? But those moments...those moments echo through your mind before shattering in front of your face like a mirror fallen to the floor. Those moments...those pieces of yourself are lost, and once you realize what has happened and you look down to see yourself as shards of broken glass scattered across the floor—

That's the second you know it's over. When both of you know it's over, even though neither of you want to say, "We're done," out loud.

Because maybe you never really started. That's the hard truth.

Because maybe when it's wrong, it's just wrong. All of it.

From the beginning to the end. This is what I'm starting to believe. How could there be any other answer?

As I lie in bed and try to sleep, my mind is filled with all of the many "wrong" Darian moments from when we were dating and married. The list seems endless now. It's too much to handle in the middle of the night. I reach out and grab my iPhone from the nightstand. Lord. It's three a.m. and I am as awake as I can be.

For the past few nights my mind has been plagued by one thought—why I stayed in my marriage so long. Thirteen years. So much time wasted. I don't understand the apparent sadistic need I had to be unhappy. I had a fairly normal childhood—as normal as it could be for a first-generation child of Iranian-American immigrants learning to assimilate into a new land. There were definitely some challenging times for me growing up, especially in high school. There were a lot of emotional moments then, but in retrospect, I find them vastly amusing. Although at the time I didn't feel that way.

But come on... Stay so long in misery? What kind of person does that?

The questions keep coming. What possessed me to continue as we were? Why did I stay? Why did he?

I tell myself it doesn't matter now. I can't go back in time and change anything. But it's hard to face such a flaw in your character.

Peace seems evasive as hell. And there's one question I can't shake: Once I find peace, how do I keep it?

CHAPTER 7

"PART THREE"

"Your ex-husband sounds like a wanker." London is unable to hide his disdain for Darian.

He insisted on knowing why we got divorced, so I gave him a brief summary. I'm happy I told him because he's just given me a new adjective to use when referencing Darian. I can't wait to share it with Pegah.

"Now your turn," I say.

Since we sat down over an hour ago, plenty of conversation and wine has flowed between us. In addition to being handsome, London is smart and successful. He works as an investment banker and travels regularly, but he's based in the UK. I discovered that he also went through a divorce five years ago. He said it had been ugly, and when I said the same about my situation with Darian, London insisted we swap stories.

"She came out," he says, taking a swig of his wine and leaning back in his chair.

"She came out of what?" It takes me a moment to understand, and then, "*Ohh...*"

"Like your ex-husband, my ex-wife was also having an affair. Lena was having one with her best girlfriend."

"Did you have any idea? Were there any signs?"

London shrugs.

"I did find it bizarre that they traveled so much together over the years," he admits. "And that she always insisted they share a room to save money, even though we didn't need to worry about that. As you can imagine, it all made perfect sense when she told me."

I stare at London's handsome face and can feel how that must have hurt.

"I'm so sorry." It's the best I can do. "Can I ask you a question?"

"You may." He gives me his beguiling smile.

"Promise not to be offended?" I'm not going to be able to stop myself.

"I think I know where you're going with this." London cocks a brow.

"Do you?"

"Is the infidelity easier because she left me for another woman?"

"You took the words right out of my mouth." I'm impressed and slightly embarrassed I'm so obvious.

He laughs and it's very sexy. His eyes lock with mine, and I can feel the butterflies in my stomach. Yes, I'm definitely attracted to him.

"Do you want to know the truth?" His gaze burns into me.

"Yes."

"It still hurt." He whispers this, and I find his vulnerability hot.

Suddenly, all I want to do is cuddle him and hug that hurt away. Instead, I keep talking. "Because you loved her."

"You know what, Ava?"

"What?"

"I did," he admits. "I really did."

"And now?" I prod. "What does she mean to you after all these years?"

"She means the same to me," London divulges, and I appreciate his honesty. "I don't know how to explain it, but Lena was a big part of my life. I was with her for seventeen years. We grew up together. Our families were great friends. We shared so many experiences. She's a big piece of my story and I see her now as the part two of my life."

"Part two?" I ask.

"Part one was childhood and my *wonder years*." He smiles devilishly. "I should clarify that and say it seemed like I was determined to drive my parents mad in my teens and college years. And I was almost successful."

"I'm gathering as much," I say with a laugh. "And from the look on your face, I'm guessing you had a lot of good times."

"I did. There are a lot of stories I'll have to share with you in more detail at a later time."

I like that he infers we'll be seeing each other again.

"Part two consisted of my life with Lena." He turns a bit more serious. "And all of the adventures, good and bad, that made up our time together."

"And part three?" I wonder.

"Part three is this next chapter. What I hope will be my last, searching for and finding a partner to live out the rest of my life with. Someone I can grow old with. A companion. A lover. A best friend."

Is he for real? These are all the right words. And I am thoroughly impressed.

"That sounds perfect," I tell him.

"I think I'm a bit of a hopeless romantic," he says coyly.

I believe him, but there's a mischievous twinkle in his eye that makes me pause. I watch his eyes darken and flicker to my lips then back to my gaze.

I can't breathe. If there wasn't a table between us, I think he'd try to kiss me. I can feel myself blush at the thought.

"I have a feeling we're both on the same kind of journey."

"Are we?" I tease.

"We're both looking for our part three."

CHAPTER 8

"SINGLE PERSIAN FEMALE"

"I'm a bit old-fashioned and would like to walk you to the door," London says to me with that confident smile. "Would that be all right?"

My heart speeds up. "Yes, of course."

He gets out of the car and comes around to my side and helps me out like a gentleman. His hands linger on my waist before he places one on the small of my back. His touch feels good. We make it to the door and turn to face each other. It suddenly becomes that awkward moment I've seen in a million romantic movies. A great date that leads up to this unavoidable ending.

"I had a wonderful time," I try to fill the silence. "Thank you."

"As did I."

We stare at each other for a beat before he speaks.

"I'm looking forward to seeing you again, Ava." London's voice is husky now. "But I have to do this before I go."

His lips are soft and sweet, and I lean in, enjoying every part of him. I decide *this* is my first kiss back from the dead—like Sleeping Beauty or Snow White. And it's pretty awesome. But I pull away before he can try anything more.

"Good night, London," I whisper happily.

"Good night, Ava." He puts his hands in his pockets and smiles politely before stepping away from me. I quickly hit the code for the alarm and step inside the house. The lights are out, so I'm assuming Pegah is already asleep. I think I might have to wake her up. I'm wound up from the kiss and can't wait to analyze every second of our date.

But first, I walk into the kitchen. I'm suddenly starving.

I open the fridge and go for the leftover Persian, helping myself to a plate. Once I'm settled at the kitchen table, I start to relive the kiss. I couldn't ask for anything sweeter for a first time back. It was nice. And pretty perfect.

Almost.

Passionate for sure.

But something was not...I don't know. Maybe I'm just overthinking it. Or maybe I'm just being too picky. I realize if I keep being so critical of every little thing, I could end up quite lonely.

I'm attracted to London!

I look over at my phone and I think of New York City. Before I can stop myself, I grab my laptop and look him up on social media.

Before I even start scrolling through any pictures or tidbits of his life, I need to double-check his relationship status. I'm not even sure why, considering I haven't seen the man in years and don't even know who he is anymore, but I need to make sure Pegah saw it right. I just do. I find myself holding my breath when I click on the link to his "About" section.

Oh shit.

He *is* single.

Goddamnit.

In less than ten seconds, I've become my stalker cousin and am neck deep in the last five years of his life. The sporadic posts he's put up. The random picture without a caption. Smiling at the camera with a strange woman, who may or may not be a relative or a girlfriend. Pieces to a puzzle that seems to have no clear picture. Here I am, staring at all of it, carefully analyzing every little detail. I look for clues to what kind of man he is. What are all of his social media posts trying to tell the world? Do they mean something? Are they clues to the inner workings of his mind?

The post about his view in Bora Bora tells me nothing, except that he has good taste in travel destinations. He posted a picture with his mom and dad. That's sweet—but that was from four years ago. And then there's a vague post about a water initiative in Africa. I kind of like that. This must mean he cares about the world—at least he does on social media. A lot of women commented, telling him how sweet he was to be so thoughtful and generous. Hmmm... maybe he posted something philanthropic as part of his game? He could be a player.

Or not.

None of this is giving me much to work with. I'm just jumping to random conclusions about his character. Jesus.

I feel crazy for even looking him up. All I know is that he was a man I had some chemistry with over thirteen years ago, when we met at a bar. And over the years we've messaged here and there—small talk. Pleasantries. Nothing real.

That's all I know. Which isn't much.

I click on the picture New York City posted with his mom, dad, and his grandmother. He looks really cute in this one. Playful and sweet, and super happy to be with his family.

I find myself smiling with him like I was the one taking the picture, instantaneously besotted, and then, the unthinkable happens—

I don't know if it's some type of social media Freudian slip or a just a dumb-person slip, but I hit the *like* button on the picture.

This is a post from *four years ago.*

Oh. My. God.

The irrational behavior of a single white female. Something Glenn Close would have done in *Fatal Attraction.*

I immediately hit *unlike*. I stare at my phone in horror.

OMG! *Did I just do that?* He's going to see it anyway...

Shit.

I hit *like* again. Then *unlike*—and *like*. What is wrong with me? It's as if I've suddenly developed an uncontrollable tick. I cover my face with my hands. This did not just happen! I want to throw up on myself from embarrassment. Will he be able to see the crazy?

It's too horrifying a thought.

I snap my laptop shut and take a few deep breaths. I tell myself it's okay—who cares? Who gives a crap about New York City anyway? I don't even know him, and besides, he probably won't even notice. I throw my phone down and promise myself I'll never *ever* check his social media again. I try to brainwash myself into believing it doesn't matter, and that he's a successful, busy man who has no time for some nonsense online. I'm sure he never even checks his social media accounts.

Just as I push my laptop away from me, I hear a soft flutter in the air.

Wings. Then silence. Then wings again. Like the sound of a Pterodactyl about to swoop in on its unsuspecting victim and bludgeon it to death.

And then Zelda lands right across from me on the kitchen table.

CHAPTER 9

"THE LEGEND OF ZELDA"

"OH MY GOD," I GASP to myself as the bird and I lock eyes.

She squawks and makes an exaggerated gesture with her head toward my plate of food. Oh no. She's hungry. I gladly push the whole damn thing over to her.

"It's all yours," I say, hoping she'll take this as a peace offering.

I watch her walk over to the plate and step right in. I hope Persian is good for her, but at this point, it doesn't matter—there is *no way* I would take the food away. She picks up a strand of the long Basmati rice and starts to go to town. She picks another, and then another, flinging them around her body in ecstasy. It looks like she's giving herself a rice-gasm, she's so thrilled to be eating it.

She chews some more and watches me. I wonder what she's thinking and if I should say something. I decide to just go for it.

"I'd like for us to be friends," I tell her as calmly as I'm capable of.

She makes an exaggerated motion with her head and continues to eat. I wonder what this answer means.

"We can coexist while I'm here," I explain softly. "I feel for you and your little brothers and sisters who all seem to have gotten the crap end of life's stick. I thought my story was bad, but you seem to have had it worse."

She shrieks loudly when I say this. I swear, I think she understands, so I continue.

"But on a brighter note, my cousin had no problem taking you all in." I try to sound as upbeat and positive as I can. "And let's be honest, this place is like the Aman Hotel for birds."

Zelda doesn't answer this time. Instead, she hops out of the pile of rice and makes her way toward me.

"Did I say something wrong?" I ponder in horror. I don't know what to do. If I run, she'll fly at me. If throw my hands over my face, she could potentially claw them off. And goddamn, I know it will hurt. This is what I like to call a *no-win situation*. So, I just wait.

Zelda gets closer and lifts her right claw like she wants me to pick her up. I stare at her even though it's clear she wants me to put my finger out.

"Is this a trick?" I ask the bird. "Are you going to bite the hell out of it? Will I lose my nail?"

She continues to lift her little claw. Since she doesn't squawk, I consider it a good sign. Zelda and I lock eyes. There's something soft I see there—if only for a second, but I swear, I see it. I realize I have no choice but to trust her.

"Screw it."

I slowly put my finger out. Zelda steps on, then hops on my shoulder so she can bury herself in my hair again. I realize I'm probably going to have to wake Pegah up to get her untangled.

I stay deathly still as Zelda moves over to my neck and cuddles up to my ear. She brushes her beak along my skin. I get goose-bumps—and these are not the good kind. She is in a position from which she can bite the hell out of me if she pleases. And my cousin isn't here to save me. So, I just go for it.

I slowly stand up; thankfully Zelda doesn't seem to mind. I grab my cell and walk with her down the hall to my bedroom. She says a few words to me that I can't untangle, and I decide it's best I don't talk back. I don't want to say anything that might instigate her. It definitely doesn't feel like she's planning on going anywhere.

I stare at my bed.

How am I going to change? How am I going to go to sleep? What am I going to do with this bird?

"Zelda, sweetie." I try to use that honied pitch Pegah does when she's speaking to the birds. "Don't you think it's time for you to go to sleep?"

She squawks at me.

"Night, night?"

I have no idea if she knows what I'm saying but I try to convince her to fly away.

"Polly want a cracker?" I wonder out loud.

She shrieks in anger when I say this. I guess that was the wrong cliché to use.

"Shit," I mumble to myself.

Zelda repeats the swear word. I walk over to the mirror and stare at the bird perched on my shoulder. I have to laugh. It is rather comical. It's like I'm Captain Hook, but with a parrot that might want to bite into me like a great white.

Since it's clear Zelda isn't moving, I start to undress, carefully leaning down and slipping off my pants. Zelda stays where she is. It's almost as if she wants to torture me. I swear that's what I think she wants to do. I reach for my shirt and start to lift it up over my head, and at that moment Zelda finally flies off of me and into the darkness of Pegah's home. As soon as she's gone, I shut the door, promising myself I won't leave the room until morning.

But, Ava, my inner voice says. *Zelda wasn't so bad. Actually, she was kind of cute.*

എ

"You kissed him?!" Pegah screeches at me like I've just discovered the cure for cancer.

Sitting in her family room, I give her the play-by-play of my night with London.

"Yes," I tell her. "Isn't that what I just said?"

"You did," she says. "But can I be honest?"

"Always."

"It all sounds very anticlimactic."

"Well, there was no climax." I laugh when I say that part.

"No," she agrees. "But you don't sound like it moved you."

"Moved me?"

"You know what I mean." Pegah rolls her eyes. "It was the first kiss after Darian. It's supposed to rock your soul."

I think about her words. There is a part of me that agrees, but then again, I don't know. I've been out of the game for so long that I don't know what's what. Maybe this is normal. Maybe it's supposed to be easy and natural and not crazy passionate. Maybe you're supposed to have a sweet interaction with someone because that's what's safe. Maybe the other stuff is what gets you in trouble.

"Do you think that kind of passion lasts forever?" I wonder.

"I do." She shrugs at me. "I haven't found it yet, but I think it's out there."

"You have way more optimism than I do."

Zelda flies over to Pegah and she's soon immersed in her own kind of lovefest with the bird. While she's busy, I do the unthinkable. I grab my phone and check social media because I'm a glutton for punishment.

New York City: I must be on your mind.

I stare at the message on my account and feel my body heat up with excitement.

He reached out. *He noticed!* Holy. Shit.

He does check his social media. Oh no. So now he knows I was stalking him! My hands cup my cheeks, and I have to force myself to take long, deep breaths.

Shit.

What do I say? My message back is going to have to be care-fully thought out. Something clever. Witty. Something that will make him wonder.

I write...

Me: Yes. You are.

Why is my heart beating so fast? I feel so stupid. I'm almost forty years old and I'm acting like a child! OhmyGod.

He starts to write back in less than thirty seconds. My heart. Stops. Beating.

But oh, does it feel good. And then...

New York City: Are you still married?

Me: No.

Technically it *is* over.

And then because I have to pretend like I didn't stalk him, even though he knows I did, I ask my own question.

Me: Are you?

New York City: It's complicated.

CHAPTER 10

"FACETIMING & SHAMANS"

"Marriage was invented by people whose life expectancy was eighteen."

Cue the dramatic pause.

As soon as I closed out of social media because of New York City's complications, my phone rang. It was my one of my best friends, Jonathan, on FaceTime. He's also gone through a dramatic divorce and I'm sure can appreciate the new theory I've been mulling over. He happens to look windblown, tan and extremely hot. I wish he was straight. I think I tell him this every time I see him.

"I believe Sam was my destiny."

Jonathan's reference to destiny makes me think of New York City's comment all those years ago...and then the message I sent him.

"It was your destiny to go through hell?" I wonder.

"You've got to look at things differently and open your mind like me."

"Well, you're looking super sexy," I say, to change the subject.

"Thanks, babe," he says as he looks me over. "Why didn't you fix your hair?"

I had put it in a tight bun on top of my head in an effort to avoid any future attempts at nesting, although I do feel more vulnerable like this. My neck and ears are definitely up for grabs now.

"I did," I tell him as I touch the top. "It looks cute."

Jonathan's eyes widen. "If you say so."

"Rude."

"Honest."

"Wait, what's that noise? Are you in a jungle?" Jonathan looks confused.

"I'm at Pegah's."

"I thought she lived in Marin? It sounds like you're in a rain forest with all those birds."

"She has a sanctuary," I tell him, trying my best to keep a straight face.

"In her house?"

"Basically."

"She needs to get laid," Jonathan returns quickly.

"I heard that!" Pegah yells out, as she comes around so Jonathan can look at her as well. Since she's holding Jasper and has another bird perched on top of her head, he gets the picture.

"You definitely need to get laid." Jonathan shakes his head as he stares at my cousin. "Is a bird hat the new thing up in Marin?"

"Funny," Pegah replies dryly.

I can't tell if she thinks it's as hilarious as we do.

"Why do you think Sam was your destiny?" Pegah asks him.

Jonathan looks to his right, then left, and lowers his voice in case someone might be listening.

"I drank that tea..."

"The tea?"

"*Ayahuasca*. With this shaman from Colombia. Luna invited me. I know you're going to think I'm crazy, but it's changed my life."

"Luna is a hippie," I remind him. "Like a full crystal-loving, sage-burning, peace and love, hippie. Does she even shave her legs or wear deodorant?"

"I'm telling you," Jonathan says seriously, "I did it a couple of weeks ago, and since that weekend I've become a different person. It sounds crazy, I know. I don't know what to say. The anger I had for Sam is gone, and now I just feel sorry for him. Sam was my choice. No one forced me to be with him. I lived with him for a reason."

Jonathan puts his hands together in front of his chest and bows. "I'm just sending him love."

"You're sending him love?" I repeat incredulously. I don't even know who I'm talking to right now.

Jonathan and Sam had one of the ugliest divorces I've ever witnessed.

"What happened to me in that ceremony was life changing." A serene look comes over his face. "I don't know what to say, Ava, I just see the world in a different way now. I see my life, all of it—from when I was young, the good parts of myself, the ugly parts—and I just accept it."

I study him for a long moment. He's not lying. He's not just saying the words, he's living them. I can see it. I can't help but feel a little envious that he found such peace. I wish there was a way I could sprinkle some of it in my breakfast cereal.

"I think *you* should consider drinking the medicine," Jonathan says, to my surprise.

"You're in the best place possible to have a mind-altering experience. I think this will help clear your path even more. Make you see yourself again and fall in love with the beauty you are. And when the time is right, you'll get to meet a man who will sweep you off your feet and you'll know right when you see him. And you'll fall in love again. Or maybe you'll fall in love for the first time." He finishes this part off with a giant, infectious smile that makes something inside me shift again.

I don't know why, but the thought of it gives me goosebumps. The way he speaks, it's like he believes it *will* happen. It sounds too good to be true, and I don't want to focus on what that picture looks like because I don't really believe it exists.

"Is there such a thing?" I ask softly.

"As love?" Jonathan looks bewildered.

I nod slowly.

"Or is it just lust at the beginning of the relationship disguising itself as love?" I know how cynical I sound. "Is it lust tricking us into believing it's that four-letter word that we've all been conditioned to chase our whole lives? Maybe it's all just one big scam."

"That sounds sad!" Pegah calls me out.

"It's not sad," I say. "It's real."

"Don't you still believe in love?" Jonathan's question throws me.

I suddenly feel unsure. I look over at Pegah, who's staring at me in worry.

"I don't know what I believe." I hate that this is my answer. I think Jonathan does too, because he takes a long moment to reply.

"Ava. Love is all there is."

Is it? I'm not so sure but I don't say that out loud, given my audience.

"Well, the shaman is up in Grass Valley!" Jonathan says excitedly. "It's like divine intervention for you. The universe is calling you. You're right there. I think you should sign up with me to do it."

"What?" I stare at him in shock. "I don't know about that…"

"Why not?" Pegah chimes in to my surprise.

"I think you can imagine the many reasons *why not*," I reply.

"Maybe we should live outside our comfort zone," she says.

"We?" I ask.

"I'll do it with you."

I'm sure my mouth is gaping open.

"I don't even know that much about it," I assert, with growing apprehension. "It sounds slightly scary."

"It's life changing." Jonathan goes in for the kill. "And trust me, from the way you and Pegah both look right now, you're in need of a healthy dose of life changing."

I grimace at him, but for whatever reason, I am more than slightly intrigued.

"It's a tea," Jonathan continues. "You'll be fine. Some people even see God."

Interesting. I do have a lot I'd like to say to God. Some of it would not be considered to be very nice.

"Seems extreme." I look over at Pegah, who looks way too eager. "I can't believe you want to jump on this bandwagon."

"Yes," she says. "It connects you to nature, too." Another bird takes that moment to fly onto her head. There are three perched there now. *Three* birds.

"I don't think you need to be any more connected to nature."

She laughs.

"I'm signing up for the weekend!" Jonathan exclaims. "We can all do it together. We'll be purging buddies!"

"Purging buddies?"

"You puke," he admits. "But you're purging your demons and the garbage in your life away. You'll purge all the negativity with Darian. Who knows? You might even forgive him."

Huh.

I look over at Pegah and she lifts her brows.

"Why not?" she returns. "It's a whole new life. And a whole new you."

CHAPTER 11

"ONE FLEW OVER THE CUCKOO'S NEST"

"Do you guys want a diaper?" Jonathan walks over to Pegah and I holding three adult diapers in his hands.

I don't know whether to laugh or cry.

"Why would I need a diaper?" I'm afraid to hear the answer, even though I have a sinking suspicion what it will be.

Jonathan takes a moment and avoids all eye contact. That is never a good sign.

"Jonathan?" I push.

"You might shit yourself," he says, like it's no big deal.

"Like, poop your pants, shit yourself?" I'm completely horrified.

"What other kind could there be?" He lifts a brow.

"You didn't tell us that part!" I cry out.

Pegah immediately gets up and takes a diaper from him.

"I'll be right back," she says without missing a beat.

I stare at my cousin in awe. I can't believe how she's embraced all of this so easily.

"I'd put one on too, babe." Jonathan tosses it on my mat and winks. "Just in case."

To be honest, at first glance, I was worried Jonathan had asked us to join a cult. With everyone wearing white and all sorts of ceremonial beads it's a lot to take in. It's how you'd imagine a hippie colony. They're all overly friendly with their huge smiles, happy demeanors, and desire to make sure you're super comfortable. I can't help but be suspicious of it all. Who really behaves like this?

"I'm excited!" Jonathan says as he looks around the room.

Right when he says this, one of the "helpers" places empty buckets and rolls of toilet paper right in front of our mats. I stare at the purge bucket.

"I'm scared." I have to be honest.

"Don't be!" He laughs at me like my concern isn't real. "It's great!"

It had better be, especially if there's a chance I'm going to shit myself.

He leaves me carrying his own diaper in hand. I wonder if I've somehow entered an alternate universe. Am I living in the upside down? One of my best friends in life just talked about willingly pooing himself as a grown adult man. Is there is still time for me to run?

I freefall into my own thoughts. Why am I here? What's this about? My mental state? My finances? My love life? Will this mysterious medicine even have time to hit all the key areas of my life? There are twenty-five other people in this room who need help, too. How can this solve all of my problems in one night?

Pegah and Jonathan come out of the bathroom.

Wow.

My cousin is wearing an adult diaper under her pants. I must memorialize this and send it to my sister and hers. Luckily, I still have my phone, so I grab it out of my bag and turn it back on.

I have a bunch of messages from friends. One is from London.

> **London:** I'm going to be back in Los Angeles in two weeks. I would love to see you.

At the moment, I don't have the urge to write him back. Right now, I don't know where I'll be in two weeks. But I'll figure it out after this weekend.

However, I do think about something else.

Of all the things I should see before a spiritual ceremony, social media is clearly not one. But I just can't help myself because...

Oh my God.

He wrote me again. I never responded to him. Somehow, I was able to hold myself back and New York City messaged again.

New York City: What? No answer?

Me: It's complicated.

I have a silly smile on my face when I shut the phone off. I realize I forgot to take a picture of Pegah. I guess it doesn't matter at this point. I get up and leave the ceremony room with my diaper. I walk into the bathroom and slip it on under the skirt I have on—it's shockingly comfortable—and decide to take a walk outside to clear my head before I drink the medicine.

Grass Valley, California, is pretty epic.

There are redwoods everywhere, and the view from the home we're in is stunningly calming. I sit out by one of the fires they have going and stare out at the scenery. It's so peaceful, but I can't seem to silence my thoughts. I can't stay out here and hide forever because that, I realize, is what I'm doing. I'm good at it. A master, really, of sticking my head in the sand and avoiding real life.

"Why are you out here?"

I look over in surprise at the young girl standing next to me. She's slender and dressed in white and looks exceptionally solemn for someone who can't be older than twelve. But something about her is soothing. I hadn't noticed her before.

"I think I'm hiding," I admit with a nervous laugh.

"From what?" she asks curiously.

Life.

I don't realize I say that out loud until she smiles at me, seeming so wise for her age. I wonder if she's someone's daughter.

"Why are you drinking the medicine?" she asks as she folds her hands behind her back.

"I'm going through a divorce," I tell her, and then, like a freight train filled to the brim with Montezuma's revenge kind of diarrhea, I proceed to unload my life on this poor girl. I don't even know where the words come from. "I was with this guy since I was in high school, and he betrayed me in every which way. But then...I don't know...sometimes I think maybe I asked for it? Maybe I was just a bad person and led him on, believing that was the life I wanted, what I needed to be happy. But I was never happy. At least I don't think I was, because in retrospect, it's all a giant pile of garbage in front of me right now. So, I don't just blame him. I blame myself too. And now I don't know how to forgive myself for wasting so many years of my own life. I *willingly* wasted a lot of my life. And I guess I even wasted his too, right? And I blame myself."

I don't know where this avalanche is coming from.

"And now, I don't know what my life is anymore. Who am I? Who is Ava? And then... I don't know. Something is missing." I say the truth that's been percolating in my heart. "Is it a man? Is it a career that fulfills me? Is it that love I read about when I was a little girl? There's just something missing that's making me want to search. But I don't even know what I'm searching for."

That last part comes out in a whisper.

The girl smiles at me like I'm *not* crazy, which is the shocker of all shockers.

"If you release the thoughts," the girl says like a wise old sage, "you will free your soul. I will pray for you tonight. I will pray for you to fill the part in your heart that *you* think is missing. But there is nothing wrong with you—nothing is missing. It is only your fear of moving into the unknown that is holding you back. What needs to be replenished and fed is the love you have for yourself. You have to fall back in love with Ava before you can find it with any-one else. The only thing holding you back from doing this is fear."

"I'm afraid to love myself?" I ask her in disbelief. Who is this astute child? When did I even tell her my name?

She walks over to me and places a hand on my shoulder.

"You're afraid to accept yourself as the rainbow you are—the good, bad, beautiful, perfectly flawed human that makes Ava. Releasing your fear is how you will find your salvation. In the not knowing. In just living each day and accepting. When you find true love within, you will be able to forgive yourself and your ex-husband and the trauma you created for each other. And then, you'll find the love of your life."

I nod my head, even though I don't fully understand the esoteric advice or what is exactly happening. A child, a girl who can't be older than twelve, is giving me the most sound advice I've ever heard. And in theory, it sounds right. Loving myself is the answer? And what about Darian? I get why I *should forgive him for completely ruining my financial life and cheating on me.* But I'm not superhuman. I'm just a regular woman with a lot of baggage, trying to figure her life out.

She smiles at me like she can see the storm raging inside. "Just *let go* tonight, Ava."

She steps over to me and takes hold of my hand.

"Dios te bendiga," she whispers. *God bless you.*

She walks away into the house. I stare after her for a moment before I head back inside to where Pegah and Jonathan are anxiously awaiting me. I wipe away what's left of my tears.

"Are you okay?" Pegah asks with concern.

"Yes," I say, picking up the roll of toilet paper and ripping some off to blow my nose. "Did you see that little girl?"

"What girl?" Pegah asks as I search for her.

She's nowhere to be found.

"She was outside. I guess she left..."

I lie down on my mat and pull my blanket over my body, taking a moment for myself, processing the fact that I spilled my guts to a child.

"Good evening, everybody," the shaman calls out to the room. "We are about to begin the ceremony."

CHAPTER 12

"THE TAO OF AVA"

Bottoms up, Ava!

I close my eyes and say a silent prayer that I'll come out alive. Then I down the medicine.

It's nasty. Like thick, gross, *nasty*. It's a taste I can't even describe because there's nothing like it—unless you're into chewing on bark and licking dirt. I wonder how I'll be able to keep it down, because we're supposed to hold it in as long as possible.

"God bless you," a stranger says to me as I walk past him.

I give him the best smile I'm capable of at the moment, which isn't much considering I want to vomit in my own mouth, and head back to my mat.

After a few minutes, the taste dissipates. I settle onto the mat and wonder if I'll fall asleep—that would be anticlimactic. I pull my blanket up to my shoulders. After a long while, I realize I'm still waiting for something to happen. I close my eyes and try to bliss out. I must have dozed off because I wake up sometime later to the loud sound of someone throwing up. This doesn't sound normal at all. Not like the regular run-of-the-mill drunky drunk night out, or even food poisoning. This sounds like something is coming from this person's soul. He is not just vomiting liquid or whatever he ate for lunch, he's wailing pain into his bucket. This purge triggers a few more and I keep my eyes squeezed shut and try my hardest not to think about the domino vomit effect that seems to be occurring in the room.

Free your mind, Ava, I tell myself over and over. Don't think about anything.

I'm beginning to have the sinking feeling that the ayahuasca isn't going to work on me. Kind of blows, I guess, but what can I do? Maybe the medicine, or the "Divine Mother," you supposedly see doesn't like me? I guess it's good that I didn't drink any alcohol and ate healthy for a week but *ohmyGod*, how am I going to fall asleep when everyone is just having a kind of vomit session, and oh shit, there goes Pegah too...

I watch my cousin bend over the bucket and start vomiting into it. I want to ask her if she's okay, but we were told we're not allowed to speak or talk to one another during the entire ceremony—something about interfering with your process. Pegah's eyes are closed, and she looks like she's having a moment.

At least it seems like *she's* getting something out of this. That, or she's in some horrendous pain.

I wonder why I haven't thrown up yet. Maybe something is wrong with me. Maybe there's some type of glitch in my DN—

I sit up quickly, dive toward the bucket, and immediately start puking in it.

This is like no other throw up I've ever experienced in my life. It's gut wrenching, like something's being pulled out from my body. I barely even ate today but it won't stop coming.

I open my eyes and cradle the bucket in my hands like it's my lifeline. I will never let it go. This bucket is my friend. No way, no how, am I moving away from it. *OhmyGod*. I can't believe I paid money to feel like this. It's like I willingly walked into a torture camp. The nausea just won't go away. I open my eyes and stare into the bucket as this black tar-ish looking liquid continues to come out of me. I don't even know where it's coming from.

What the hell is happening to me?

I think I need a doctor.

They need to call 9-1-1 for me...

Or an Uber. I need to get out of here.

Holy shit. Is that a vine I see in the bucket? It's a vine…no, it's a picture of a jungle. What's a jungle doing in my bucket? The visual morphs into more greenery. I look to the left and am about to ask for help when I see a giant boa slithering its way toward me.

For a second, I'm mesmerized, but then sanity kicks in. I realize the boa could very well try and bite or eat me because it looks large enough to do just that.

I try to scream out for help, but my voice is trapped. I fall back on my mat and close my eyes and pray. Please God, don't let the boa get me. *Please God,* I'll never ever do anything like this again. God, if you just let me get out of here in one piece, I promise I'll never complain about anything in my life again.

A white light flashes before me and then something shifts.

What is happening to me?

I'm suddenly being transported through space. I have no idea where I'm going but it's like I'm flying on my own through the solar system. The stars and planets are vivid and seem real. A feeling of peace comes over me. I don't know what I'm seeing or what any of it means, but a sense of calm is moving through me, taking away the fear that had engulfed me earlier.

It's going to be all right, Ava, I hear a voice say.

The voice sounds like the girl I met earlier in the night.

Come with me, she says.

Somehow, I'm able to follow the voice. I'm taken through space and time back to my high school, to the moment I first met Darian. It's jarring for a second, and then I'm flooded with a feeling of nostalgia. I see Darian leave a rose and a love note in my locker. He used to do that a lot back then. I remember my friends thought he was so romantic. I see myself find the gift and watch the genuine joy come over my face. I had forgotten how special those little gestures would make me feel.

The scene shifts again, and I watch the moment Darian first kissed me. We were outside the drama classroom, and it was after school. To me, he was the most handsome boy around. I couldn't believe he liked me.

I watch as he steps toward my younger self and then somehow, I'm her—in *her* body—and he's leaning down toward me. The feeling of that moment floods every part of my soul. I am so excited...so enamored.... I can't wait for his lips to touch mine, and when they do, it's perfect. We melt into each other's arms.

That kiss changed the course of my life.

The love I had for him moves through my body and I can feel tears streaming down my face. I see flashes of us in high school laughing, holding hands, waiting for each other after school... sneaking around behind my parents' backs—the excitement of that first love buzzes through my body like an electrical storm.

"Ava," I hear Darian's voice say. "Will you marry me?"

I'm with him in at a hotel in Cabo, and he's so solemn as he says the words. I'm so happy even though I can remember the rollercoaster of emotions that made up our relationship. There was a time when Darian was so safe to me.

Something turns my attention to another place and time. It's years later and I'm in our family room with one of my girlfriends. Darian walks in from work, and I see myself barely saying hello to him, immersed in my girlfriend's problem. Darian is holding flowers and the steak I asked for, but I barely acknowledge him. I see his face fall. I continue ignoring him, and then he kind of shakes his head and walks away.

I'm appalled by my behavior.

The tears really fall now and sobs rack my body. I can feel how hurt he is by the way I ignored him. I can feel it in my soul. I want to yell at my younger self, tell her to get up and kiss him and give him love, but the moment changes again and I see us on vacation.

I'm leaving for the pool and he's still in bed. He wants me to stay with him and fool around, but I want to lay out in the sun. Instead of responding to his gesture of romance, I leave. I see his face when I close the door. It's the kind of look a man has when he feels like he's been massively rejected.

It cuts deep.

I see how my behavior hurt him and I am so sorry for it. So incredibly sorry for it.

I cover my face with my hands and sob like my life depends on it. I am so overcome with emotion and sadness for the moments I was just shown.

But it wasn't all bad.

There was good too. There were moments that were special and loving, moments that made me want to be with him—that made me want to fight for us. And I did love him. And he loved me. And I still feel that love. It's different, but it's there.

Before I know it, I'm pulled away and suddenly have wings, and I'm soaring across the sky. The feeling is exhilarating. I fly for what seems like forever until I come to land in the middle of the jungle. I stand in front of a full-length mirror.

The wings disappear; behind me all the greenery moves and sways in an ethereal way. The colors are so vibrant, they're mesmerizing. I watch as a tiger moves out of the jungle and walks slowly toward me. For some reason, I am not afraid. The tiger sits next to me and I can hear it say, *look at the mirror again. Ava.*

So I do.

And I see myself.

It's like I'm naked, but I'm not. I see my hair. My eyes. Nose. Mouth. The contours of my body. I can even see my heart beating strongly in my chest. Everything becomes more amplified, and a light starts to emanate from me. I'm almost breathless over the beauty I see.

Suddenly in the mirror, I'm staring at the girl I met earlier in the evening.

And I realize she was *me.*

Adult Ava was meeting child Ava. We're both curious, but younger Ava seems so much happier. She seems so free. I've forgotten what it's like to feel that way. To be filled with an endless capacity to love and accept. To find joy in the simple things. To just be happy just because.

I have forgotten.

I want to stay forever in this place of pure love. I want it to exist outside of this space we're in, outside of this ceremony. I want it to manifest into the real world. I never want it to go away. I want to be filled with this feeling forever.

I want to be love.

CHAPTER 13

"HIGHWAY TO HEAVEN"

For two days Pegah and I don't discuss what happened in the aya-huasca ceremony.

There is a lot of silence in her house—minus the birds—as we both process our own spiritual journeys.

The first change I notice about myself is that I'm no longer deathly terrified of Zelda. Rather, when I see her, I feel compassion and love for the animal. Maybe it's the energy I'm giving off or the perma-grin that seems to be glued on my face, but Zelda becomes tranquil around me and has preferred to sit on top of my head instead of Pegah's. A few other birds even join her, and I don't mind. I feel kind of honored.

In some inexplicable way, I understand her. I understand why she shrieks the way she does, and I understand why she's a little angry. I would be too if I was robbed of a life of freedom and sold to a human to possibly live in a cage for a lifetime.

That's one thing ayahuasca has brought me: a connection to the earth. I find myself staring at the nature outside Pegah's house and contemplating how the trees, shrubs, and flowers are truly *alive*. They're not just aesthetic beauty to me anymore; they are sentient beings.

The second change, which is the most profound, is that I don't seem to have any anger left for Darian. None. Even when I think about everything he did—cheating, gambling, *lying*—there is nothing there but a strange understanding, and a sadness that we were unable to make our lives work together. I've shed many tears the past two nights over how the love we had for one another went so awry. The anger that lived there is replaced by sorrow and a strange sort of reconciliation that I can't yet explain. But I'm still not ready to see or speak to him.

The third change hits me in the gut: the way I see myself when I look in the mirror. I see my younger self flashing before me, and what I would usually pick apart is ignored. I only have love for who I am.

"Mind if I join you?" Pegah asks as she sits in the chair across from me.

"Not at all."

We both stare out at the trees that line her property and take it all in.

"It's so beautiful here," I tell her. "You're lucky to have all of this."

"I know." She nods her head. "I realize that. I've taken so much for granted. Even my mom and her annoying pestering of me to get out of the house and find a husband..."

I nod in understanding. It's the same feeling of empathy that has come over me for Darian.

"I'm just emotional." Her tears start. "I'm like this raw wound that's healing. My mind hasn't stopped racing. I've done a lot of dumb things in my life, Ava—and to myself."

"But you can't change anything," I say, then reference the principle in *The Tao of Pooh*, one of my favorite books. "You can only try and flow like the river now."

"I know," she agrees. "I saw the pain I inflicted on myself and it's staggering."

"You're not alone in that department," I share. "I too have been studying the book of Ava. And let me tell you, I've got some greatest hits."

Pegah laughs, then shakes her head. "We just have to work on ourselves every day. I don't think it'll be so easy when we come out of this bubble of bliss that's come over us, because real life never is."

"No," I agree. "Real life never is."

"I'm so sad you're leaving. Zelda's going to miss you."

"Shocker of all shockers…" I admit. "I'm going to miss the little pterodactyl too."

We laugh, and then Pegah asks me, "Are you going to see London soon?"

"When I'm back in LA," I say. "But I feel like it should be something more, you know? I remembered my first encounters with Darian, and I remembered what it felt like to want someone so bad—"

"And London doesn't make you feel that way?"

"It's not that." I try to find the words to explain as best as I can. "Because I *am* attracted to him. But I'm at a different age and it's a different time—and I'm not running into it with that same excitement I initially had with Darian. I don't know…maybe if I see him again it will be different. Maybe I'm overthinking it."

"And what about New York City?" she asks.

I cock a brow and immediately feel my temperature rise.

"Maybe he's a big fantasy. That moment we had could've just been that."

"Maybe." My cousin shrugs. "But fantasies are good for the soul."

A bird's screech makes me look up, and we see two hawks fly across the sky. They move in circles then soar high and land on a tree.

"Are you excited to go see Gia and Will? I think it'll be fun for you out there in Idaho," Pegah says.

"I am, but I'm sad to go."

Pegah takes a sip of her tea and looks out on the horizon.

"The dots always line up the way they're supposed to."

࿔

New York City: What's your number?

I'd be lying if I said his message doesn't affect me. There's something about this man that makes my blood rush—that's always made my blood rush—every single time we've connected. And it's annoying.

Here I am, having just had the most profound spiritual experience of my life, and all I'm doing is obsessing about New York City and when I'll hear from him.

What is the deal with that? Is it a woman thing? Or is it just an Ava thing? My instinct tells me no, this is not just *my* issue—it's one that plagues many women out there. We're all on the same quest, searching for satisfaction, for something that feels right. Hunting for what we know will be our match. For the person that clicks.

For that *perfect* partner.

And the angst and all-consuming thoughts won't stop until we find what it is we're looking for.

I stare at his message for a second longer, then type in my number and press send. Once it's out in the universe, I put my hands to my cheeks and feel myself heat up over the thought of him texting or calling me.

Easy there, girl. He could have changed. He could be a total douche, for all you know.

But I decide I would like to find out. Firsthand.

I click open an app for a diary program I downloaded to be able to jot down notes about my nomadic summer. The notes are all about people, events, or sayings that move me.

Memories I feel like I should hold on to.

Memories that I might memorialize later on my blog...or in a book? Who knows.

I think about my time up north with my cousin, and of course, the ceremony I had.

I think about what came from all those different moments.

I learned that sometimes we willingly walk into a cage of our own design and stay there because it feels comfortable and safe.

I learned that sometimes by saving another person or creature you end up saving yourself.

I learned that a love that fulfills you doesn't have to be the love you feel for a man. It can be for friends, family, or even animals. Maybe even love for yourself.

I learned that I must stop chasing after the next moment and instead, live in this one.

And as Zelda cuddles into my neck and rubs her beak against the very area she took a giant bite out of when I arrived.... I learned that patience is key, and love really can conquer all.

83833
GOZZER RANCH
"GOOSE JUICE"

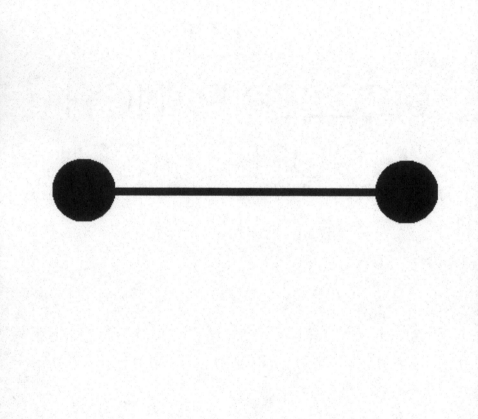

CHAPTER 14

"HUNTERS AND GATHERERS"

"HERE'S YOUR LATTE, AVA." WILL, my girlfriend Gia's handsome husband, literally a dead ringer for Superman, offers me the drink as I sit under a cozy blanket on their expansive veranda and stare out on Coeur d'Alene Lake, in Idaho. The area has become a hotspot for LA natives looking to disappear from the busy city life. With the mountain trees and perfectly manicured lawns and golf course, it's picturesque.

Gia is currently with their seven-year-old son, Daniel, helping him get ready for the day while Will and I catch up on life. Since the day Will and I have met, I've called him my "brother from another mother." He was also friends with Darian, but as with all divorces, people tend to pick sides. Will chose mine.

"Thank you," I say gratefully. "The foam looks perfect."

"I've mastered the skill since being here," he says, sitting on the comfy looking chair across from me.

"This view is everything." I stare out at nature. "I would never leave."

Gia and Will spend their summers here with fellow Angelenos of a certain means, and I don't get out to visit enough.

"You can stay as long as you want," he tells me. "We love having you."

"Well, I love spending time with you guys, so be careful what you put out there," I warn as I take a sip of the latte. "OhmyGod, Will, you could become a barista if the whole uber successful businessman entrepreneur thing ever goes south."

He laughs.

"Wait until you try my pasta tonight. *Then* you'll be impressed with me."

I take another sip of my drink, enjoying the moment.

"Tell me how you're doing, Ava." He turns serious and protective. "Are you and Darian speaking yet?"

When I decided to leave Darian, Will was one of the first people to call and ask twenty questions about my choice. He wanted to make sure I was making the right move and that I was positive I wanted to walk away from all the years Darian and I spent together. He was adamant about me doing a lot of soul searching before I made my final decision.

"Not yet. I'm not ready...but soon."

"We worry about you, Ava."

"I know, but I'm fine. I promise. And I'll be even better. Now tell me how you've all been."

"We can't complain," he says, gesturing out at the scenic view. "What else can we ask for?"

"Nothing, really," I agree.

Gia takes that moment to make her grand entrance and walk outside without their son. In true Gia form, she shakes her thick, long chestnut colored hair and dramatically rolls her almond shaped brown eyes before making her way to me on the couch. She smiles at me in pleasure and as usual, I'm taken aback by her natural beauty. She's a girl's girl and a guy's girl, the kind of woman that is comfortable in any setting and always manages to become the center of attention without even trying.

"The tutor is here, thank God," she says as she gets under the blanket, pulls it up to her neck, and looks over at Will. "That kid is hard."

I laugh.

Gia is one of the funniest people I know, and also the bestie I've known the longest. She's like a sister to me. We met each other in our early twenties and were inseparable. She's Italian, so we have a lot in common with the way we grew up and our families' meddling ways. She's loyal down-to-earth, and funny as hell. She'll have you pee-laughing in no time. She's one of the few people who knows everything about me. I mean, *everything.*

And she's still here.

As couples, we did a lot of traveling together, so she also knows my relationship with Darian very well. I'm sure she saw the many flaws, but being the loyal friend she is, she kept her mouth shut and supported me.

"Before you and Ava become immersed in your catch up, did Daniel eat his breakfast?" Will asks.

"Barely." Gia shrugs like it's not her problem. "He's in a mood. He'd rather hang out with us than do summer school." Gia and Will have Daniel in a summer "get-ahead" program. "Maybe we should let him have the day off?"

"That's not the way school works...he's not ditching like you might have done in Italy."

"He's just a kid." Gia sounds annoyed. "He's got so much homework, and it's the summer. It's insane. I don't remember ever having that much to do."

"That's because you probably didn't do it," Will says knowingly.

I laugh. Luckily, Gia doesn't mind the comment. "Maybe. But it worked out just fine for me."

And it did. Gia is an extremely successful TV personality who's got multiple businesses and juggles them all like a pro. She's always been ambitious and driven, working hard to make all of her dreams come true.

"I'd like our son to finish his homework before he plays," Will says. "The reward comes after the work."

"Fine." Gia rolls her eyes in jest then looks over at me. "How happy are you that you never had a kid with Darian?"

"I am very relieved we never had a child," I agree with a laugh. "That would not be too fun right now."

"No, it would not. Kids are not easy. And add a divorce in there…"

"No, it would not have been fun."

"OhmyGod, I have to show you something." She pulls out her iPhone. "You're going to die."

"What is it?" I'm instantly intrigued.

She swipes through a million different text messages before pulling one up. She studies my face. "Before I show you this, how do you feel about Darian right now on a scale of one to ten? One being you can't remember what he looks like and couldn't care less what he does, and ten being you envision terrible, terrible things happening to him."

"I'm a solid four," I say, without hesitation.

"Then I can show you this." She points to her phone, displaying a screen shot of Darian's new online dating profile. He's smiling at the world and looks quite handsome. It says he's an entrepreneur looking for a companion to travel the world with.

"How did you get this?"

"He matched with Alice." Gia's eyes are wide. I can't tell what she's thinking. "Did you notice anything interesting about the profile?"

I stare down at the screen again. "He spelled entrepreneur wrong."

We both laugh uncontrollably.

"You two." Will shakes his head. "Give the man a break…he made a mistake in his excitement to sign up."

"Let us have this moment," Gia pleads.

"No," Will says. "It's not kind."

"Fine," we both say at the same time. I study Darian's profile picture.

"Is this the new normal?" I ask. "Is he going to start matching with our friends on dating apps?"

"Probably," she says after a while. "What about you…are you on one yet?"

"No," I say, shaking my head. "I can't bring myself to do it. Not after I saw one that had a video montage of pictures to a song by Demi Lovato. I don't even know what my theme song would be."

"Any song by Leonard Cohen."

"That feels super depressing," I say.

Gia gives me an *if the shoe fits* look.

"The good news is that I think there are some great guys up here for you!"

"Ava doesn't need to rush into anything. She's just getting out of a long marriage." Will holds out his hands. "Slow down there, girl. Give her time to adjust to her new life."

"My girl is single and ready to mingle, and *Darian's* been having a good time," Gia retorts.

"I am ready to meet someone, but I don't feel the need to *actively* search for them," I clarify. "But I did meet a guy from London while I was in Marin."

"That's too far," she chides. "You can't move. Your family will never let you."

"I'm a middle-aged woman. I don't think my family can tell me where I can or cannot move."

Even as I say the words, I know they're a lie. My mom can get anyone or anything to do exactly what she wants, and she doesn't even have to try that hard.

"You should see the look on your face." Gia laughs. "You're as scared of your mom as I am of mine, who, by the way, can't wait to talk to you. We'll FaceTime her by the pool later. She has *a lot* to say about your marriage."

"Can't wait." I am expecting a reaction similar to my own mother's. I'm sure it's going to be a lot of swearing about Darian. But I do love both of Gia's parents.

"Should we change and go for a hike?" Will claps his hands together and stands up. "Let's do that, and then we'll get everyone together and go out on the lake."

"Sounds fun," I say. "And very ambitious."

Will walks back inside and Gia grimaces. "He always wants to be active."

I chuckle. "It's healthy."

"Maybe," Gia brushes her long hair away from her face. "Ava, I need to hear everything. And I want to know all about the London guy."

"Oh, I'll tell you everything. Promise. There might even be an ayahuasca story mixed into all the craziness...."

CHAPTER 15

"MOOSE MUNCH"

AN HOUR AND A HALF later, Gia, Will, and I are on what I now believe is the hike from hell.

What started off as an easy, breezy, beautiful nature walk has turned into an episode of *The Amazing Race*. Will is so fit that sometimes I think he forgets that the rest of the normal human population can't walk ten miles in a day, and if they try, they might very well fall over and die. Gia and I trail far behind him on our trek up what seems to be Mt. Everest. I'm grateful I'm not the only one struggling.

"I can't do it," I say to her as my breath comes out in gasps.

At that exact time, Will calls out, "Come on! You two are walking like little old ladies!"

Now I know he really is Superman.

"Just leave me here," I whimper, panting as I look around at the trees and shrubs, "and think of me fondly."

"He's like the energizer bunny." Gia shakes her head at me.

"Do you walk like this every day?"

"Yes," she says. "I mean, not this exact walk, different kinds of exercise but the same type of exertion."

"Then why are you struggling?" I wonder. "You should be good to go. This should be a walk in the freaking park for you."

"I go at my own pace, and sometimes...okay most of the time, he finishes before me and just turns around and meets me, so I don't have to complete the trail with him," she admits.

"I don't think I can do this every day." I'm so out of breath.

"You know there is no way he'll let you skip. It's all for one, and one for all. Always."

"With everything?"

"Yes," she says. "We do it as a family or we don't do it at all. That's a William Rutherford motto. We do everything together."

"Lord."

"Annoying," she returns in humor, but I know she doesn't mean it because I see a soft smile come over her as she stares out at Will.

"Looking good, Rutherford!" she calls out to him, pulling out her iPhone to take a picture.

"I spy the look of love," I proclaim, grinning.

"What can I say? Him and Daniel are my guys. I want to be with them all the time. I'm kind of addicted."

She's not lying. Over the years, Gia has never been one to take a girl's trip or leave Will for any extended period for work. Even before Daniel, they've always been a unit, doing everything together or not at all.

Will suddenly stops and turns toward us. He motions in silence for us to hurry but to do so quietly.

My eyes widen in fear. "It's not a bear, is it?"

"If it was a bear, he'd tell us to turn around," Gia says.

It takes us a minute to reach Will's side, and the second we do, the torturous hike is worth every painful step. Will points at a clearing with a small lake. There's a giant moose drinking from the water along with two of her babies. The sun shining on the water makes it sparkle. It's nature in its purest form and everything about it is spectacular.

"Wow," is the only profound word I can manage.

"Aren't moose dangerous?" Gia sounds worried.

"We're keeping our distance." Will uses his soothing voice.

"Are you sure?" my friend persists, and I giggle as quietly as possible.

"What are you laughing at?" she asks me.

"You're a total chickenshit," I say. "You're legit afraid of a moose?"

"Look at the antlers on that thing." She points at it. "What if it charges us? They look hungry."

"They are herbivores, honey," Will says with a laugh.

"Hungry animals do desperate things," Gia insists, then narrows her eyes at me. "You're just as scared as I am."

"Not really," I say. The moose takes that moment to look over at us, and she's definitely checking us out.

"Oh shit, Will." Gia's voice is shaking. "She's staring at us. I'm getting out of here."

I'm definitely going to do the same, but I don't want to be as dramatic about it as Gia, considering I just declared my fearless attitude to both of them.

"Ladies." Will shakes his head in disappointment. "Let's take in the moment right now. This is incredible. Look at her babies. This is the beauty of Mother Nature. I wish Daniel was with us to see this. We'll have to bring him up here tomorrow."

"Take a picture for him and let's go," Gia says as she slowly begins to back up. "That moose is making eye contact with me."

Will reaches out his hand to her.

"Stay for a second, honey," he pleads. "You know I would never let anything happen to you. Or to Ava."

For a second, I think Gia might reject him, but after a moment, she reluctantly gives him her hand. "Fine," she mutters.

He pulls her up against his body and plants a kiss on top of her head. "Isn't it beautiful, Gia?"

"I guess," she grumbles like she's annoyed, but from the look on her face, I know she's appreciating what she sees. She moves into Will some more.

The intimate moment makes me smile. There's something great about watching happy couples. It makes you hope that it can happen to you too.

Gia extends her arm and I move in so I can cuddle up to her side.

"We're like *Three's Company*." I laugh, but the moment is great in every single way.

"How are you doing over there, Ava?" Will asks considerately.

"Pretty perfect."

CHAPTER 16

"SAD MONA LISA"

GIA CALLS HER MOM ON Facetime to surprise her.

We're laying out at the club pool while Daniel plays tennis. After letting loose in Italian for a few minutes on Gia, the first words out of her mouth were—

"I never trusted him!" she yells with her thick, Italian accent.

"You sound like my mom," I say.

"Your mom is right!" She speaks both English and Italian to me, even though she knows I can't understand a word of what she says in the foreign language. She happens to be as funny as Gia. Maybe funnier.

But I would never tell my best friend that.

She turns to Gia and lets loose again. I think she's cursing Darian up and down a storm, because I hear her call out his name a few times and Gia is laughing like a loon.

"My mom says," Gia finally tells me, "she wasn't happy with him at your wedding. She didn't think it was right that he went home to sleep at his mom's house."

I burst out laughing. I had forgotten about that. Darian slept over at his mom's house the night of our wedding instead of wanting to be with me; we were leaving on our honeymoon the following day and he wanted to spend time with her before we left. I hadn't thought twice about it, but it must have looked very strange to the outside world.

"I guess that should have been a sign." I nod my head at her mom.

This prompts her to spit out another monologue in Italian.

"Mama," Gia says. "We get it. You're mad at him too."

"You're gonna find a good man," her mom says to me. "One who deserves you."

"I hope so, though I'm not in a rush."

"You have to be!" she yells back, and shakes her head vigorously. "You're not getting any younger."

You have to laugh. So Gia and I do. We fall over, we laugh. You gotta hand it to the mamas from the old world—they do know how to make you feel good about yourself.

"I thought you could find love at any age?"

"No!" Gia's mom screams this out as she moves her hands around in annoyance. "No. No. No. You have to move fast. Men like younger women."

"I'm officially dead," Gia says. "Mama, come on. Ava's a catch and she still looks great. She'll find someone."

"Yes, she is a good girl, but she has to be quick before the wrinkles start to show," her mom lectures. "Are there any boys out there for her?"

It's official. All moms from the old world have one common goal for the women in their lives—to see them married off.

"Matthew arrived with some friends today," Gia says as she looks over at me. "I think there are some singles in the mix."

"Make sure she looks good," her mom orders. "And that she smiles."

"I'll make sure, Mama," Gia promises, and I know it's costing her everything to try and keep a straight face.

Gia hangs up with her mom a second later and we burst out laughing.

"Who knew she felt that way about Darian?" Gia looks at me.

"That was a serious opinion," I return in awe. "I can't believe she was able to hold it in for so many years."

"To be honest, neither can I. My mom loves you, so I think she just wanted to keep her mouth shut and not rock the boat. But she did always tell me that you looked like a sad Mona Lisa."

"She did not!" I scream out. "My mom said the exact same thing!"

"It must be some old-world analogy," Gia shrugs.

"I guess," I return. "I'll never look at that painting the same again."

"I'll definitely be picturing you from now on."

"Rude."

"You love me," she says.

"Maybe."

Her friend, Brianna, that I just met before we settled into our lounge chairs, walks toward us in her barely-there bikini. Gia and I both stare, and I know we're thinking the exact same thing.

"Her body is sick." I'm the first one to say the words.

"Legit," Gia agrees.

"Hiieeee!" She waves at us. "What're you gals doing?"

Brianna is that all-American girl with blonde hair and blue eyes and playmate body that is enviable. I have the sudden urge to cover mine up with a towel.

"Just talking to my mom," Gia says.

"Oh." She cocks her head to the side. "I love her. She's so *Italian*."

"She *is* Italian," Gia says.

"I know! So, what are your plans for the rest of the day?" she asks us. "Are you going to sit out here and lounge around or go out on the lake?"

"We were supposed to go out on the lake," Gia tells her, "but we took a long hike this morning and are exhausted, so I think we're going to save the water sports for tomorrow. Will wants us to golf though."

I look over at her.

"I'm only familiar with miniature golf," I warn.

"I suck at it too." She waves me off. "But it's fun to drink wine on the golf carts and drive around and watch the guys play."

"I'll just have to trust you."

"This is kind of perfect!" Brianna exclaims. "Because I have a surprise for you gals."

"What's that?" Gia asks.

"I made my famous batch of goose juice," she explains. "And it's been soaking up the goodness for eleven days now."

"Goose juice?" I wonder out loud. "Sounds Grey Goose-y?"

They both laugh.

"It is, and then some," Brianna says. "Trust me. You've never had anything like it—it's so good it's dangerous. I think we should head over to my place on my golf cart and have some. Let's party!"

Brianna sounds positively titillated by this possibility.

I look at the time. "I guess it *is* five o'clock somewhere...."

Gia ponders it for a second or two then agrees. "I'll let Will know where we're going. We can meet up with him and the guys on the golf course. He wants to celebrate your arrival, so he booked us a special dinner tonight at the club."

"He's the best," I say happily.

"Yay!" Brianna jumps up and down in delight. "Ava's going to love goose juice!"

⌘

Three cups in and I'm definitely a fan of goose juice.

Brianna's special brew is a concoction of Grey Goose infused with berries and pineapple. It's so sweet it tastes like candy, which is why the drink is highly deceptive. Gia and I have helped ourselves to the goose juice, and to everything we could find in Brianna's pantry. We are the no shame sisters.

"I feel like I'm buzzed," I say, stating the obvious out loud.

"You are," Gia agrees. "And so am I."

"Did you text Will and tell him?"

"Hell no. He'll see us when we meet him out on the golf course in twenty. He'll get the picture."

Gia and I proceed to take a million terrible drunken pictures of ourselves before Brianna interrupts our photoshoot with what seems to be the phone call from hell.

"Ugh!" Brianna screams into the phone. "You are such a loser, Zack!"

It's like that moment when the music scratches in the club and all eyes turn to the one who dared turn the fun dial down. Gia and I glance at each other before we stare at a rather drunk Brianna, who puts the call on speaker.

"Stop spending my money!" Zack screams back at her.

She looks over at us and points at the phone like it's possessed. I think if she was sober, she wouldn't want us to hear this.

"I only spend as much on myself as you spend on your mistresses!" she rages back at him, then gives us both that bitter smile.

I'm too afraid to even look over at Gia.

"You spent twenty-five thousand dollars on one Amex card last month!" Zack is so loud that I'm sure the neighbors can hear. "On one! I'm afraid to look at the other accounts!"

"And?" Brianna slurs into the phone. "That's what's due to me after having to spend the last ten years sucking on your small little cock!"

Gia grabs hold of my arm and squeezes. I look at her. We are both wide eyed and riveted. I know it's not funny, but then again, it kind of is.

"I've had to lick your tiny dick and your miniscule low hanging balls," she says, going on a rampage. "Do you have any idea how that makes me feel?"

"Your pussy is as wide as a freight train!" Zack yells back at her.

Gia squeezes my arm harder.

"A real man could keep me satisfied!" Brianna rants on, totally unaffected by his insult. "Those poor women who have to pretend like you're pleasuring them just so you'll buy them a cheap pair of Gucci flip-flops."

"Are you forgetting the way we met, dear?" He screeches. "One-eight-hundred-dial-a-hooker. I should have realized what I was getting since your price was so low."

Oh. My. God.

Now I am officially dead.

"Screw you," Brianna retorts. She doesn't seem bothered that she was outed at all. She looks over at us and points at the phone like he's the crazy one.

"Trust me, you'll be doing that tonight when I arrive," Zack promises.

And just like that, Brianna changes her tune.

"Oh baby," she says, sounding sultry. "I can't wait to see you and give it to you so good you'll forget what planet you're on."

It must be the goose juice because I don't understand what is going on. How in the world did the conversation go from one extreme to another? Is this their weird version of foreplay?

"I land at ten," he promises. "Be ready and naked in bed."

"Promise." She kisses the phone for good measure. When she hangs up, she looks over at us and smiles.

"I love my boo."

CHAPTER 17

"DRUNK 'N LOVE"

BRIANNA BOUNCES OFF TO USE the bathroom, and Gia and I stare after her in silence.

"Am I drunk, or did that just happen exactly like I think it did?" I ask out loud.

"You are drunk, but it did," she confirms. "Every single second of it."

I look over at her and take a sip of my goose juice. "Is that normal for them?"

"Yes. They have the craziest fights and then suddenly turn it off and want to bang each other after hurling the most insulting things you could imagine at one another. It's unlike anything I've ever seen."

"Well, I don't need to imagine," I point out. "I just saw and heard firsthand. And if you had told me that story, I never *ever* would have believed you."

"No, I guess you wouldn't have," Gia agrees and takes a sip of her drink. "That's what I like to call the crazy kind of love."

"Would you even call that love?" I wonder.

"It seems to work for them," Gia says. "Even though Zack has that perpetual angry look on his face whenever he stares at her, he's sticking around for something."

"Unreal" is the only word I can manage.

Even in our ugliest moments of fighting, Darian and I never spoke to each other in such a disrespectful way. I've never been a fan of hurling insults that you'll probably regret later; it's never been my style.

"I guess that's a different kind of marriage," I say. "And a different kind of foreplay."

"Sure is." Gia takes another giant sip of her drink and then we both laugh.

Brianna must turn the music on because Dua Lipa is suddenly blasting through her home and I immediately start to dance. Gia picks up her cell phone and starts taking videos.

"Are we going out in public?" I ask Gia over the blaring music.

I don't even mind that she's filming me. Since she's cackling hysterically to herself, I'm going to assume my dance moves are not that great.

"Give me some belly dancing moves," Gia urges me. "We can put this on your dating profile later so the men can see how well you shake your hips."

"Not going to happen," I say, but four seconds later, I'm doing just that. I blame the goose juice.

We dance around Brianna's kitchen island. And then, one by one, genius ideas start to come to us. First, we FaceTime a few hundred of our friends to let them know how much fun we're having and, of course, for them to see us in our extraordinarily drunken state. I am pretty sure we will regret many of these calls when we sober up, but right now, it feels good.

Next, we have even more goose juice, and Gia decides that she needs to do my makeup. She makes Brianna bring out all her cosmetics and my friend starts to paint my face.

"You look so sexy," Gia slurs at me.

"But you can't see well," I remind her with a laugh. "Don't make me look like a clown."

"I'm a TV personality!" she yells at me, sounding somewhat offended. "I know how to apply makeup."

"Let me get Ava one of my little sundresses." Brianna claps her hands together in excitement. "I have one that I know will look *so* good on her!"

Since Brianna happens to be wearing a skimpy sundress that shows more than an ample amount of cleavage and bum, I start to wonder.

"I am *not* walking around this place with my ass out," I warn Gia.

"Live a little, Ava!" she urges me, like it's no big deal. "You've got to meet a guy. And stop moving around, I'm not done applying this eyeliner."

"I'm scared," I whisper to her. "This feels like a lot of makeup."

"You'll love it," she promises.

Brianna returns with a white sundress that looks like dental floss. It's about two feet by two feet and there are a lot of strings and holes.

"Is that underwear?" I ask.

"I'd call it underwear adjacent," Gia says as she laughs hysterically.

"It's a dress." Brianna hands it to me. "The last time I wore it, I drove Zack crazy. Go put it on."

I stare at it for a long moment and then I kind of shrug. What the hell? Conservative dressing Ava is about to become hoochie Ava.

"I'll be back."

Five minutes later I'm staring at a complete stranger in the mirror. I don't know if I look more like Robert Smith from the Cure or a sultry vixen, but I decide to just go with it. Ava has left the building and in her place is her hussy doppelganger raring to go with makeup and a white sundress that dips down to her navel, barely covers her ass and is open in the back with strings hanging down. This is a whole new me.

"Come out!" Gia demands before walking right into the bathroom. "Holy. Shit. Look at you, girl. Sexy mama."

I cover my breasts.

COLET ABEDI

"I feel naked," I tell her.

"Let's have another drink," Gia urges. "You'll feel better after that."

She's not wrong.

Another cup of goose juice and I'm feeling comfortable with my new look. I even feel like I should take a picture for my Facebook profile...New York City could see!

"Will's texting us," Gia says as she looks down at her phone. "We need to go and meet him out at hole seven."

"Sounds like a plan," I agree. "Should we take a roadie?"

"The correct answer is no," Gia says pointedly. "But I'm going to give us a pass this one time and say yes, we need one."

We fill up our cups with even more goose juice and head out of Brianna's place. She promises to join us soon, but I have a feeling she's going to sleep the drinks off and get ready for her sex-a-thon with Zack. I come to this deduction after she admits he likes to be tied up and whipped, so she wants to get the room ready.

"She's like the real-life *Fifty Shades of Grey*," I say with a giggle to Gia as she drives the golf cart.

"She's fifty shades of something..."

"Are they happy together? I mean...that was all kinds of crazy town."

Gia shrugs.

"It seems like they are," she says. "She doesn't look like she cries herself to sleep, but then she has his money to comfort her, and she clearly knows how to spend it."

"I don't know if I would want a relationship like that. Even with all the money in the world, it seems too volatile."

"No. That's definitely not something for you or your delicate sensibility."

We laugh.

"I wouldn't survive that for a day," I say knowingly.

"Neither would I," Gia concurs. "But to each his own. I've learned something by spending our summers here and watching all these couples—everyone has their own deal. Their own rhythm. And some of them work well, even though you'd think it would be the opposite. You just have to find whatever floats your boat."

CHAPTER 18

"CALL ME TIGER"

SOMEHOW GIA AND I FIND Will on the golf course.

Honestly, I don't know how it happened because we're both pretty loopy. Not to mention busy scream-singing old school songs that Gia keeps playing on her speaker. She even played "Please Don't Go Girl" by New Kids on the Block. That almost brought me to tears. Happy ones. Right now, it's, "Crash Into Me" from Dave Matthews and I'm singing it like I'm auditioning for *The Voice*.

We pull up on the golf course and there is a group of guys huddled around, talking. No one looks that serious about the game. It's like they're using it to congregate and *bro-out*. Gia and I tumble out of the small vehicle. I try to sober up considering I'm basically wearing cheap looking lingerie and should at least sound respectable. Luckily, I had the wherewithal to keep my bathing suit bottoms on underneath. But still. It's definitely a ho-ho-ho kind of situation.

Gia makes her way over to Will as gracefully as possible. Even in my state, I can tell he's aghast by what he sees.

"Hey, babe." She kisses him on the cheek...or at least tries to. She giggles at him. He doesn't look so amused.

He narrows his eyes. "Did you goose it up with Brianna?"

"We did." Gia turns and points at me. "And we gave Ava a makeover."

Will takes in my new look for a long moment. He doesn't seem too impressed. Five seconds later I can confirm my suspicion.

"You turned her from a pretty, wholesome lady, into a woman of the night!" Will holds his hands up in shock. "No offense, Ava."

"None taken." I can't say I disagree. "Totally get where you're coming from."

"Brianna gave her the dress." Gia leans over and laughs uncontrollably.

"Are you okay to drive the cart?" Will looks into Gia's eyes. "You smell like a liquor shop."

"It's Brianna's fault," Gia explains. "That was some serious goose juice."

"Did you shower in it?" he asks.

"Pretty much." We both say this at the same time.

"Should you both go sober up at home for our dinner tonight?" Will continues, like a protective dad. "It might do you some good... and then Ava will be able to wash her face."

"Honey!" Gia gasps, but is still laughing. "I'm offended. I think I did a great job."

"Hey, Ava!" Gia's good friend from work, Matthew, comes over. He checks out my new getup. I feel like he has the same opinion as Will. "Looking...good."

I smile awkwardly and hug and kiss him hello on the cheek.

"Gia did this." I hope I don't sound too drunk, because I definitely am. Times three.

"Nice." Matthew looks over at Gia with wide eyes. "On purpose?"

"Yes!" I tell him.

"Well, I want to introduce you to my friend, Ryder," Matthew says to my horror. Meet a man? Looking like this? And highly tipsy? Before I can ask him to wait, he calls out to his mysterious friend with a hot name.

Ten seconds later, a tall, built, dark-haired gentleman walks over to us. I try to pull my dress down to cover up more of my legs and rear end, but it's completely impossible. I am going to have to own this.

Up close, Ryder lives up to his hot name. He's got that perfectly chiseled, rugged look. His eyes are piercing, a startling bright blue against a tanned face. There's something about him that makes me think he's an East Coast type. One who grew up playing rugby, or was captain of the crew team in the ivy league school he attended.

Yes, I deduced all of this from one look. What can I say...I have an active imagination.

He smiles politely at me, making sure to keep his eyes on mine instead of the various naked areas of my body. There's a lot he can choose from, so I give him credit.

"I'm Ryder," he tells me, reaching out his hand.

"I'm Ava," I return.

Our hands meet and eyes lock and I admit I'm interested.

"Nice to meet you." With that accent, he's definitely from the East Coast.

"You too," I say, and look over at Matthew, who's glancing at the two of us with a knowing grin.

"Gia just gave Ava a makeover," Matthew says, almost like he's trying to explain why I look the way I do.

"You look beautiful." Ryder clearly grew up with manners.

"Thanks." I know I sound awkward, but I can't help it. I'm feeling super vulnerable here—drunk, practically naked, and wearing full hooker makeup.

"When did you get in?" Ryder asks me.

"Late last night," I say. "And you?"

"A few hours ago," he says with a smile. "My first time here and I'm already loving it."

"There's a lot to love."

"Do you play golf?" Ryder continues the questions.

"Some." I decide to lie. I don't know why I lie because I've only hit a golf ball three, maybe four times in my life. But I know I am good at miniature golf, which is almost the same thing. *Right?*

"Do you want to hit this round for me?" Ryder's smile is infectious. "I'm up next and I'm happy to let a beautiful woman take my turn."

"You don't have to!" I quickly rush out. "I can hit another time. I'm a bit rusty."

Understatement of the century.

"Come on," he teases. "It'll be fun."

"Just hit one, Ava," Matthew encourages to my horror. "I feel like I've seen you hit a few balls before. You're decent, right?"

"Of course."

Lie. But then I think, honestly, how hard can it be?

"Come on, then," Ryder encourages, and I find myself following him out to the putting green.

Will and Gia watch me with wide eyes. I look over at my girlfriend and she gives a subtle nod in Ryder's direction. I know her well enough to know what the secret signal means—she's telling me he's cute and looks good and she knows I think the same.

When we reach the area, Ryder runs over to his golf cart and pulls out a few clubs. I'm guessing he's trying to see which would be the right fit for me.

"I think this will work," he says and hands me a club.

Honestly, I have no idea what the difference is between the clubs.

"How does it feel?" he asks when I take hold of it.

"Like a golf club should?" I say. This makes him laugh. He takes a step back and encourages me to go.

"Show us what you got!" he orders, like an excited coach.

"Go for it, Ava!" Gia shouts out in glee, and I know, I just *know* if I turn and look, I'll see her filming this moment to memorialize it forever. This will be part of her *best of Ava* reel. There are already some real gems on that album—just from today.

It's unfortunate that she calls out to me, because suddenly silence falls over the entire group. They all stop to watch me take my shot. I think back to the last time I tried my hand at this with an instructor in Mexico. What advice did he give me?

You got this, Ava, I think to myself.

The alcohol has fried all my brain cells, because I can't remember even one nugget of wisdom. So instead of a professional instructor's advice, I think back to all the times I played miniature golf in high school. I was good at it. Sort of. I *know* I was incredible at ski ball—no, it's not the same thing, but it's the same idea of putting a ball in a hole.

I stare down at the golf ball and focus, trying my best to drown out the silence and pretend no one is watching me. I think about how I was able to clear my mind in my ayahuasca session. If could do that there, how hard can *this* be? I take a small swing once, aiming for the ball, just to make sure I'm going to hit it. Then again, for good measure. I feel like this is what a professional would do. Finally, I swing with all my might and go for it, thinking—what's there to lose?

Apparently, the club.

CHAPTER 19

"GOAT"

THAT'S RIGHT, I DON'T JUST swing hard—I swing and *throw* hard.

The club goes flying out of my hands. And it flies far. I'm impressed I gathered that much velocity behind my swing.

I look down and notice how the golf ball is still sitting right there on the tee, exactly where Ryder put it. Then I hear a loud snort and I know it's Gia. I look over at her and she's bent over to the side, laughing her ass off and yes, holding onto her iPhone. Since I can't bring myself to look at Ryder, and it *is* funny, I join in as well.

After a long while, Ryder reaches out to help me up.

"I am so sorry about your club," I tell him, and rub the tears away from my face. I hope I don't smear my makeup—but I'm pretty sure what's happening on my face is a lost cause.

"Chris went to find it. I've never seen anything like that before. That's one for the books. I'm impressed."

"Stick with me and you'll be bombarded with all sorts of tricks like that." I smile in embarrassment.

"I can't wait to see what else you have in store," Ryder flirts.

"Be afraid," I warn.

Gia and Will walk over to us and they're both shaking with laughter.

"I caught it on camera," Gia tells me.

"I noticed," I say. "I'm never going to live that down, am I?"

Will shakes his head. "No. Definitely not."

"I think we should go back to the house and freshen up for dinner." Gia throws me a bone. "Since Will's planned a special night for us."

"Totally," I agree, simply wanting to get out of there, wash my face, and pretend like this whole situation never happened.

I glance at Ryder and he's observing me with a small smile on his face. It's like he thinks I'm cute. Or funny. Maybe a combination of both.

"Looking forward to seeing you again, Ava," he says to me. "Maybe I can give you a private lesson while we're here. I can give you a few pointers."

"If you're not too worried about losing more clubs." I can feel myself blush.

"I think I'll be all right."

"You must be brave."

"And willing." His look is slightly intense.

"To?" I raise a brow.

"See."

*

Gia and I go back to her place to sober up for Will's dinner. Once I'm in my room, I shower and scrub my face clean. I'm happy when I see the old Ava again. I guess she's not so bad. I slip on my pajamas, jump into bed, and think about Ryder. He is definitely hot. And confident. A lethal combination for me—for any woman, for that matter. I reach over to the nightstand and grab my phone. There's a text message from a number I don't recognize.

Lord almighty.

New. York. City.

My heart leaps out of my chest. I immediately feel nauseous.

> **New York City:** I'm going to be out in LA in a few weeks. I would love to see you for dinner to catch up.

He wants to see me.

In a few weeks.

That's fast. I feel a stupid smile creep up of its own accord. Since I'm still pretty buzzed and have proven to have no inhibitions where he's concerned, I write back immediately.

> **Me:** I would love to. I'm in Idaho now.

I put my phone down. It pings. I'm surprised he writes back so quickly. But I'm not going to lie, it does give me a rush.

> **New York City:** What are you doing in Idaho?

> **Me:** Visiting friends.

> **New York City:** Send me a picture.

Bold. *Very* bold. But I answer his request by sending him a scenic picture I took this morning from our hike.

> **New York City:** Gorgeous. But I want one with you in it.

My heart slams in my chest. Who does this guy think he is? I kind of like it.

> **Me:** Presumptuous.

> **New York City:** Always.

> **Me:** I'm not sending you my picture. You'll have to wait to see me at dinner.

I have a goofy smile on my face now. How does a guy I haven't seen in years even do this to me? *And what is this?*

> **New York City:** You're going to make me wait.

> **Me:** Yes.

And then, because I can...

Me: And you're still in a complicated relationship.

He takes a moment to respond to this text.

New York City: It's over.

Me: But?

New York City: I'll explain at dinner. Any food pre-ferences?

Me: None.

New York City: Then I'll pick. I'm looking forward to seeing you, Ava.

Me: Me too.

He sends me a heart emoji and it makes me spin. Does this mean that he's into me? He must be, right? Yes, I tell myself, *this* who you become after having zero dating experience.

And then it dawns on me...

OhmyGod. I'm going to see New York City. I'm going to see him in person and not just stare at his social media posts, wonder-ing about his life...after how many years? It starts to sink in. Before I can obsess about it or call my sister, Layla, and let her in on the news, I thankfully fall into a drunken slumber.

☙

Will really went all-out for dinner.

He booked us a private table at the club with our own chef, saying he wanted to do something special for my visit. Will's always been super caring like this. It's in his DNA. Gia lucked out in the husband department, because this guy is even incredible to her friends.

We're sitting outside at a table that overlooks the lake, enjoying the ambience. Will interrupts the quiet moment.

"Honey, if you don't mind," he says. "I'd like to check in with you."

Gia looks over at her husband and cocks a brow. She seems surprised. "Yes?"

He takes a second to mull his words over before he speaks.

"Do you think having a gallon of goose juice was such a good idea on a Tuesday afternoon, when we have our son to think about?"

I wasn't expecting that. I don't think Gia was either. I giggle into my napkin when I check out the look on her face.

"It was Brianna's fault," Gia responds innocently.

"Did she force you to drink that excessively?" Will asks.

"No. But she was *very* persistent."

"She was," I chime in, defending our booze fest. "And that stuff is lethal. It works fast and is very deceiving."

"So is Brianna." Gia helps herself to some of the bread on the table. She dips it into the olive oil with gusto.

"I get it. I just felt like I needed to check in with you." Will doesn't sound annoyed or angry, just matter of fact. "That's all."

"I hear you, Rutherford," my friend grumbles. "Point taken."

"Thank you." Will reaches out, takes her hand, and kisses it.

I study them for a moment. The energy around them is calm and loving. Sadly, I don't believe Darian and I ever exhibited these qualities together. We were always tense—like waiting for a bomb to go off—especially in the last few years of our marriage.

I can see now that we were never in sync.

It's a wonder we lasted so long.

CHAPTER 20

"NO RESERVATION"

"Do you two do this a lot?" I ask. "Check in with each other?"

"All the time," Gia says.

"I don't think I've ever seen it happen before."

"It's our way of making sure we never hurt each other or do something inconsiderate," Will explains.

"This way we don't hold any grudges," Gia says.

"Or fight," Will finishes.

Huh. Come to think about it, they are one of the only couples I've never seen fight. They've had funny arguments in front of me before, but nothing significant. Is this why?

"It's a great idea," I say.

"It works for us," Will says. "But everyone has to find their own rhythm."

"Seeing is believing." I smile at them and help myself to a piece of shrimp from the paella.

"How do you like the food?" Will asks as I fill my fork.

"Delicious," I say. "This is my second or third plate. I've lost track, I've eaten so much."

The private chef made us paella and various other appetizers that have been equally amazing. Since Gia and I have sobered up and I'm now dressed in my normal clothes, I feel a lot better about things.

"So, what's going on with work, Ava?" Will asks.

"I'm figuring it out. I think I'm going to get my blog going again."

"That's a great idea. I'm assuming you're going to tell your audience about your marriage?"

"Yes...it'll have to become the single girl's travel blog."

"That feels better," Gia says. "And you'll have more fun."

"I won't take that personally." Will laughs. "Is there anything else you see yourself doing?"

"I don't know." I shrug then make a joke. "Write a book about my divorce?"

Gia's contemplating my words.

"I'd read it," she says pensively. "Cover to cover."

"I would too," Will agrees. "And I'm not into chick lit."

"Awesome. I have two sales already. And I definitely have some other friends and family that would be more than willing to take a look."

"Darian would die," Gia says after a moment.

"Totally," I agree.

"But do we care what he thinks?" she asks me.

The scene I saw in my ayahuasca session flashes before me. The one of Darian arriving home and being hurt by me ignoring him. Where there was anger for him before, I only feel sadness and some remorse for my role in hurting him.

"Yes." I sigh. "Despite it all, I wouldn't want to devastate him."

"That's a new attitude you've got going for you." Gia seems impressed. "A month ago, you couldn't find a nice thing to say about him. You think it's just a time thing?"

"I think I'm starting to accept my part in the demise of our marriage," I admit ruefully. "He wasn't perfect by any means, but neither was I."

"Ava, I'm impressed." Will leans back in his chair and crosses his arms. "That's very adult of you."

"If the shoe fits..." I laugh.

"No," Will says. "In most of the divorces we've seen, people can't get over the pain and anger and just want to place blame on the other party."

"Look, I was there too. And like Gia said, a month ago, all I wanted to do was blame him for everything. But as time goes by, I'm seeing things in a different light. I realize that everything in our marriage wasn't all bad."

"No, it wasn't, and I'm proud of you for admitting this." Gia smiles. "There were a lot of good moments and we shared some of those with you. Think about all the fun we had on the trips we took together. Those were some good times."

"Yes, they were." I'm hit with a wave of nostalgia as I think back to all the times we traveled together. There were so many laughs. "But let's be honest, a lot of the time it was just me hanging with you guys while Darian was on his computer or in the room."

"True," Gia admits.

"It's all in the past now. And I'm sure he's doing some soul searching of his own. Let's make a toast to new memories," Will says as he lifts his wine glass. Gia and I are still nursing water.

"Here's one right now," I say gratefully. "Thank you for having me."

"Of course," Gia says. "You're family. We'll always be here for you."

"Now tell us about the ayahuasca." Will commands with fascination.

I tell them the whole story about my night of embarrassment and enlightenment.

"I don't think it's for everyone. But what can I say? Desperate times..."

"Desperate measures?" Gia laughs.

"I'm definitely desperate for something." I chuckle. "I just don't know what that something is yet."

"You'll know when you find it," Gia says. "And I think the more you obsess about it, the more you'll spin. Look at you now. Honestly, I've never seen you look better—there's something different about you, an energy that didn't exist before. Just see where the journey takes you."

"When did you become the Dalai Gia?"

"You know me." She winks in my direction. "I've always got a few tricks up my sleeve."

"I can see that."

"And you also know I don't take anything too seriously. And I don't allow negativity to enter my orbit."

That is the truth. Gia has never let anything or anyone take her down. She is fierce like that and forged in fire. Over the years, she's taught me to be stronger and to not let the little things get to me. Her attitude is one I wish I could always emulate.

"I'm working on it. But it's not easy."

"You do you, Ava," she says softly. "As long as you know you're doing your best, that's all that matters. Everything else is just noise."

CHAPTER 21

"MORE THAN AYAHUASCA"

"I LOVE CHEATING IN MY mind," Brianna tells me as she takes a giant gulp of rosé out of her two-year-old's sippy cup. "That imagination stuff is legal as fuck."

I look over at Gia to gauge her reaction, but her face gives nothing away. She's a statue and I'm impressed.

Meanwhile, I'm still trying to come to terms with the fact that Brianna is a mother to three children under the age of five. Thankfully, they were nowhere to be seen yesterday when we were indulging in goose juice—I guess they must've been with the nanny.

I've also had the pleasure of meeting Zack. He's not at all what I'd pictured for Brianna. He's older and about five foot three, a good two heads shorter than his wife.

We're currently on Gia and Will's boat on the lake with Daniel for a day of water sports. Brianna and a couple of other women have joined us for wine and to watch the guys wake surf. The nannies are all on kid duty. Ryder is part of our crew but is on Matthew's boat partaking in a healthy competition they've decided upon. From what I've seen, he's pretty good at all the activities so far, which is another notch on the hot factor belt.

"Honey!" Brianna screams out to Zack. He's slathered in sunscreen and has on a Cuban hat that I personally don't find to be a good look for him, but who am I to judge?

"Zack!" Brianna's voice is shrill.

Zack is standing at the back of the boat watching Will come in from another successful go on the water. He waves his wife off like she's some pesky mosquito and doesn't even bother to turn around.

"Can you top us off?" She tries another angle, but he ignores this attempt as well. It's like he doesn't even hear her this time.

"He's so funny." Brianna laughs it off and grabs the bottle of rosé herself. "I think he's tired from last night."

"Totally." I hate that I immediately picture Zack and a montage of whips, chains, and bondage balls. But I do, and I have Brianna to thank for that.

"You want some more?" She holds out the bottle toward me.

I shake my head and cover my cup. "I'm good for now."

"Boring." She pouts at me. "I'll make you change your mind later."

"You're up, Ava!" Will shouts from behind me, looking fully invigorated from his round on the lake.

"I don't think so. I've never done wakeboarding before."

"It's so fun and I know you'll love it," he encourages.

"There is no way I can do that." I can't even believe he's promoting this. But then, who am I kidding? It's Will—the guy who wants you to *really* live every second of your life.

"You can!" He sounds like he believes it. "I'll help you, and we'll keep the pace slow on the boat."

I look over then and see Ryder wakeboarding like a pro.

"No." I shake my head. I have embarrassed myself enough in front of him. "Way."

"You should try, Ava." Gia speaks up, but I know it's only because she wants to videotape me and capture what will surely be a disastrous go on the lake.

"Why don't *you*?" I narrow my eyes.

"I have already," she says. "And I'm not good at it. But this could be something you might excel at. Remember our conversation last night?"

"How is wakeboarding surrendering to life?"

"You're living outside your comfort zone," she explains.

"I've been doing a lot of that lately," I say defensively. "But that scares me."

"More than ayahuasca?" She lifts a brow.

I have a feeling I'm going to hear those words a lot.

"Come on, Ava," Will cajoles. "We're not taking no for answer. If Daniel can do it, so can you. Be brave!"

I look over at their adorable son. He gives me a giant smile and waves.

"You can do it, Auntie Ava," he says and gives me a thumb's up.

"You can even use Daniel's board, since you're almost the same size." Gia loves to make this joke about how petite I am.

"Rude," I say.

"True."

"Maybe..." I say, dragging out the word. I let out a frustrated sigh and look over at Will. He's not going to give up. "Fine. I'll try it once. But you have to bring me back in when I want."

"Deal!" Will claps his hands together. "Let's get a life jacket on you."

I strip off my sundress and stand there in my bikini, suffering through Gia's cat calls. I hate that she's drawing attention to me so the world can look—but I guess my outfit yesterday on the golf course was pretty much just as naked and definitely more scandalous. I notice that Ryder is now done with his turn wakeboarding and is getting back into Matthew's boat. I cringe. He's about to witness my next folly.

First, the golfing.

Now, the wakeboarding.

This is not a good look for me.

Will hands me the life jacket and I slip it on. He starts giving me directions. Of course, I don't hear a word he says and just nod. At this point, he might as well be speaking Swahili. The only part of his tutorial I understand is that I have to hold onto the handle that will be pulling me on the wakeboard. That's key.

Don't let go.

"Ava! You've got this!" Will tries to pump me up, but instead of feeling any type of excitement, a sense of doom envelopes me.

"What if I break a leg?" I ask him in rising panic.

"You won't."

"But is it possible?" I continue. "Or an arm? Or neck?"

"You won't, kid. You're freaking yourself out for no reason. I promise you're going to have a good time out there! I know you—you'll like this."

I look over at Gia.

The iPhone is already rolling.

"Say hi, Ava!" Gia waves at me.

"These could be my last moments." I give her a dirty look.

"Before you eat it in the water, yes," Gia agrees. "I promise to capture every second of it. I think we should start uploading these to all of your social media accounts. Maybe you can meet men this way."

"That doesn't dignify a response." I take a deep breath.

"Try to be semi-decent." She lowers her voice. "Ryder's watching."

Wonderful.

I look out on the back of the boat and stare at Daniel's wakeboard. Will reaches out and helps me find my way on it. And since I know Ryder is watching, I'm even more nervous and more awkward, because why would it be any other way? It's me, Ava—the girl whose autobiography will be a compilation of one embarrassing moment after another.

But I can't think about that now. I only pray I'll live to write it.

The water is crisp and not as warm as one would hope. Still, freezing to death is the least of my problems.

The visual is this—me on all fours on the board, just floating in the cool water, panicking that I'm going to die. I give Will a look of fear.

"You've got this, Ava," Will reassures me, while trying his hardest not to laugh in my face.

"I think this is as far as I should go," I manage between my clenched teeth.

"Just remember everything I told you," he says, trying to remind me of the conversation I wasn't listening to. "I think you'll be a natural."

Gia finds that comment hilarious.

"You think?" I wonder how in the world I'm going to get myself to stand up.

"I'm going to take it slow," Will tells me. "And you'll find your groove."

"I will?" Terror overtakes me. This is the same feeling I would get as a teen before the Freefall rollercoaster ride at Magic Mountain. I'd be screaming as soon as the countdown to takeoff would begin.

"Yes!" Will should have been a coach. "I believe in you."

I look over at Gia. The phone is firmly in place.

"I hate you," I whisper to her.

"Love you!" is Gia's response.

It takes me a second, but I'm slowly able to crouch and then stand. I grip the handle Will gave me. There is too much chop and I don't like it one bit. Why can't it be like glass today? Isn't that what lake water is about? Will takes the boat's wheel and turns to watch me. He looks so excited for me I almost feel bad.

Almost.

He gives me a thumbs up and I realize he's ready to go. I don't return the sentiment. Only nod. There is no way I'm letting go of this handle.

When the boat starts to slowly take off, I close my eyes and hold on for dear life. If I can't see, it's almost better. The terror isn't as gripping. I'm just counting the seconds until I'll be done with this torture. How long can it last?

The screams come naturally.

Kind of like the way you would scream if you had a surprise run in with the Loch Ness monster. Real fear is belting out of me—this is some hell.

Like real hell.

"Open your eyes!" Gia yells at me from the boat.

They're squeezed so tightly shut that I don't know if it will even be possible.

"Ava!" she yells again, but I try my best to ignore her.

"You're. Missing. Out. On. Everything!" The words come belting out one at a time.

Something rattles in my soul. Her words reach out and grab my heart and squeeze. *You're missing out.*

My eyes open immediately.

Something clicks. It's like my brain is Tetris and all of the pieces suddenly fit. Everything makes sense. It's not about missing out on watching the lake zip past me, or doing a sport I clearly do not have an ability for—it's something deeper and more profound. If I keep my eyes closed, I'm going to miss out on the rest of *my life.* Even if it's not always pleasant.

And I've missed out on enough already.

I've wasted enough time being miserable. Being sad about one situation or another. Wondering why Darian and I went so wrong. Why my life was shaken so badly and turned upside down.

Gia is right. It's time to surrender and live *my* life.

I open my eyes wider and stare out at my friends on the boat. Gia and Will are fist-pumping the air, they're so proud I've lasted this long. I know they can't believe it. I look over at the other boats and everyone seems happy for me, but what's more, *I'm* happy for me.

Surrender *is* the answer.

Living *is* the answer.

This moment is what life is all about. Here right now. Me, on a wakeboard, scared as hell but kind of loving it.

CHAPTER 22

"HARVEST MOON"

"IF YOU HAVE ONE REGRET from your marriage, what would it be?" Ryder asks as we take a stroll by the lake that night after dinner.

After our boat trip, our whole group went out to dinner together. Since everyone was exhausted from the sun and action-packed day, we called it an early night. Shockingly, I felt invigorated. I took a few more turns on the wakeboard and might now be a fan. I'm not admitting that to anyone yet, but I had a great time.

Ryder stealthily came and sat next to me at dinner, and we had a great conversation. He's smart and funny and had me laughing almost the entire meal. He had to take a call from his brother and is going back to LA in the morning. I learned his father has been battling cancer for years and is not doing well, so Ryder understandably wants to hurry home.

He surprised me when he asked if I'd like to take a walk with him by the lake. Since I'm surrendering, I said yes.

"Only one regret?" I laugh.

"Just one."

I don't have to think about my response. "My one regret in my marriage is that I didn't see."

"See the demise coming?"

"No. That I didn't see how separate our lives were. Or how unhappy we both were. I kept the shades on and ignored it."

An ostrich comes to mind.

"That's easy to do," Ryder says after a moment. "I think every person is guilty of that at some point in their lives."

"True," I agree. "But you asked me what I regret."

"I did." His tone is flirty. "But I don't want you to feel badly about it."

"I don't." I feel my face flush.

"You sure?"

"I'm done feeling bad about everything. I've lived in that place for too long."

"How do you mean?"

"Personally and culturally, as well," I explain. "For better or worse, I was raised very conservatively, so everything I did was analyzed under a microscope by my family and my community. It didn't help that my sister conformed to all of their norms and expectations."

"She's the perfect child?"

"I'm definitely the black sheep."

"You probably had more fun," he says, winking at me.

"Maybe now I am," I laugh. "But I'd been with Darian forever, so my fun was pretty limited before."

"It's never too late to start over." Ryder's tone is light. "I predict this round will be like finding a penny heads up—only good things for you now."

"I think you're right," I say optimistically.

We both share a smile.

"And you?" I ask him.

"Yes?"

"Since you've never been married," I say. "What's your biggest regret in life?"

"Not spending enough time with my father when he was healthy," Ryder answers quickly. "There were so many times I should have been there, and I wasn't for one reason or another. But now, when he's sick and dying, I am. If you think about it, it's absurd. We both lost out on memories we could have had together...and it's because of me."

There's a sensitivity I see that I find attractive.

"That's my biggest regret. Every time I see him—it's the first thought in my head. What the fuck were you thinking, Ryder?"

I can tell how tormented he is over this, and I'm sad for his pain. It makes me think about my own relationship with my parents. I'm guilty of not spending enough time with them, especially in the past few years when I've been too immersed in my own problems and misery. The thought of being in Ryder's position is frightening.

My voice is soft as I say, "Somehow life always seems to get in the way."

"Family *is* life," Ryder's says, emphatically. "Without family, in whatever form they come, you've got nothing. That's something I understand now."

I think about my crazy family. I mean, they *are* crazy and amazing and funny and loud and in-your-face and just...I guess, kind of perfect in every way.

"You're right," I agree. "Family *is* life."

"I take it you're close to yours?" he inquires.

"Yes. Uncomfortably close."

He laughs.

"They know everything," I tell him. "Aunts, uncles, cousins, Mom, Dad—they always all know everything—it's like they're on speed dial and need to tell each other what's going on with everyone at all times. And they're always in your face about your life, giving their opinions and advice, which is just their way to tell you what to do. And if you don't listen, you're a naïve idiot who's going to have the wool pulled over your eyes."

Ryder's laughing hard.

"And I'm not exaggerating one bit." I put my hands up.

"I love your culture." Ryder chuckles over at me. "I have a lot of Persian friends."

"And let me guess," I say with a knowing look. "You know a few words."

"I do. But somehow, I don't think they're appropriate to share with you."

"I like your answer."

"I like you."

His words make my heart stop. Ryder stops walking, forcing me to do the same. He turns to face me.

"You don't really know me," I say, the girl with the most uncool responses to men ever.

"I like what I've seen so far." His voice is husky now and the vibe completely changes.

He reaches out and puts his arm around my waist. His touch is soft and warm, and I like it more than I want to admit.

"You're very beautiful." His gaze sweeps over my face. "And surprisingly, I don't mind that you're embarrassingly bad at golf."

We share a smile. He takes a step toward me, closing the distance between us.

"And I'm going to kiss you now," he whispers, before his lips brush mine. The kiss is warm and cozy. Like a perfect summer day. There is something more to it than London's kiss.

With the shimmer of the stars on the lake and the moon in the sky the moment is especially romantic, and I memorize every second of it. We kiss for a long while and when we pull away, Ryder holds me in his strong arms. I can admit that I like the way they feel.

"When can I see you again?" he asks me.

"When I get back to LA," I say. I can't believe I have two—no *three*—dates now, when I'm back home! How did this even happen?

He pulls away from me and looks down at my face.

"It's a date?"

"For sure."

CHAPTER 23

"UP CLOSE AND PERSONAL"

"*Maman!*" I yell at my mom over FaceTime. "Hold the phone back! I can't see your face!"

For some reason my mom cannot grasp the concept of where the camera is on her iPhone, so the only thing ever visible when she calls is her eyeball, brow, or nose. Sometimes I get lips, but that's rare.

"Yes, you can," she tells me like I'm making it up.

"OhmyGod." I give up. I realize there's no use in trying to argue with her, because she's adamant that the picture on FaceTime is as it should be.

"Don't, 'ohmyGod' me," she says, her accent thick, her tone annoyed. "How are Gia and Will?"

"They're good," I say.

"Vhen you come home?"

"I'll be in LA next week," I assure her.

"Vhen you come here?"

"Mom, I already told you, I'm going to see a few other people before I come stay with you."

"Ah-ha," Mom says, and I wonder what she's secretly thinking. She's quiet for too long, so I know it can't be good.

"How was the *meh-moon-ee* (party) you and Dad went to at Shaida-joon's house?" I ask, hoping to distract her from whatever thoughts are percolating in her head about me.

"Food vas very bad." My mom's answer is predictable. "But she bad cook, so your father and I eat before ve go. Nobody touch her food. Very sad. But, I am so mad at your fadher."

"Why?"

"He goes and eh-sleeps in dhe car vone hour into party!"

I try my hardest not to laugh. This is one of my dad's most famous *ghost* moves. When he's done at a Persian party, which is usually after food is served, he disappears—either on the longest walk known to man or to take a nap in the car.

"Your khaleh says you vent out on date." Mom changes the topic like a pro. "How come you don't tell me dhat?"

"Because I knew she would," I return dryly.

"He nice guy?" Her eyeball stares right into my soul.

"He's British," I say. "And he was nice."

"No, no, dhat's too far," my mom proclaims, like it's the law. "You can't move to England."

Gia was right my family not approving a move across the atlantic.

"Mom. We just went on a date. He didn't propose."

"Ah-ha," she says, suspiciously. "You pick bad guy again?"

I laugh. "I must have bad taste."

"You do," she agrees.

"How are you feeling?" I change the topic because Darian is not a rabbit hole I want to go down with my mom, and this question will get her going.

She proceeds to tell me in Farsi how her back hurts, her blood pressure is high, she's eating too much—but that's because of my dad—she hopes she doesn't get "lopez disease," which I realize is lupus sometime later, and she doesn't understand how she's survived under this stress for so long. The unspoken sentiment is that I am the cause of most of her ailments.

"You need to take care of yourself," I say, and can't help but think of my conversation with Ryder by the lake.

"I try," she says, then her tone changes to something uncharacteristically soft. "Ve miss you very much."

"I miss you guys too." I smile at her nose. "Thank you for letting me take care of myself the way I want. I know it's killing you to stay quiet."

"No!" I think she shakes her head, but thanks to the camera angle, I can't be sure. "Vhat kills me is vhen I see my daughter sad. Or crying. Dhat is vhat kills me. You be happy and I am happy."

"I'm getting there." I feel myself get emotional over my mom's comment. She's never been super flowery or sensitive, so when she shows that side, it's always a moment.

"You looks good," she says as her one eye checks me out.

"Thanks, Mom."

And then...

"But you are too skinny and too tan. You get wrinkles." The words come out fast and furious. "Cover your face. You get old too fast. And I don't like dhose earrings...."

☙

I'm sitting outside by the lake, staring out at Will and Gia as they play with their son on the banks. They're laughing and enjoying themselves. Their family is such a tight unit, and it's nice to watch and pick up a few tips for whatever the future brings. We've had a relaxing few days, and it's been so nice and peaceful here that I don't want it to end.

I pick up my phone and open the diary app.

I stare at the lake and think about my trip here in Gozzer with Will and Gia. Time is moving fast and it's hard for me to keep up. I feel like I just got here. But Gozzer has proven to be a surprisingly impactful stop for me. Something shifted out on that lake when I was so overcome with fear—maybe it was the culmination of everything I've experienced so far during my couch-surfing summer, but a switch was flipped. And I need to make sure the light stays on.

I don't want to forget.

So, what did I learn from my friends and my experiences here?

I learned that the right friends are teachers who can open your world in ways you never thought possible; they can push you to live outside your box and change you for the better.

I learned that in nature, you can find peace.

I think about Brianna and Zack. It's not a relationship I would want, but one that is right for them. Watching the two taught me there is no real magic formula. Different things work for different marriages. And even if it seems bizarre to me, it can be the most perfect way for that couple. I mean, those two obviously keep coming back for more. Something is working in their favor.

I look over at Gia and Will.

I learned that being a unit is a must in any relationship. The family that does everything together, stays together.

I learned that *checking in* with your partner is something I'm going to adopt in my future relationship, whenever that might be. This one idea truly resonated with me.

But I want a specific question. I want him to ask me the one that's the most important—the simplest of all.

Are you happy?

That's my checking in question.

That's the question that's going to move me. That's the question that means everything. And when he asks me, I want to say, "*yes.*"

And then I want to ask him the same question back. And I want him to say—"Deliriously, Ava. I'm deliriously happy with you." That's what I want. That's the fairytale.

Happiness.

90210
BEVERLY HILLS
"THE SECOND WIFE"

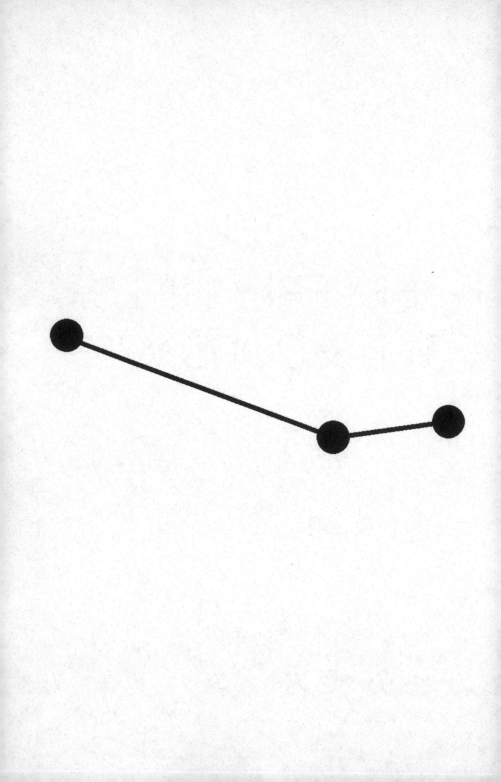

CHAPTER 24

"PARCHED"

"WE ARE GOING TO CALL you *the second wife*," Nick Sherman, my friend Faith's husband, says to me on my first night at their home.

It's sunset and we're sitting outside having a cocktail and staring out at their multi-million-dollar view of the sprawling city of Los Angeles, dotted with palms and the rolling hills of the Santa Monica Mountains. The panoramic views stretch out to the ocean.

"Tell her why," Faith urges him with a laugh, as she hands me another vodka soda. I'm super grateful for her heavy pour as I take in my surroundings and sigh in pleasure.

I am indebted to the Shermans for inviting me to stay at their paradise. Faith and Nick's home is like something out of *Architectural Digest*. It's a twenty-thousand-square-foot modern masterpiece. The home has an indoor/outdoor design with sliding glass doors throughout that open to the spectacular view. They have an indoor koi pond with a bar that emerges from the luxurious stone floor that is used seamlessly inside and out. Building the house was a labor of love for Faith. She meticulously picked every last detail and turned this into her very own dream home. I think it's fair to say that for 99 percent of the population this would be their ideal home too.

I feel blessed she urged me to stay here and for as long as I want. But that's just Faith. She's one of the most giving women I know. My girlfriend is in her late forties and with her sun-kissed blonde hair, tanned skin, and big green eyes, she is a showstopper.

Her and Nick complement each other perfectly. He has always reminded me a bit of Jack Nicholson. They have the same swagger, same kind of demeanor and same flirty appeal. I can see why Faith was drawn to him. Though he's thirty years older, he doesn't look his age and he's a kid at heart. He's also super successful. He's self-made and amassed his vast fortune by importing goods from China.

He happens to be the baller kind of rich. *Sick rich*...as in sick, wet your panties, *rich*.

It comes as no surprise that Nick is still absolutely enamored with Faith and either lovingly or begrudgingly supports everything she does. He might nag (as all men do), and sure, she'll bitch about him, but I've always felt like they're both genuinely happy in their marriage. That they do love each other.

"In Chinese culture you have a first wife and you have a second wife," Nick explains with a happy smile.

"Isn't the second wife equivalent to a concubine?" I raise a brow.

"Usually, yes," he returns good-naturedly. "But in your case, you'll be exempt of all those kinds of duties...if you know what I mean."

"I do," I return with a laugh. "So what duties will I have?"

"Helping me plan a menu." Faith winks at me in jest. "Providing conversational entertainment with guests we have over."

Nick pulls out the fattest looking joint I've ever seen. I'm pretty sure my eyes have lit up like a Christmas tree. "Faith is so boring."

"I think I can handle all of those duties." I'm not mad at my situation at all.

"I might like this, Faith," Nick jokes.

"I'm fairly confident you will." She grins and takes a sip of her drink.

"But Ava should know that I'm also on the hunt for a second wife who will perform the *real* duties," he says, glancing my way in jest. "Considering that in order to make love to my wife I have to be washed, dried, and fumigated."

"I have a yeast infection!" Faith scowls at her husband, then locks eyes with me. "I rejected him last night and his feelings are still hurt."

"Every one of your holes always has something going on." He sounds mildly annoyed. Nick is also that guy who says exactly what he's thinking...and boy, does he have the balls to do it. Sometimes it sucks, like for his wife, who happens to always be polite, gracious, and overall, freaking wonderful. Through the years, I have personally witnessed times she's wanted to smash a platter or two over his head.

Her husband lights the joint and takes a long hit.

"So I want to talk to you about something," Nick begins slowly as he waves over at Faith. "My wife's going to be pissed at me for saying this the first night you're here, but you know me...."

Yes, I do. I mentally prepare myself.

"I never liked the guy," Nick blurts out.

"I'm not surprised," I say with a laugh.

Darian's favorite thing to do was not show up. Like ever. And when he did, he was the most antisocial person around. He never came to a dinner with me. He hated going to parties, so I was pretty much always by myself at any social gathering. It became a normal occurrence over the years, and my friends got used to it. In retrospect I can see how that was such a flaw in our relationship.

"I didn't like how he always made you go places alone," Nick continues, a combination of mind reader and protective older brother.

"No, that definitely wasn't fun," I agree.

"Pretty lonely if you ask me," he continues.

"Are you trying to make her cry?" Faith cuts in, sounding more than annoyed.

"And I always told Faith I thought he was up to something," he says, ignoring her. "I just didn't realize he would be up to *so* much. Multiple asses. Multiple sets of tits. The whole shebang."

"Tell me about it." I know I should be sad by his words, but the way he says them is kind of funny.

There is a definite warning in Faith's voice. Honey, none of us could have predicted this for her. Ava, please just ignore him."

"I'm fine." I wave off her concern. "Really. He's not telling me something I don't know already."

Faith scowls at him then gives me a gentle smile. "Have you heard from Darian at all today?"

"He texted me an early happy birthday," I admit. Biggest ass-hole text of the century:

> DARIAN: *Happy early birthday, babe. A year older...I've been thinking about all those years you complained about all the things that were wrong in our marriage. Well, here's my birthday gift to you...you don't have to worry about that anymore. Xoxo Darian*

I don't know if I want to share the contents just yet. If ever. But it's making me rethink all the new and kind sentiments I have for him.

"It would be a happier birthday if he gave you some of your money back," Nick says calmly.

"Can't you go easy on her for just tonight?" Faith sounds exasperated.

"Ava loves me," Nick states without concern.

"I do," I agree, then change the topic myself. "So what are the house rules?"

"The only rule we have is if you're home, dinner is at six-thirty." Faith sounds like a protective mom. "And we like to sit down together as a family every night—that includes you."

Huh. Sitting down for dinner at a scheduled time was not something Darian and I regularly did. With our calendars and always-plugged-in lifestyle, we didn't make eating together a priority.

Nick claps his hands together. "Now let's talk about the fun stuff."

"Like?" I raise a brow a bit fearfully.

"Getting you laid." I know I shouldn't be surprised, but I am. And he doesn't stop there. "I can get you someone up here, no problem. My gift to you."

"*Get* me someone?" I manage.

"You know, a male escort to get your juices flowing," Nick says, like we're talking about the weather. "If I had to bet, I'd guess you haven't gotten laid in a long while."

Accurate assessment.

"Maybe," I admit.

"What kind of man do you want? It's on me."

Faith can't hold her laughter in.

"Woah now, this conversation feels real." I narrow my eyes.

"It *is* real," Nick returns. "This is my divorce gift to you. I just need to know your type."

"I'm good."

"Boring!" Nick flickers his hand at me. "You've got to get back on top and ride that saddle...or else."

"Or else what?" I ask with a laugh.

Nick has no shame.

"You could dry up down there."

CHAPTER 25

"WAR AND PEACE"

THEIR CHEF INFORMS US THAT dinner is ready.

I'm surprised to see their two children, Leigh and Mark, join us. It's Friday night and I would have thought for sure they had other plans.

Leigh is a junior in high school and is at the age where she's over everything—mainly her parents. She can't wait to graduate and start her life as a model. I would love to tell her that she shouldn't be in such a hurry to get away from the safety of being with her mom and dad, or the general splendor of her home, and that she should enjoy this moment of her youth...but I know it would just be a useless conversation. When you're that age you think you know what you want, and you think you know everything. I remember all too well.

Their son, Mark, is in his mid-twenties and a permanent fixture in West Hollywood's trendy scene. He's super popular and loves to go out. He's also handsome, funny as hell, and we happen to get along great. I'm glad he's around for my first official dinner as *the second wife*.

Mark sits next to me and gives me a broad grin. "Selfishly, I am so glad you're staying with us. Think about all the fun we're going to have."

"We definitely will," I agree.

Their chef brings out the food, and I notice I'm given the biggest helping of pasta.

"So what's going on with you and Scott?" Nick asks Mark about his boyfriend of two years.

"Why do you ask?" asks Mark.

"He hasn't been up here in over a week." His father doesn't hold back. "Seems strange considering how hot and heavy you two have been up until now."

"Well, thank you for noticing, Dad. We're taking a break." Mark's announcement is met by collective shock. I'm even surprised. They've been together for so long, and as far as I knew, they were a picture-perfect couple.

"Oh no, honey." Faith looks genuinely upset. "Are you doing okay?"

"I'm fine." Mark gives the group a fake, bright smile then glances down at his plate. *Uh oh.* I know that look. It's been a permanent fixture on my face for over a year. I'm pretty sure he's anything but okay.

"We don't have to talk about it," Faith says considerately.

"I'd like to," Nick asserts.

"Well, not tonight." Mark looks over at me and rolls his eyes.

"We are going to respect our son's wishes." Faith gives Nick the stink eye. "Leigh, why don't you tell us about your day, sweetheart."

"It was fine." Their daughter doesn't sound like she wants to offer anything more.

"Just fine?" Nick wonders.

She shrugs her shoulders. "It was school."

"Doesn't a lot go on in school?" He's relentless.

"Not really."

Wrong answer, Leigh. *Wrong* answer.

"I pay more than fifty thousand dollars a year for a school that's got nothing going on?"

She shrugs again. "I guess."

It takes everything I have not to burst out laughing when I take in the look on Nick's face. I glance at Faith. She has a *what the fuck is my daughter thinking* look on hers, and I'm pretty sure I do too.

"You guess?" Nick's voice is suspiciously low. "Well then *I* guess we have to pull you out of this school that I'm just burning money paying for, and stick you in another."

"Dad." Leigh rolls her eyes, completely unaware of how she keeps poking the bear. "Don't be so dramatic."

"Leigh." Faith tries to warn her.

"Are you insane?" Mark is way more blunt. His voice is incredulous. "Do you even realize what's coming out of your mouth?"

"What?" Leigh says indifferently. "It's the truth."

I respect Leigh for her bravery, but get this girl a shovel because she's digging her own grave.

"Then I'm not paying anymore." Nick stares her down. "There's no reason for me to pay for a place that's got nothing going on. You can go to public school your senior year."

"Okay, Dad." She rolls her eyes, not believing him for a second.

"I don't like your tone," Nick says.

"What's wrong with my tone?" Leigh looks around at all of us, completely oblivious to how she might have upset her dad.

"Honey," Faith says, turning to her daughter. "I think you need to quit while you're ahead."

"She's not ahead. She's behind." Nick sounds pissed. "I suggest you excuse yourself from dinner."

Leigh stares at him for a long moment before standing from the table. I can't tell what she's thinking but I don't think she's bothered. To be honest, she looks relieved that she gets to leave.

"Sure, Dad," she says flippantly as she walks out of the room.

The silence at the table is palpable. I'm afraid to look up from my plate. Nick finally looks over at his wife and he looks pissed.

"I'll handle it," Faith says, with surprising calm. "Don't worry, honey. She got into an argument with Nancy today. She's just testy. I'll take care of it."

I don't know if it's her tone or just the overall serene way she speaks to Nick, but somehow, his entire demeanor relaxes and the whole room does as well. I have some mad respect for Faith right now. She's so calm and collected that she manages to rub right off on to those around her.

Like magic.

We finish dinner and Nick and Mark leave to talk about the family business in Nick's office while Faith and I linger at the table. When I know they're safely out of earshot, I pin my friend down.

"It was impressive of you not to let Leigh rattle you," I tell her admiringly.

"I try." Faith smiles in satisfaction.

"And your ability to make everyone feel calm around you..." I say.

"It's what I do best. Why should I let my teenage daughter's oblivious comment ruin our lovely dinner tonight?" She gives me a wink and continues, lowering her voice in case anyone can hear. "I'll tell you a secret. I've learned how to let the little things go. And ninety-eight percent of the time, what irritates us day to day is just little things. By allowing myself to get worked up over them, I would just ruin my own life."

I let her words sink in.

During my marriage to Darian, and if I'm honest, even while we were dating, I found it very difficult to just *let things go*. Everything little thing mattered so much to me, and it was always so important to be right.

Looking back, always needing to be right—even about silly, little things—seems like such a waste of time now.

"I think it's easier said than done," I slowly say. "When Darian made me angry, I was never able to be that calm."

"Christina once told me something many years ago that I will never ever forget." She mentions a friend of ours who happens to be the embodiment of perfect mental health. "And I've adopted it as my life's motto."

"What was that?"

"I'm addicted to peace."

CHAPTER 26

"HERE'S TO YOU, MRS. ROBINSON"

"You don't even look your age," Faith says to me as we lie on the lounge chairs in the submerged shelf of her heated infinity pool.

"Oh my God, why does hearing you say that I don't even look my age make me somehow more depressed about my age?"

"It shouldn't," she says, her eyes lighting up. "You need to start talking to more men. Single, hot men. Young ones. In their twenties. Have some fun. Live outside your box...let them into *your* box. And do different. You'll experience a lot of new excitement with a younger man, and he'll help introduce you to the new world. He'll teach you everything you need to know to become the queen bee out there."

"What kind of excitement are you talking about?" I ask, even though I know exactly what she's talking about.

She cocks a brow. "The good kind."

"You want me to be Mrs. Robinson?" Even though it should be very appealing to me as a newly single woman, I'm not remotely interested in her idea. In reality, I'm slightly appalled by it.

Depressed by it, even.

"Why the hell not? You will have a great time!" Faith sighs and then fans herself as she thinks it over. "A *really* great time."

"Don't you even know me? Me? Avalie Monfared. The woman you found sobbing under her dining table in a fetal position because she didn't know how the hell she was going to survive her life.... *This* Ava Monfared that you're looking at right now, dating a *younger* guy?"

"And?" She stares at me like *I'm* crazy. "Older women date younger men all the time. There are many successful relationships I can give you examples of."

"I think all a younger man will do is make me sad." I try to picture myself with some twenty-year old. "I don't even think we speak the same language."

Faith laughs. "What I have in mind requires no verbal communication."

"You and your husband are shameless."

"I promise you it will work."

I'm sure she can see the skepticism on my face.

"This is the new you!" Faith sounds so passionate and excited about my circumstance that I wonder if I'm missing something.

"But the new me still doesn't want to date a twenty-five-year-old that's going to think I'm some old lady trying to get off."

"At least you'll be coming."

"Faith!" I can't help but laugh.

"What? Ava, you're the perfect kind of young—still beautiful but with wiser eyes, a better lens, and a greater understanding of the way life works. You're smart. You have a career that might be rocky right now, but you'll be back. So what if you're in a holding pattern financially? You're getting a second chance to do it right and make your own way, to make it yours. Think about it. Do you know how lucky you are?"

"I don't know what to tell you. It still feels scary."

"Of course it does," she returns. "But that's also part of the adventure. Isn't that what this nomad summer of yours is about... adventure?"

"I guess it's supposed to be," I admit. "But it's not easy. I am still mourning something I lost. I won't be able to run from that. I have to go through the stages."

"Ava, you've been mourning Darian's loss for quite some time now. I don't care what you say, you knew you were leaving him years ago. You wanted to put the house up for sale—you and I both know you were using that as an excuse to get out of the marriage because you were unhappy. When you hired someone to look into him and learned about his double life, that may have been the universe conspiring to push you out the door."

"Maybe," I say, but I can't deny it. Faith is right.

I had been unhappy for so long. I had no bearing. I just knew I couldn't, and Darian and I *both* couldn't, go on as we were. But making the leap was hard to do. After being with someone for so long, you get comfortable. Getting out isn't easy. How can it be? It's a life you built together. But as his lies surfaced, it became an unavoidable truth—like Faith said, the universe *was* showing me all the signs and I couldn't ignore them any longer, even if all I wanted was to keep my head in the sand. But only because it was easy and familiar.

I guess I had been so busy being mad at Darian for every perceived wrong he did to me that I forgot to be mad at myself for allowing it. For living the way I was, which was not living at all. And now, I'm remembering how to do it. How to live.

Am I ready to have something new with a man?

"I guess I just can't picture it," I confess after a moment.

"That's the biggest travesty I've heard. Once you start meeting more men and putting yourself out there, you'll realize what you were missing. And you'll remember how good it feels—to be wanted. To be *desired*," she says. "And because you're so damn difficult, Nick and I will find you some men to choose from who are older than you. You must let me know how old you'll go."

I have to laugh.

"What if I end up with another version of Darian on my hands?" I wonder out loud. "Like a Darian 2.0, 3.0, 4.0, or any other version for that matter."

"Not all men are going to be Darian—3.0 or 4.0 version," she says firmly. "Now, go and get your phone."

"Why?"

"We are going to download a dating app," she commands.

"Not happening right now," I say, getting up off the lounge chair and practically running away from my friend. "I'm having lunch with my mom and sister tomorrow."

I flee to my room and check my phone before I jump in the shower. I have text messages from Jonathan and Pegah.

And Ryder.

And New York City.

Seeing his name on my phone makes my heart rate pick up in a really good way. I save his message for last and answer Pegah and Jonathan first. Then I open Ryder's message.

> **Ryder:** Hey Ava, how are you today? I'd like to see you soon. How about dinner on Sunday?

I think about my affinity for New York City, but then mentally stop myself. I don't even know if we'll have the same chemistry together...it could all be a fantasy in my head.

> **ME:** I'm doing well. How is your father feeling? And as for dinner, I'd like that.

I click open New York City's message.

> **New York City:** Happy birthday, beautiful.

The goofy smile on my face should be outlawed. But I can't help myself. I like him.

> **ME:** Thank you.

As soon as I write back and hit send my phone pings and he messages right back.

New York City: I hope you're spoiling yourself today.

ME: I'm going to have more of a relaxing day.

New York City: Well, I can't wait to spoil you in person.

My stomach drops.

ME: When will that be?

I boldly ask, suddenly overcome with the need to see him as soon as heavenly possible.

New York City: Soon.

CHAPTER 27

"DICK PIC"

"YOU LOOK LIKE YOU'VE BEEN in the south of France," my sister Layla says as we hug and kiss.

Her and my mom drove up from Newport Beach together and are taking me to lunch at our favorite Italian restaurant, II Pastaio, for my birthday. While my mom is in the ladies' room my sister and I have a moment alone together. Layla looks on point, as usual. She's dressed conservatively in simple black pants and a cashmere sweater. She always looks put together by a stylist. Her straight, thick, black hair is cut into a sleek bob. No matter what time of day it is or what's going on in her life, it always looks like she came straight out of a salon. Her face is stunning, with incredible green eyes she inherited from our father. In high school, the boys were always knocking on our door for her. Of course, she was never allowed to date anyone or talk to them in front of our parents, but she was wanted and popular.

I, on the other hand, looked like a gremlin. Some Persian girls go through an awkward coming-of-age phase...and I was definitely one of them. I had skin issues; my nose was too big for my face at one point, and my hair was a frizzy mess. Sometimes I wonder what Darian was initially attracted to, because I'm telling you, the situation I had going on wasn't pretty.

Like me, Layla married her first boyfriend. Thankfully, her situation turned out much better. Her husband, Ben, or Fariborz—a lot of Persians like to give themselves American names that are of no relation to their given name—is a gem and truly an older brother to me.

"My tan is courtesy of Faith's pool," I tell her.

"Well, you look great."

"Thank you," I reply. "How have you been? How's Ella?"

"She's good and misses her auntie," my sister says pointedly.

"I miss her too."

"So when are you coming down to stay with us?"

"Soon." I know I sound defensive and possibly bitchy, but I don't want to feel guilted into anything in this moment in my life. And my family has a tendency of doing that.

"Just asking." Layla holds up her hands. "Don't get all agro on me."

"Sorry," I mumble. "I'm just testy."

"Any reason why, besides the obvious?" she asks.

"I went to the bank and it was super depressing to see how I have nothing monetarily to show for my life up until now." I try to shake the gloomy feeling. "I'm just waiting for the day when it won't be so jarring."

"People go through rough patches all the time. Do you know how many of my friends have pulled themselves out of bankruptcy to come back as multi-millionaires?"

"I know, but it's not as easy as it sounds," I say. My sister is a successful attorney, so she's always had it all together. "I'm still trying to figure my career out."

"What career?" My sister asks deadpan, then starts to laugh. "I'm joking! You should see the look on your face!"

I decided then to admit my secret to her. "I think I'm having a midlife crisis."

"You're just exhausted from the last six months of your life," my sister says, surprising me. I was certain she was going to lecture me on how I needed to put my big girl pants on and figure myself out. "This is completely normal. You want a break. I get it. We've all been there. Don't worry. We'll help you."

"You can't." I shake my head. "You've already done so much for me financially this past year. I'm not going to take anymore. I have some money. I just have to be frugal and figure my blog out...or a book, who knows?"

"Ava." My sister's voice is sympathetic. "This is what family is for. Good and bad times. And let's be honest, you're just going through a shitty one."

We laugh, both seeing the humor in the situation.

"I really am."

My mom takes that moment to sit down and join us. She moves a hand through my curly hair. I know she prefers it straight.

"It's vild." My mom tries to pat my hair down.

"I like it."

"That's all dhat matters." There's an awkward silence as she picks up her menu and looks it over.

"Okay," she says. "Vhat you guys vant to eat?"

"I need a glass of wine," I say without hesitation as I try to make eye contact with a waiter.

"Really?" Mom stares me down in a way that makes me feel like I'm sixteen again.

"Yes." I have to remind myself that I'm a grown adult. "It's my birthday."

"Hmm," is the response she gives me before focusing back on the menu.

"So Ava," Layla says, "you need to start dating."

"Oh God," I mumble, hoping the waiter gets to us fast. "Please do not tell me to get on a dating app or to go out with a younger man."

"Absolutely not!" My mom's voice sounds like it comes from the heavens.

I turn to look at her.

"Why, Mom?"

"Vhy?" she asks. "Because it's eh-strange. You meet eh-man face to eh-face."

I happen to agree with her, but I feel like giving her a bit of a hard time.

"Everyone is doing it," I say innocently. "That's how you meet a guy now, Mom. People send pictures to each other too."

"Pic-sher?" When she's annoyed, her accent gets thicker.

"Yes, you send pictures to each other." I keep my voice even and try my best not to laugh. "Naked ones."

My mom looks like I just asked her to eat glass.

"*You do dat?*" In a manner of seconds, I watch my fall from grace. I go from being her beloved Avalie to a harlot.

"She is going to spontaneously combust." Layla tsks me, but I know she thinks it's hilarious too. "Look at her."

"No, Mom, I don't do that," I say reassuringly. "But everyone gets on dating apps now. There's nothing wrong with them."

Mom doesn't look like she believes me.

The waiter comes by, and we all quickly order. My mom even asks for a beer. I'm shocked, but then I guess being in my presence must be doing wonders for her mental health.

☙

"Hey Ava, it's me. I was just calling to make sure you're doing okay. I wanted to check in on you. I know I was kind of a dick yesterday on your birthday, but you know, I think I'm still hurt. I know you are too. And I know there's so much between us...all the years together. Just take care of yourself, okay? You know I'll always be here for you no matter what."

I listen to Darian's voicemail and feel the familiar pit in my stomach. I can't wait for the time when he won't affect me anymore. Will it ever come? I turn off the lamp on the bedside table and snuggle into the bed. Just as I'm about to settle in...

My phone pings with a text.

My heart speeds up at the possibility of it being New York City again. But when I check, it's from London. Unfortunately, I feel a bit deflated. I'm surprised he's texting me so late.

London: Are you up?

I decide to engage.

ME: Yes. About to try and sleep.

London: Are you in bed??!!

His overuse of punctuation marks causes me to pause.

ME: Where else would one sleep?

London: What are you wearing?

I can't believe he asks me this. It feels too bold of a question after having only been on one date together. But then, maybe this is how it's done now.... Am I supposed to tell him that I'm wearing lingerie? Lace? I choose humor.

ME: Clothes? And you?

When he doesn't answer right away, I think I must have killed the moment for him. He obviously doesn't think I'm that funny.
A second later, I realize I'm wrong.
London gifts me with a belated birthday gift I'll never forget....
My very first dick pic.

CHAPTER 28

"ALPHA OR BETA"

"HERE WE GO AGAIN...ANOTHER DOG with another problem I'm going to have to pay for," Nick grumbles as he stares at the adorable picture of the rescue dog Leigh wants to pick up from the shelter in the San Fernando Valley.

I'm sitting on the couch in their family room reading *The Tao of Pooh*. I've been rereading it lately, in an attempt to see the world through a different lens and embrace *The Way*, as Taoists call it. *The Way*, as I understand it, is to exist with the knowledge that all living creatures are yin and yang, and our goal in life is to be one with nature and to go with the flow in the universe. To just be. I'm guessing that Laozi, the father of Taoism, obviously didn't take divorce into consideration.

Or Persian mothers.

"How much is this dog going to cost me?" Nick asks Faith, who's busy scrolling through the pictures of the puppy, completely lovestruck.

The family are all in the kitchen hovering over Faith's desktop. Nick looks so irritated that I have to lift my book up over my face so I can silently giggle into the pages of *Pooh*.

"It's just a hundred dollar pickup fee, honey," Faith states calmly.

"Not buying it, no way." Nick shakes his head adamantly. "I just paid eight thousand dollars for Teddy's doggie LASIK, when you said he was going in for a routine eye visit."

"Daddy." Leigh crosses her arms and looks mad. "How can you say that? It's *Teddy*. He's family. He's your son."

Their four-legged *son* is currently snuggled up against me on the couch. I pat his sweet little orange poodle head, and I have to say, he stares up at me with the clearest eyes a dog could ask for. I think he might even have better vision than me.

"He's a traitor," Nick blurts out as he points at me. "He's been sleeping in her room since she got here."

"At least he has good taste," Faith says.

"Who pays for him?" Nick all but bellows.

"Don't be jealous," his wife replies. "Teddy adores Ava, but you're his number one. You have nothing to worry about. You're the alpha, love. You're the man of the house and Teddy knows it."

Ooh. That was definitely a good comment for Faith to make. Nick crosses his arms and uncharacteristically doesn't make a sharp retort. I think his chest might have puffed out as well.

"Now, what do you say about the dog?" Faith asks.

"I don't want to talk about this right now." Nick waves the two off, but his tone has definitely softened. "I'll think about it."

Leigh gives her father the biggest smile. "Thank you, Daddy!"

"I didn't say yes," he quickly replies.

"Can I please get the puppy? It's a Mitzvah," she says to her dad.

"Smells like a money pitzvah for me."

She laughs, then kisses him on the cheek and runs out of the room. Nick sighs out loud.

"Why do I feel like I've been had?"

"I'd like to have some more of you." Faith gives him a sexy wink, and Nick blushes. I can tell he loves the innuendo.

"We need to prep for the party." Nick looks over at me. "What are you cooking?"

"Whatever you want me to," I say, still taking in Faith's magical way with her husband. I am so impressed how she just managed a new dog for Leigh. And make no mistake, *she* did. Even if Nick didn't agree out loud, he agreed inside. Look at him—he's like putty in her hands.

"I want Persian rice," he tells me. "Extra crispy. With the pota-toes on the bottom."

"I think I can handle that," I reply.

"Good. We invited a couple of single men for you. You can impress them with your culinary skills. Maybe you'll be excited about one—or more—of them. We told them we have a hot, sin-gle, Persian woman with some crazy hair."

I know he's not making this up.

ॐ

Sometime later, I find Mark sitting at the counter scrolling through his iPhone.

"What's up?" I say as I open the fridge and start to pull out what I need to make the food for dinner.

He looks right at me with tears in his eyes.

"Mark?" I walk over to him, worried. "Are you okay?"

"I don't know how you're acting normal and not crying all over the place," he admits as his voice breaks. "Don't you miss sleep-ing next to Darian? Don't you miss eating with him? Just waking up in the morning and knowing you have someone there? Putting aside all the garbage between you two...how can you not miss the familiarity?"

His question throws me.

It takes me a moment to answer. "We had a strange marriage. We were both there, but we weren't, you know? I don't know how to explain it other than I think we were just checked out. I think we were both ready for something else. There was this deep unhappi-ness between us that permeated every breath we took. It was that energy that was inescapable."

"But you've known him since you were in high school," he says with disbelief. "How can you just let go?"

I stare off into space, not seeing anything but faint images from our lives together. Seems like a lifetime ago. Even events that occurred between Darian and I only a few months ago feel like something from another world. How does that happen so quickly?

"I guess it's like a death in a way. Even though the person is physically here still, they're not. And you're not here together... Our marriage died."

A tragic, painful serial killer-esque kind of death.

"I guess I wasn't expecting my relationship to die. That sounds so morbid!" Mark's voice is sad. "I didn't want to give up on him or on us together."

"Sometimes it's not our choice." I hate to break the news to him. "And it sucks. And it's painful. And you think you won't survive. But then, somehow, you do."

Mark is quiet.

"Can you change anything?" I ask him softly.

"No."

"Can you stop living?"

"No."

"Then grieve his loss and have faith in your future." My voice is strong, and I wonder where the words come from.

"Do you listen to your own advice, Ava?" Mark inquires after a moment.

"I'm trying to," I say sheepishly. "It's easier to guide everyone else. When it's your own life, all you find are roadblocks."

"Ain't that the truth," Mark mutters. "Maybe we should both see a healer?"

"What kind of healer?" Mark knows about my ayahuasca experience.

"My friend told me about this incredible woman who heals you through breathwork. Want to try it with me?"

"Do I have to consume any strange substances?" I ask in trepidation.

He laughs. "No. It's only about breathing."

"If that's it, I'm in."

"I'll book us a session." Mark starts to study me as I chop toma-toes. "Ava, I think you need to have three tiers of dating."

"Three tiers?"

He nods, then explains, "Lowest rung is a young, hung hot-tie who will just come over and have his way with you." I stop chopping when he says young and hung. I immediately think of London. "And then he'll leave because you don't want to have a conversation with him. Not enough brain cells, but that's okay."

My mouth is open now.

"Stop staring at me like you're a virgin." He waves off my look.

"I feel like I kind of am," I return.

"*Do not* say that out loud again!" He looks horrified.

"I'm afraid to ask what the second tier is."

"Middle rung is a dateable/potential friend zone guy who you like but you don't know where it's going."

I immediately think of Ryder.

"Lastly, we have the upper rung," he says with flair. "This is your goal. This man is the pinnacle of your desires, and you'll do whatever it takes to get him. And when I say whatever—I mean, *whatever*."

New York City comes to mind.

"That sounds lethal."

"All's fair in love and war, my beautiful friend." He smiles devilishly. "And trust me, it's a war zone out there. I'm talking the Thirty Years' War kind of destructive."

His words scare me.

"But do you see what I want you to have?" Mark sounds excited. "With this strategy every part of you is satisfied."

"Very true." He has a point.

But before he can say any more...

"Are you making my food, or what?" Nick claps his hands as he walks in the kitchen.

"I'm giving her dating advice," Mark explains.

"Wait until you see who I invited over for her today." Nick looks like the cat who caught the canary.

I shake my head in worry. "Please, just tell me you didn't pay for any gigolos?"

Nick's smile puts me in a full panic. "That's for me to know and you to find out."

CHAPTER 29

"KABOB"

....

"AVA?" I HEAR FAITH CALL out to me as she knocks on my door.

"Come in."

Faith is dressed up and ready for the afternoon pool party with their friends.

"You look beautiful," I tell her. "I'm sure Nick is loving the cleavage."

"I did give him a morning surprise to set the mood for the day." She winks at me. "It works every time."

"A blow job before you have company?" I have to laugh. Now their earlier interaction makes even more sense. No wonder Nick was walking around the house with such a big smile this morning.

↩

Two hours and four sangrias later, I find myself sitting at the edge of the bar with a man Nick did, in fact, invite for me. The party is in full swing, and as usual at the Shermans', people are having a blast listening to music, eating good food, and having great conversation.

Gus, a real estate mogul, is nice enough and very eager to get to know me. I didn't feel any type of spark when I was introduced to him, nor do I now, but in the spirit of being open to anything, I'm engaging in small talk. Gus is in his late fifties and kind of reminds me of Bill Gates. He even wears a pair of those same nerdy glasses. Not exactly heartthrob material, but I'm still here.

"Nick tells me you're Persian," Gus says, giving me a big smile and revealing what I'm pretty sure are a very expensive set of pearly white veneers.

"I am."

"Interesting." He smiles again and his teeth are almost blinding. They take up a lot of his face. "I know a few Persian words."

Uh oh.

I pick up my drink, thinking I'm going to need a refill because I know what's coming. I'm about to get a list of all the swear words Gus knows. And I'll bet anything that some, if not most, will be highly offensive.

"*Cos-kehsh*," he says.

Bingo.

Direct translation—"one who pulls on a vagina." The worst, if not *one* of the worst insults you can say in my culture. It is a taboo phrase.

I smile politely.

"*Mah-dar sahg*," is the next one he gives me. This means your mother is a dog. Another gem.

"It's all coming back to me!" he says excitedly.

"Awesome," is all I can manage before taking another sip of my sangria.

"And *jendeh*!" He laughs hard at this one and kind of points at me. I wonder if it's intentional. Jendeh means whore—a real nasty one, in case you were wondering.

"Your knowledge of *Farsi* is quite impressive. You know a lot," I say, unamused. I help myself to Nick's cheese platter.

"I grew up in Beverly Hills and had a ton of Persian friends. They taught me all the words and phrases that matter. They were great," he says, taking a sip of his drink. "I'm trying to remember one more...I'm sure it'll come."

"Can't wait." I infuse more than an adequate amount of sarcasm in my tone so he might take the hint. "It seems like your friends were quality."

"We had some good times," he remembers fondly, then he shouts out, "*Goh-eh-saag!*"

Dog shit. Awesome.

Gus clearly doesn't know how to read a room. He slaps his leg and laughs. I can tell he's taken with himself.

"And we always went for koobideh together," he reminisces. "I love the food. Especially the beef kabob. It's my favorite."

I'm not surprised. It's practically what we're known for. That, and our crispy rice.

"You know, Persian women remind me of koobideh." He points at me and smiles like he's giving me the compliment of the century. "Little and juicy."

I laugh. I *have* to. Right in his face. It's just too much.

"I didn't offend you?" Gus asks, but I swear he doesn't look like he cares if he did.

"No." I shake my head with a wide grin. "You're good."

"So tell me about Ava." Gus changes gears and sips on his rum. "Why are you staying here with Nick and Faith?"

I think about how to answer for half a second, then just go for it.

"My husband cheated on me with a ton of prostitutes, gambled our money away, and completely screwed me over in every which way." I let out the first mouthful. "So I basically don't want to be alone, because if I'm left with my own thoughts, I might freak out. Or have a nervous breakdown, if you know what I mean? And I don't want to move in with my family because we tend to end up fighting. So, I'm a nomad for the summer...possibly the foreseeable future. Who knows where life will take me?"

Either Gus is drunk, doesn't care, or doesn't understand a word I said. Whichever it is, he continues as if he never asked the question.

"So, are you dating anyone?"

"No."

"I'd like to take you to dinner." He leans in nice and close when he says this. It's unfortunate for him because I instantly spot an abnormally long white hair poking out of his eyebrow, and it happens to be staring straight at me. It's suddenly all I can focus on.

"Let me take care of you." He eyes me up like a piece of that koobideh he just mentioned. "Come out to dinner with me."

From his tone I realize he thinks I should be honored.

"Oh, funny!" I pretend like it's not a real gesture.

"I'm serious." He brushes his arm against mine and I freeze.

I don't exactly know how to come back and be nice about it. The white hair in his eyebrow begins to flash in front of me like some psychedelic trip, urging me to just say no.

"So?" He's relentless, I'll give him that.

But it's all I can see. This white hair. I wonder why he's never plucked it.

"Ava?" Gus says.

As if heaven sends an angel, Leigh magically appears behind the bar.

"Ava," the teenager says with the sweetest smile I've ever seen. "Dad wants you to cut up more fruit for the sangria. We're out."

Now I know why everyone I ever encountered encouraged me to have a child. This is the moment that makes it all worth it. Leigh isn't even my kid, but she saved me.

"Totally." I hop out of my seat so fast I'm sure Gus's head spins like the exorcist.

I follow Leigh out of the bar, and when we're safely in the kitchen, I reach out and pull her in for a giant hug. I don't care if she hates it.

"You saved me." I know she can hear my passion.

"I know," she says with a knowing smile. "He wasn't cute. He creeped me out. I can't believe my dad thought he'd work for you. I couldn't let you suffer."

I have to laugh. What is it about being a teen that makes you not give a damn what comes out of your mouth?

"You're the best." She laughs when I squeeze her tight then shakes her head at me.

"You've got to be open to everything, Ava," she says, like a wise old sage. "But not *that* open."

CHAPTER 30

"I DID NOT INHALE"

THE PARTY HAS PRETTY MUCH cleared out.

Now it's just Faith, Nick, their friend, Charlie, and I sitting on the couches facing their infinity pool. Thanks to their staff, most of the party has already been cleaned up. We've kept a few flavored bottles of Ketel One, beers, and the cheese platter close by. Even though we've done nothing but eat all day, I still find myself grazing. It might be because of the vape pen Nick made me smoke (okay, maybe he didn't have to *make* me).

Whatever concoction he purchased has made me feel like I'm floating. I know Charlie is on the same—if not similar—planet as I am, because he's eating all the cheese with a vengeance.

Faith is sitting at the end of the couch. She's only had a few drinks and is watching Charlie in disbelief.

"There's dinner, too," she warns him.

"I'll be good." He waves off her concern.

Nick shuffles around on the couch and lifts up part of his shirt.

"It's hot, isn't it?" he asks as he leans back into the couch and closes his eyes.

"It's not that hot, honey," Faith disagrees. "But you are pretty loaded."

"I didn't drink much." He sounds tired. "Just a glass of sangria. Wasn't feeling it."

"It's probably all the food." Charlie's southern drawl is particularly pronounced as he cuts another piece of cheese and places it on the cracker. "I'm so stuffed and I can't stop eating."

We all laugh at the absurdity of his comment. Then I lean into the platter and dig in for some of my own gratuitous snacking. Faith joins and grabs a cracker for Nick, who is suspiciously quiet.

"Would you like some, honey?" she asks her husband.

He doesn't respond.

"Nick?" She starts to stand. "Nick!?"

Nick's head falls back on the couch. Something is wrong. My heart races as I run over and get behind the sofa and hold his head up. Faith is trying to get him to respond.

"Charlie! Call 9-1-1!" Faith shouts as she continues to speak to Nick, asking him to respond to her. Faith leans in and shakes his chin, whatever she can, to bring him back.

He's giving nothing.

My body trembles in fear and I start to pray. I look over at Charlie and he looks back at me, frozen with terror, his phone in his hand.

"Charlie?" I prod.

"I don't know..." He sounds aghast.

"You don't know what?" Faith yells over her shoulder.

"I don't know what the number is for 9-1-1."

It is a moment I'll never *ever* forget. Ever. The look on his face. How high he is. The gravity of the situation. The absurdity of his statement. I don't know whether to laugh, cry, or cut myself another piece of cheese.

"Charlie." I keep my voice as calm as I can. "It's just the numbers, *9-1-1*." I hope this makes sense to his foggy brain.

I look down at Nick with worry. He's definitely not in the hands of the A-Team—we're more like the Z-Team.

"Are you kidding me?!" Faith screeches at Charlie. She holds out her hand. "Give me the phone!"

"They're on." Thankfully, Charlie understood the memo and is speaking with the dispatcher. Thank God for small miracles.

"It's a man," he drawls out. "He's not doin' well. He might have had a stroke or something. I don't know what else to tell you...but can you get here? You just need to get here! That's all I can say. Get here. Now."

I look over at Faith, who is gently moving Nick so that he's flat on his back on the couch. I run around and try to help but she knows what she's doing. She props his feet up on two pillows and starts to fan him.

"Nick," she says soothingly. "Can you hear me? Focus on my voice."

Nick mumbles incoherently, and I let out the breath I've been holding. At least he's responding. Minutes go by but it feels like hours before the paramedics arrive. Charlie and I huddle together as Faith speaks to them and they work on Nick. I watch them look over the incriminating scene of the party.

Alcohol. Joints. I can only imagine what they're thinking.

"Were you smoking, sir?" one of them asks Nick as they transfer him to the stretcher.

"He was," Faith says, then points at Charlie and I like accomplices. "And so were they. Those two are stoned!"

What the hell?

Charlie and I look at each other in a panic and hold our hands up like we're about to be arrested. All I can think about is what I'm going to tell my parents when they have to bail me out of jail. Fortunately, the medics remain quiet, but the look on their face says it all. They are judging. And I can't say that I blame them.

They begin to transport Nick out of the house. As they roll him out of the side gate, I hear one of medics ask him in awe, "Is this your house, man?"

"Yes, it is," Nick says.

"Pretty dope."

○○

"He's being such an asshole." Faith sounds uncharacteristically grumpy as she stretches out on the sofa and pulls a cozy-looking blanket over her legs.

I was surprised she joined me today considering she spent half the night with Nick in the emergency room. Thankfully, the diagnosis is good: he only suffered heatstroke. Still, he was dehydrated, so they insisted on keeping him overnight for monitoring. Faith told me they also want to run tests on his heart this morning just to double check that everything is okay.

Nick did not appreciate the news one bit, and according to Faith, made sure everyone in the hospital knew it as well.

"I can't tell you how relieved I was when he fell asleep." Faith looks like she's exhausted. "I think the nurses and doctors were grateful as well. I'm sure they couldn't understand why the sleeping pill took three hours to work. They just don't know my husband's will."

"He *is* stubborn." I have to laugh.

"You have no idea," Faith concurs.

"In his defense, he did have a traumatic afternoon."

"Still," she says, annoyed. "He refused to accept that the hospital was full and had no private rooms. He wanted me to do something about it. I think he half expected me to try and grease someone to move him around."

I laugh. "Faith, I'm not surprised. Are you?"

"Not at all," she says, then glances away from me before her shoulders start to shake in mirth. "Oh my God, can we talk about Charlie for a second?"

We both fall over on the couch in hysterics.

"That was a moment I will never *ever* forget," I manage to say between gasps for air.

"Never," she agrees. It takes us a while to calm down, but when Faith speaks next she is serious.

"But God, Ava, was yesterday scary for me. I felt so helpless seeing the man I love like that. The way I saw our life together just flash before my eyes."

Her voice is small, unsure.

"Nick is my life." Faith's eyes brim with tears. "He's my whole world. All of the family's lives, really. We feed off his energy. He's this force of nature...and to see him like that—to see him so vulnerable. It was a moment for me."

"I can only imagine," I whisper in understanding. "He's always so strong."

"He is." I can see the love radiating from her eyes.

This is real—this feeling she has that seems to permeate from her soul. This is a culmination of a lifetime together; through good and bad, there's still this passion between them. It's palpable. I see it and I'm sure every other friend can as well. They make each other whole.

"All I could think about is what would happen if I lost him." Her voice trembles. "Because of our age difference, and the natural progression of life—Nick going before me...it's something I've always known in the back of my mind. But now, it's something that somehow feels more real."

I hadn't thought about how that part must have felt for her. Nick's so youthful that it never even crossed my mind.

"Maybe this will make you appreciate everything you have even more," I tell her softly.

Faith wipes a tear away.

"Especially time," she agrees.

CHAPTER 31

"BREATH OF STRIFE"

THE NEXT DAY, MARK AND I are sitting inside the sacred temple of Shaman Azria.

She specializes in breath work and according to Mark, is a miracle worker. We're currently sitting on two plush mats covered by matching white duvets.

"Welcome, sacred souls," Shaman Azria says rather dramatically. "Thank you for coming here and choosing this path of breath and life. I know it will change you in a profound way as it has for me and the hundreds of clients I see. I promise you two children of the great Mother Earth, from this day forward, nothing will ever be the same again for you. Breath is life. And life is breath. And in this divine temple we will connect to the source again."

Shaman Azria is dressed in a boho neon printed cape and has giant feather earrings. She's wearing all sorts of beaded bracelets that I'm sure have some sort of spiritual significance.

"I'd like you to close your eyes and open your arms wide like the majestic eagles you are," she says passionately, "so that I may sage you of all impurities."

She walks over to me first and proceeds to wave the sage all around my body while chanting an indecipherable prayer. The smoke is intense and a giant whiff of it bursts into my nose, singeing any thick hairs that might live there and sending me into an uncontrollable coughing fit.

"It's the darkness leaving you," Shaman Azria explains as she waves the sage around my face. "I can see the energy fighting to stay inside. Just let it out and let it go."

I want to tell her I'm choking because she literally blew smoke up my nose and it was too much to take in at one time, but I think better of it. I am here for healing, and who knows? She might be right. Maybe all the negative energy from my marriage and everything else in my life is on its way out. One can only hope.

She moves on to Mark, who suffers no coughing fit. I'm guessing the shaman thinks he doesn't have my darkness.

"I'd like you to lay down now and get under the duvet," she says as she dims the lights. "There will be soft music playing in the background that will help your brain waves while I guide you through the breathwork. The most important thing to remember is to let go. Let the breath consume you. Let it guide you to where it wants you to go. And above all, let it heal you."

Shaman Azria starts to play peaceful music—an orchestra of gongs and chants and humming that kind of vibrates through my body. We listen to the music for a few moments before she begins the process.

"Now I want you to follow my lead while I show you how this healing works," she says, again rather dramatically. "Breathe in through your nose and hold, and out through your mouth and hold."

She moves her arms with her breath and closes her eyes. She has us imitate her a few times to get the technique down before she tells us we're ready.

"Remember," she says before we begin, "to just *let go*."

We begin to breathe deeply with her. For the first few minutes, I can't seem to get out of my own head. My one reoccurring thought is—why did I pay two hundred dollars to have someone blow smoke all over me so I could learn what I came into the world knowing how to instinctively do? I thought I had pretty much mastered the art of breathing. I've been breathing on my own for almost forty years and I'm still alive.

"Allow your thoughts to float away as you keep focusing on your breath," Shaman Azria says, as if she's reading my mind. "Let go!"

Easy for you to say, lady.

"Nirvana will come if you free your mind." Her voice is softer now, beckoning me to think about that state of bliss. "Free. Your. Mind."

Free your goddamn mind, Ava! I repeat in anger to myself.

I think I will it to happen because something suddenly shifts.

It's either because she raised the volume or because she basically yelled at me, but I'm suddenly breathing in and out with Shaman Azria and Mark, totally lost in the process. All I can do is concentrate on taking in these deep breaths and feeling the mystical sounds thud in my chest.

My breath becomes my focus. It's like it's trying to take me somewhere. What the destination is—I have no idea. There is suddenly a relaxing lull in knowing that I don't have to know; I can just "let go."

And then...

I see a moment from my childhood, a scene buried in the recesses of my mind. My father is leaving on a plane to Los Angeles and I'm scream-crying and banging against the window of our house, begging him not to go. My mom pulls me away, holds me close, and tells me he has to go for work but he'll be back. The moment feels so sad to me. Like I'm somehow being abandoned by my hero, even though I know he's leaving because he has to. I can feel the pain it brought me as a little girl.

The memory breaks my dam.

I go from breathing with the shaman and Mark to scream-crying.

Like...wailing out loud. Shaman Azria rushes over to me and soothes my forehead, lovingly rubs my face, and tells me to let it out. That it will all be okay. For the life of me, I have no idea what

I'm letting go of, but I listen to the shaman and cry for that young girl not wanting her dad to leave her. It feels so unbelievably painful to me now. I'm so devastated for her—for me—and the emotion is overwhelming. But I let it out and let it go like she's guiding me to do.

After she's able to calm me down, I get back into the breathing, and a serenity that I can't really explain consumes me. I feel lighter, having somehow released something painful that I didn't even know I was holding on to.

When the breathwork is done, the shaman leaves Mark and I on our mats with our own thoughts so that we can process our experiences. I cover my head with the duvet and bury myself in the cloud that has enveloped me. I feel spent. Like I just had some intense therapy session.

I think about growing up in Utah and those times my dad would leave us for a business trip. The environmental work he was doing kept him away for long periods of time. He really wanted us to move to California because that's where his job was based, but my mom liked the ease of Utah and the comfort of having a close circle of friends in Salt Lake City, which has a large community of Iranian expats. I never realized how much his absence impacted me. My dad and I were always close—the sun rose and fell on his shoulders. He was everything to me. He still is. And every time he left, especially because it would be for so long...

It was an absence I felt in my soul.

I don't know why, but I start to cry again and my mind wanders. *Is this just therapy 101, Ava?*

I missed Dad in my younger years, then clung to the first man who seemed somewhat stable. A man who was there, but wasn't. One who would come and go for work—or whatever the hell else he was doing—but who always, *always* came home? Was this the deep-rooted issue behind why I stayed with Darian for so long?

"Girl, you had a serious moment there," Mark states the obvious, disrupting my reverie.

"Did I ruin yours?" I ask.

"No, but I did worry about you for a second. Then it seemed like Shaman Azria got your shit together."

"She helped for sure."

"What happened?" Mark asks. "Only if you want to share, of course."

"I just saw these pictures from my childhood that popped up out of nowhere," I tell him, still processing it all. "And I was almost transported back in time. I don't even know where the memory came from. It was crazy. Did something like that happen to you?"

He shakes his head.

"No," he says. "But during the breathwork I found myself saying goodbye to Scott. I was using this method I've heard about that essentially has you cut cords—so I did that with him."

"Cut cords?"

"Yeah, it's a spiritual release I read about online that you should do after a breakup," he explains, like it's the most logical thing in the world.

I can't help but giggle. "You do realize how ridiculous that sounds?"

"Any more ridiculous than you bawling your eyes out just because you were breathing harder than normal?" Mark raises a brow.

"Fair enough. Tell me about it."

"So apparently you need to visualize yourself with the person you want nothing to do with anymore—in your case, Darian—and then you picture cords that attach the two of you together and you cut them in your mind."

I envision cords and a giant pair of scissors.

"Huh. I'll think about it."

"I'm telling you," he says, "people swear by it."

"Maybe I'll try it one day."

"I think it would do wonders for your situation." Mark studies my face.

"You *just* cut your cords," I remind him politely. "It's not like you've seen results yet. Maybe we should wait and see how it works out for you before I start cutting?"

"I think it'll work for you." Mark is dead serious. "And I think you should do it on the full moon."

"Are you serious?" I suddenly picture myself running around naked like an ancient pagan priestess during the full moon.

"Full moons are powerful times." Mark suddenly sounds like Shaman Azria.

"You're a Jewish kid from Beverly Hills. What do you know about pagan rituals and the moon?"

"*Everyone* does full moon rituals." Mark looks at me like I'm the crazy one. "Duh."

CHAPTER 32

"FATHERS AND DAUGHTERS"

IT'S BEEN FOUR DAYS SINCE I've heard from New York City.

I can't even count the number of times I've checked my phone for a message. It sucks that I haven't heard from him. The whole dating app situation is starting to look appealing now, since none of Nick's picks worked out for me and I've excommunicated London because of the unsolicited dick pic. Even though I'm going out with Ryder tomorrow night, I'm not expecting that to lead to anything more serious.

I pull up into the cul-de-sac that leads to my dad's favorite hiking trail in Malibu. This is the longest I've ever gone without seeing my father. I know he's dying to talk to me face to face and make sure I'm okay. I've been avoiding him, and he knows it. But I've never wanted my dad to see me as weak or as a failure, and I feel like both right now.

My dad is standing at the edge of the trail waiting for me, wearing a smile that always tugs at my heart. Dad is the kind of man who is always smiling. Even if there's no reason to smile, he does. He's optimistic and happy, always pushing my sister and I to be our best in every way. He's our biggest champion.

My dad is wearing his signature white t-shirt and khaki shorts. He has his glasses on and his thick white hair is looking good from a new haircut.

I can't seem to stop myself from running over to him.

When I'm close enough, I move into his arms and let him pull me in for one of his bear hugs I close my eyes and let his presence soothe my anxiety. He gives the best hugs—the kind that engulf you in a sea of love and take away your pain, if only for a minute.

"Hi, Daddy." I sigh against his chest, feeling the familiar sense of peace I experience every time I'm around him.

"Honey," he says, with the lightest of Persian accents, and kisses me on top of my head. My dad, unlike my mom, doesn't have a thick accent. I think it's because he worked in the corporate world for so long and wanted to assimilate into American culture.

He pulls away so he can study my face. "Did I tell you I love you?"

"No, you haven't yet." This is my favorite thing my dad says to me, and he's said it since I was a little girl.

"I do," he tells me, with all the love in the world shining from his eyes. "You and your sister are my hopes and my dreams. You are the apple of my eye and the sunshine of my life."

Usually I tease him, but today I revel in his words. They feel like home.

"I'm glad you still have faith in me." I know he can hear the emotion in my voice.

"I've been very worried about you," he tells me, and the second he says this I burst into tears. He pulls me in close and hugs me tightly, whispering that everything is going to be all right, he's sorry my marriage turned out the way it did, and he loves me. He says these things over and over.

"Ava, your life will turn into something beautiful." He sounds like he believes it. "These kinds of journeys are put in front of us to teach us something. I promise you, love. This is just a moment of growth for you. I can clearly see your bright future."

I wipe my tears away.

"How do you know?" I whisper.

"Because I believe in you."

His words make my heart smile, working just as he likely intended.

"I love you so much, Daddy."

"I love you too." He pats my cheek. "Now, let's walk."

We start off and soon I can't help but admire the ocean view as I deeply inhale the scent of wild sage bushes lining the trail. This hike along the cliff is one of my favorite things to do, especially with my dad.

"So how are Faith and Nick?" he asks after a moment.

"They're good," I answer. "Happy and wonderful." I decide I won't tell him about the visit to the hospital. It will only upset him.

"They are nice people," he says. "They have been incredible friends to you."

"They are," I agree. "I'm very lucky."

"Very lucky." Dad is quiet for a moment, then asks, in a voice tinged with amusement, "So, how do you like sleeping on the couch?"

I look over at him and raise a brow.

"After this summer, you will be a professional at it." He laughs when he says this.

I can appreciate the humor he sees in my situation. "But I'm not on a couch. I have my own suite, and it's nicer than my room at the house I shared with Darian. Life could be worse."

"I'm only teasing."

"I know. Don't worry, I'm not going to start crying again."

"Your mother and sister think that's all you do lately."

"Well, it was...for a while," I admit. "If you could get a PhD in crying, I think I would have been able to receive one."

"With special honors," my dad agrees.

"Perhaps." I laugh.

We're quiet for a moment before Dad brings Darian up.

"Have you talked to him?"

"No."

"Why not?" he asks.

"I'm not ready to open communications just yet."

"Well, he called me."

I look over at him in shock. Darian was never close to my father, but he did respect him. I can't believe he had the balls to reach out to him. I would have thought he'd be too embarrassed by his actions.

"When?"

"A week ago," he admits. "We spoke for a few minutes."

"And what did he say?"

"He apologized." My dad's tone softens and I'm not surprised by this. He's always so kind and gives everyone the benefit of the doubt. "He said he was sorry you couldn't make each other happy. He wanted me to know that he would always love you and he wouldn't hurt you anymore. We just have to give him time to make it right."

"Interesting."

I keep my gaze glued on the ocean.

"Do you believe him?" I ask my dad.

He takes a moment to answer. "I think he believes what he's saying. I don't know if he will follow through, but I think he wants to."

"I thought it was supposed to get easier as we got older, Dad?" I look over at him. "Why do I already feel so tired of it all?"

"Sometimes, life does that to us. But you have to keep getting up and moving on."

"When will it stop raining on me?" I ask, knowing I sound like a whiny little girl.

"When you finally see the sun."

His words make me wonder if all I've been looking for are clouds lately.

"I can see your future, my love, and I know you're going to have a life you never imagined possible."

My dad believes in me.

"But what is that life?"

"Look forward to the adventure," he says then locks eyes with me. "Don't you remember the stories I told you about my life? Where I came from, and how hard I had to work to get here, to America?"

"Of course I remember."

I know how hard it was for him. He left home as a child and made his own way in life. He wanted something more than being a farmer like his father, and he worked hard to make his dreams come true as a successful environmental consultant.

"I wanted my family to live in this country," he explains. "I wanted my girls to have every advantage and opportunity they could. I wanted you to be seen as the equals you are to men."

"We are so grateful for all that you sacrificed for us," I say, and it's the truth. He worked his butt off for everything he has, for the life he gave us.

"It's not a sacrifice, when I see you and your sister thrive," he says with all the kindness in the world. "I had so many setbacks, so many obstacles thrown at me through the years, and I just kept going. I still keep going because that's what life is. When you stop moving or doing, that's when your soul dies."

I let his words sink in for a moment.

"You're right."

He points out at the view. "Look at what you get to see right now."

I take in the splendor of the blue ocean. "I am very lucky."

"You are, Ava. And your mother and I can't wait to watch you shine."

CHAPTER 33

"BLOW ME"

"She hated giving me blow jobs."

"I'm sorry?" I pick up my glass of wine and take a long sip. When I asked Ryder why he broke up with his girlfriend of nine years, I wasn't expecting this answer.

"I'm a blow job kind of guy." His face is flushed, and he has a grin that alcohol and a good time bring.

I don't know how to respond.

"Sorry to be vulgar," he says, somewhat sheepishly. "But it's the truth."

"I appreciate your honesty." I avoid eye contact by putting a dollop of humus on my plate.

We're having dinner at Avra and the evening has been easy and fun. Ryder's sense of humor is great, and he hasn't stopped asking me questions. Up until this comment, there hasn't been one awkward second. But now we're on a second bottle of wine and he's tipsy.

"I feel like I need to be honest with you about my needs," he says, leaning forward.

"I get it," is the only thing I can muster.

His blue gaze bores into mine with an intensity that I understand. Ryder wants to hook up. I'm guessing he wants me to give him one of those blow jobs he loves. It's as clear as day.

"I'm easy, Ava." He winks at me. "Give me a blow job that satisfies me, and I'll go down on you for hours."

I'm sure my mouth is hanging open (no double entendre intended).

"I'm sorry?"

He smiles. "I'll make you come. All I demand in return is loyalty, honesty, drive, and unconditional love."

That's all?

"That's quite a list."

"Not really. It's simple. My needs are simple. Feed me. Blow me. Fuck me. And be a lady when we're out with my friends."

Alcohol is the best truth serum. I watch him pick up his glass and drink some more. I wonder what else is about to come out of his mouth. What could he possibly say to outdo this last statement?

"I've been told that I have a magic tongue...just like a magic Persian carpet."

There it is.

"I'd like to go down on your carpet if you'd allow me." He says it so earnestly that I can't be mad or offended.

"I-I'll take that into consideration," I stutter out with an awkward smile.

"Shall we check into the Beverly Hills Hotel?"

"Maybe next time."

Or never.

Dating apps here I come.

○○

This is my last dinner with the Shermans before my caravan of one journeys to the home of my girlfriend, Lisa, and her husband, Travis, for a few weeks. The Shermans went all out for my last night here by having an extra special dinner.

"What time are you heading out?" Nick asks as he cuts up his chicken.

"I'm leaving in the morning."

"We're going to miss you," Faith says as her eyes fill with tears. "You know you're a part of our family and can come over whenever you want."

"Are you sure the husband is okay with that?" I say, teasing Nick.

"You're wife number two for eternity." His voice turns soft. "I felt your loving hands on my head when you all thought I was about to kick it."

"So are you saying we didn't scare you off?" Faith asks me later that night, when the two of us are sitting outside by her firepit sipping on our usual cocktails.

"You didn't scare me at all."

"You sure?" she teases.

"On the contrary," I tell her, "you gave me hope."

Later that night, while I'm lying in bed thinking about my stay at the Shermans', I'm surprised by how fast the trip went by. It feels like yesterday that I arrived, and now here I am, leaving for my next destination. Time really does fly by when you're having fun.

I glance over at my iPhone and pick it up, opening the diary app for my stay with the Shermans.

It's cleverly titled (insert sarcasm): *What I learned from the Shermans*

I skim over the list and add a few notes. I let my own words seep in as I read over it...

I learned that peace comes when you realize you don't have to fight the little things. And with that peace comes happiness.

That opposites can attract. There is no magic formula in a relationship. It just exists when it's right.

That life can be beautiful. That it's all about perspective, and all you have to do is sometimes flip it around in order to see it in a different way or lens.

That time is precious, and we have to do our best not to take it for granted. You can lose what you love in a second and there's no going back. This moment is the only one that is guaranteed.

That breathing in and letting go can do wonders for healing old wounds. Just breathing can change the entire feeling in your body and soul.

And one of the most important lessons...

That a dick is a man's best friend, and a blow job really does matter.

91302
THE ESTATES
"EMO VS. PHYS"

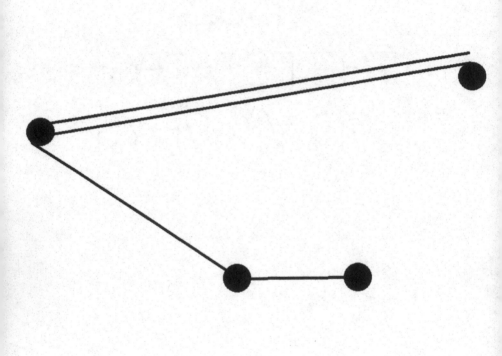

CHAPTER 34

"MARS AND VENUS"

IT'S HOT.

Like *valley* hot. And if you've ever crossed the 405 at Ventura Blvd and hit the 101, you know exactly what I'm talking about. The second you leave the west side the temperature rises by four hundred degrees (I exaggerate, but not by much). Thus, making the valley a land of eternal controversy.

There are those from California who believe it is *the* place to live—with its rolling hills and horse pastures and space... Endless, *endless* space. And then there are those who believe the valley is where Satan took up his primary residence—hence the reason for the scorching temperatures. Whatever side you might fall on, there is one thing that all Angelinos agree: when you go north past Mulholland Blvd, heat awaits. Uncomfortable, scorching heat.

"The problem with your relationship with Darian was you were an Emo and a little bit of Phys, and he was just Phys." My girlfriend Lisa gives me this piece of insight as we watch her two young children play in the pool with their friends.

"There were so many problems with my relationship...the emotional verses physical couple theory is probably just one of the many flaws," I say, slathering sunscreen on my legs as I wipe sweat from my face. "I've analyzed it to death and it's really exhausting."

"At least you're not crying anymore." Lisa smirks at me and brushes her brown hair away from her pretty face.

Out of all my girlfriends, Lisa is my newest addition and one that has been a godsend. We met through a mutual friend and clicked immediately—it was as though we had known each other forever. She's an incredible human who's super loyal and generous to those she loves. Lisa and her husband are also two of the most giving people I've ever known. She's no-nonsense and unemotional, and is the one friend who gives me as much tough love as my sister. There have been many moments I've thought they must be the same person.

"To be honest, every single time I cry now, or am about to, I think about all the wrinkles I must be creating—so that alone stops me. It's not because I've grown in some exponential way and have had some epiphany. It all boils down to vanity."

"If it works, I like it." She nods her head in approval then shouts out to her son, "Austin! No dunking your sister underwater!"

Her cute eight-year-old gives Lisa an innocent look.

"I saw you," Lisa says, pointing at him. "You can't put one over me."

He gives the kind of devilish smile that makes me worry for Lisa. This one is going to be a handful. At least I know she's completely aware of it.

Lisa is displeased. "He can be such an asshole sometimes."

"Men," we both say at the same time and laugh.

"He's exactly like Travis and just as stubborn. Sometimes I think I must be raising my husband."

"You probably are."

"Great," she says, looking at me and rolling her eyes. "Just what I wanted."

"Why is it that every single time a kid misbehaves they're exactly like the parent not present?" I wonder out loud.

"Because I don't have the same issues as my husband," Lisa says passionately. "And you know I'm way more easygoing."

She sounds more annoyed than easygoing right now, but I'm not one to call a friend out.

"I think you should look at this like a blessing. If you see any of Travis's flaws in Austin, you'll get to fix them at a young age. Imagine what a catch he'll be for whatever partner he finds later in life."

Lisa squints her eyes like she's actually contemplating my words.

"Your children are fresh canvases," I tell her as we watch them play. "They are ready to become masterpieces."

"Okay, Michelangelo," she says sarcastically. "You make it sound so easy."

"Children never are," I respond.

"What child-rearing experience do you have that I don't know about?" Lisa asks.

"I'm just observant."

Sylvia, her adorable four-year-old with a cherub face, gets out of the pool and runs over to us, cupping a ladybug in her hand.

"Look, Mama!" She shows us the tiny little insect crawling around. "I saved it from drowning!"

"You're such a good girl." Lisa pulls her in for a hug and gives her a ton of kisses. "You have such a kind heart. Do you think you should go place the little ladybug on the flower over there?" Lisa encourages her. "It might be hungry and want to look for its family."

"It has a family?" Sylvia wonders in awe.

"Of course it does, honey! It's got brothers and sisters and a mom and dad."

Sylvia's eyes are round. "And a grandma and grandpa?"

"Yes," she tells her.

"I'm going to help the ladybug find its family again!" Sylvia runs off excitedly.

"No running!" Lisa yells after her, and her daughter immediately slows down.

"She's the cutest," I remark.

"She's my sweet little angel. I mean, just look at the difference between Austin and her. Boys and girls. Mars and Venus. It's unbelievable. Seriously, watch them."

Sylvia is at the bed of roses placing the ladybug on a flower. She is so gentle and innocent. She's even talking to the bug. She's a delicate little thing—all ethereal with those angelic smiles of hers.

"Mom!" Austin screams out, drawing my attention away from the serene moment. "Watch this!"

He runs and does a cannon ball in the pool, successfully splashing us and every dry item in the immediate vicinity.

"Again!" he shouts out in glee when he comes up for air. He and his friend scream with joy at the mayhem they just caused.

The difference between Austin and Sylvia is remarkable.

"Right on time!" Lisa looks over at me and shakes her head.

"That was kind of perfect," I agree.

"Changing the subject," Lisa says, "I forgot to ask if you have everything you need in the guest house? Are you comfortable there?"

Lisa's guest house is a two thousand square foot abode that sits on her enormous property. She and Travis live in one of the most exclusive areas in the valley. With over three acres of land and a home that could comfortably house a small village, their living space is idyllic. Even though a lot of their neighbors are celebrities, the community has a different vibe from the city. It's more laid back and family oriented. If I could describe it in one word, it would be chill.

"I am more than comfortable. The place has everything I need."

"Good. Just let me know if you need anything."

"I will."

Travis comes out of the house and walks over to where we're lounging by the pool.

"Hey, Ava." He leans down to give me a hug and kiss on the cheek "It's nice to see you."

"You too," I say to Lisa's hubby. Travis happens to be one of my favorites. He's a ton of fun and very easy to talk to. He never judges anyone, and sometimes I think he might even be sympathetic to a fault, but that's one of the reasons he's so loveable.

"You didn't want to get in the pool?"

I look at the water and shrug.

"It's ninety degrees," he coaxes. "Just the way you like it."

"All Persians, honey." Lisa smirks.

I laugh. Yes, Persians are known for liking especially hot pools. We won't get in the water if it's not at least eighty degrees.

"You should take a night swim," Travis says, then looks at Lisa. "They called from the gate and Brenda and Kayla are here. I'll watch the kids while you ladies do your thing."

I look over at Lisa.

"Are you having a party I didn't know about?"

"Not a party. I've just got some girls coming over that I want you to meet. You're going to love them. And...I ordered a ton of sushi from Sugar Fish," she says to my pleasure.

I'm curious as to why Lisa hasn't revealed this plan to me sooner.

"Just relax. This will be good for you!"

I look over at Travis. "Should I be worried?"

He gives me a small smile and shrugs.

"Maybe."

CHAPTER 35

"FIRST WIVES CLUB"

"I LEFT HIS ASS OVER two years ago and I'm still having to relive all the trauma he caused. This divorce is taking everything from me!" Brenda Cranston, the ex-wife of one of the most famous NFL players in the country, says to me between her bites of sushi.

"Please," the British-born Kayla says as she holds up her hand, "I think I take the cake with my deadbeat. I have to pay him fifteen thousand dollars a month in alimony, plus the cost of the nanny *and* the chef he needs to take care of the kids when he has them, because the loser stopped working the last two years of our marriage. Convenient for him, is it not?"

"I don't know why you ever let him stop working," Brenda says, shaking her head in disappointment. "That was a dumb move."

"He said he wanted to be a stay-at-home dad." Kayla is possibly the hippest-looking mom I've ever set eyes on. She's wearing leather pants, a leather crop top with a jacket, and looks like she just had her hair and makeup professionally done.

She seems to be offended by Brenda's comment. "I was trying to be sympathetic to his needs."

"You were just being stupid," Brenda throws in her two cents.

"I like to think of it as a temporary leave of mental fortitude," Kayla says defensively.

I think I might adopt her saying.

I stare in fascination at the two women. They are both larger than life. Kayla is a highly successful trader—basically a baller in her own right—and Brenda is whip smart and beyond cool. She dedicated her life to her kids and her ex-husband's crazy success-ful career—although it's evident the latter didn't quite work out as anticipated.

Jennifer, another one of Lisa's newly divorced friends and someone I've met a few times before, has just arrived. She's busy fill-ing her plate with sushi, but that doesn't stop her from chiming in. She's slightly overweight, a bit disheveled, and extremely likeable.

"Brenda's right," she says over her shoulder. "Everyone knew that letting your husband quit his job was a bad idea the sec-ond you told us, Kayla. Especially when you let him hire that Norwegian au pair. For God's sake, she had double Ds and was way too hot. I don't know what you were thinking."

"Have you seen my breasts? They're perfect. Even after three kids. And they don't sag the way hers do," Kayla proclaims, sound-ing insulted.

"Your breasts are pretty perfect," Lisa agrees.

"Thank you," Kayla nods at her. "And he was my husband. I married him, and I trusted him unfortunately."

"Mistake number one." Brenda takes a shot of the sake. "You can never trust a man with a large bank account and a single woman who knows it."

"That's not true." Lisa rolls her eyes. "You all just picked men you were supposed to procreate with, not live out the rest of your lives with."

"That's not the way I went into my wedding," Jennifer says as she joins us at the table. "I thought I was in for happily ever after."

Last time I met her, Jennifer admitted that her husband left her for a man. She's trying to be friends with him and his part-ner but it's hard, because she's clearly still in love with him, which makes my heart ache for her. Jennifer's predicament makes me think of London. The two would have a ton in common. She might even enjoy a dick pic from him.

"You had past-life karma you had to end," Lisa says, as if it's the most logical explanation in the world.

This is why I love my friend. Even though she's type A squared and one of the most realistic and no-nonsense women I know, she still believes in past lives, karma, and soul destiny.

"Do you really believe this crap?" Brenda looks offended by Lisa's words. "I did not pick this jerk in some heavenly space, only to allow myself to be shit all over, because he's a lying, cheating asshole. I reject that theory on principle."

"I kind of do as well," I chime in and look over at Lisa. "Darian and I don't even have kids, so there's no one I was supposed to bring into the world with him."

"You picked Darian." Lisa looks unfazed. "And you picked Devon, Brenda. You made a soul contract."

According to Lisa, a soul contract is an agreement you make when you're dead to come back and fix whatever past life negativity you might've had with a friend, lover, or family member. The whole theory is based on the idea that every single one of your relationships is predestined and that we keep coming back to the same people in different lives, with different roles, to learn lessons and become highly elevated souls so that we don't have to come back again. Basically, earth is school, and we keep coming here until we finally get it right and graduate.

"I'm still not buying it. I mean, there are moments I think Darian acted more like my son than husband, but I would never have chosen *this*. What kind of crazy person would?"

"I second that," Brenda says.

"Third," Kayla says and raises her hand.

"Fourth," Jennifer pours some sake for herself.

"It's so simple." Lisa is looking at us like we're the idiots. "You don't see it yet. But you will."

"Girl." Brenda shakes her head. "That's a tough pill to swallow."

"It is," Lisa agrees. "But if you start changing the way you look at things maybe you'll see your ex like a life lesson and not an albatross."

"Oh, he was a life lesson, all right," Brenda says, with an edge to her voice. "He was a lesson on what *not* to do. At least now, I'll be able to steer my girls in the right direction. Help them pick a man who deserves them."

"You hope you'll be able to," I mutter as I take a sip of my sake.

Brenda pins me with her gaze.

"What do you mean by that?"

I shrug. "I'm sure your ex was charming when you met him," I start. "People tend to be on their best behavior when you first start going out. Ted Bundy didn't give away that he was a serial killer when he smiled at his victims. They thought he was just a handsome, normal man."

"Honeymoon phase," Jennifer adds. "Ava's right. Every relationship has it. I even lied and hid the fact that I have chronic IBS from Josh. For the first two years of our relationship, he thought I was a robot who never had to use the restroom. He always wondered why on every trip, I would disappear to the *gift shop* multiple times a day."

We all laugh.

"I met my ex when we were in high school," I tell them. "He was so different then. And to be fair, I was too. I'm pretty sure my opinion of him would have been different if we had met in our twenties or early thirties."

"You still would have married him. It was your soul destiny," Lisa states adamantly.

"You and this soul destiny thing." I shake my head at her. "I reject the idea that all of us beautiful, intelligent women would willingly pick this kind of suffering to learn a lesson."

"And why do we need to learn this lesson again?" Kayla asks as she takes off her leather jacket. "What's the purpose?"

It's over one hundred degrees in the valley. Thank God she took the jacket off, I think. I was getting hot just looking at her.

"To graduate to the next level," Lisa says.

I still have no idea what she's talking about.

"What's the next level?" Brenda wants to know.

"Higher consciousness," Lisa says like it's the clearest thing in the world.

"What does that even mean?" Jennifer says in frustration. "I'm sorry but my days are filled with Mommy and Me classes, Kumon, Russian math for my kids, and piano—I don't have time to read about my consciousness. I'm lucky I make it to bed at night. Sometimes I fall asleep on the couch. Sitting up."

"Wait." I hold up my hand. "Back up. What is Russian math?"

"You don't want to know." Brenda rolls her eyes. "It's some serious shit."

"We got off easy," I say sympathetically. "I don't think I would have ever graduated if I had to do any of this stuff."

"No," Jennifer contests, "you would have graduated, but you would've had grey hair at eighteen."

"A full head of it," Kayla agrees. "Kids these days have about five hours of homework a night. I pretend that I don't feel sorry for them, but secretly, I'm horrified and think I might be robbing mine of their childhood."

"Me too," Jennifer agrees, then turns to Lisa. "So, I'm sorry I don't have time to think about my consciousness between kids, school, and thinking I'm a bad parent. My soul karma is the last thing I'm worrying about."

"It's at the bottom of my list too," Kayla agrees.

"It's not about where it is on your list." Lisa sounds frustrated. "It's just about the lessons, and why things happen the way they do. And just accepting them. You'll find peace that way."

I ruminate on her theory for a moment. According to Lisa, Darian hurt me in this life to pay back some awful deed I did to him in another. And this is something I just had to go through to learn a lesson.

It kind of sounds brutal.

"I feel like I was always a nice person in all the lives I've lived," I admit to my friend.

"I was definitely a Pharaoh or a queen," Brenda announces with conviction.

"Right," Kayla says sarcastically. "God forbid any of us were peasants on the streets in ancient Rome."

"I think I might have lived a life like that." Jennifer raises her hand and I laugh at the serious look on her face. "I don't feel like I was a queen."

"I think you might have been one," I encourage. "You never know."

"Know thyself." Jennifer slowly shakes her head then narrows her eyes at me. "I really don't think you were a queen either, Ava."

"Really?" I don't know whether to be offended or to laugh. "I kind of feel like I might have been royalty in another life. I mean, I am Persian after all, and I like nice things."

Apparently, this statement is funny as hell. Everyone is laughing.

"What?" I'm offended.

"You're Persian and like nice things?" Lisa mocks me. "What does that have to do with anything?"

"It means everything!" I exclaim. "What Persian do you know who isn't wearing some type of designer clothing, shoe, belt, or bag?"

The group gets suspiciously quiet.

"Do you know any Persian who doesn't own gold, platinum, and some type of precious stone?" I continue. "And I would venture to bet you'd find most wearing these items at all times."

Dead silence. And so, I must go on.

"Do one in three Persians name their child after a designer brand, or a car, or a famous Italian?"

We could be in a deep space. There's not one peep from any of them.

"*Now* do you understand why I know I had to have been some type of royalty?" I ask rather dramatically. "We like nice things. I am positive my past lives were filled with them."

"Point taken." Jennifer claps. "That was a clear, concise, well-thought-out argument regarding your past life hierarchy as a Persian."

"Thank you." I smile in appreciation.

"You should have been a lawyer like Layla," Lisa agrees.

"Maybe I was in another life."

CHAPTER 36

"PAST LIVES & KARMA"

AFTER THE LADIES LEAVE AND because the weather is so insanely hot, I retreat to the guest house and blast the air conditioner. This is unusual behavior for me because I hate AC. Every part of it. I hardly ever put it on. Fortunately, Darian felt the same way, so that was one thing we never argued about over the years.

My thoughts pause on him for a moment.

I wonder what he's doing, and more importantly, if he's okay. At times, Darian did battle with bouts of depression, and when they would come, they were intense. I hope that he's not going through any of that. I close my eyes and send a quick prayer out into the universe and wish him well. With all things considered, and as I try to continue to grow as a human, this is the best I can do.

My phone rings and it's an unknown number. I send it to voicemail. I immediately think of New York City and the fact that I still haven't heard from him. I decide to take the plunge and do something completely uncharacteristic.

> **Me:** Hi. How's your day?

When I don't hear from him within two minutes I start to spin. Why did I send a message? What was I thinking?

And then...

> **New York City:** It's been crazy for me. I haven't figured out my dates yet, but I'll let you know as soon as I do. How are you?

Me: I'm good. I'm in the valley. It's hot.

New York City: You're hot.

I can feel my cheeks flush.

New York City: I'm sitting down for a work dinner now. I will hit you up later.

Me: Have a nice night.

New York City: You too, beautiful. Before I go... I've been thinking a lot of about that thing called destiny.

My heart pounds. I put the phone down and stare at it like it's possessed and then it pings again. I grab it quickly and try to temper my disappointment that it's Lisa.

Lisa: Pizza for dinner. Any preference?

Me: I'm easy.

Lisa: Says the woman who can count the number of sexual partners she's had on one hand—only one finger to be exact. PLEASE be easy!

I laugh.

Me: Hoping to be in the future.

I see Lisa immediately start to text back.

Lisa: We need to immediately sign you up for a dating app. I'm not taking no for an answer. Come back to the house when you're done relaxing. I'll be with the kids.

Me: Will do.

She texts again.

Lisa: I almost forgot—I had Norma leave a book for you while we were having lunch with the ladies. It's by your nightstand. ☺

I send her a heart emoji back and walk into the bedroom. I glance at the nightstand. *Many Lives, Many Masters* by Brian Weiss.

Of course Lisa sent this. I'm not surprised.

I pick up the book and quickly read the back blurb and am intrigued. It's about a psychotherapist who puts his patient under hypnosis, and the patient begins to recall different lives. Because of his pedigree, the story sounds incredibly fascinating. It's not that long either. I lay down on the bed and decide to give it a go.

One hour leads to two, then three, and I am so riveted I lose track of everything. I'm immediately pulled into the story. I fly through the book in one sitting. When I'm done, I close my eyes and try and absorb everything I just read. This book was written by a well-respected doctor and the manner in which he stumbled upon the patient's memories feels very real. I contemplate the idea for a long time. If there *is* such a thing as past lives...

Could Lisa's theories be possible? Is she right?

Are we souls who keep reincarnating together? Maybe Darian *was* my son in another life? Or an aunt or an uncle? What if I did owe him something for a sin I committed against him in a past life?

Have we now paid our karmic debt to each other? Is there really such a thing?

For Hindus, Buddhists, and Sikhs, reincarnation is the foundation of their beliefs. They live their lives according to that doctrine. It's a hard idea to contemplate, especially for someone who sees things more black and white, but it is quite a beautiful one. To know that you'll always reconnect with your loved ones in one way or another is comforting.

But then, the idea of coming back again and again...

And again.

Who wants that?

I certainly don't.

I want a heaven, with pearly white gates and angels opening the doors, telling me, "It's going to be all right now, Ava. For the most part, you did well. On a scale of one to ten, I'd say you were a solid eight. Some days maybe you were a two or a three, but overall, you were good."

I look up at the ceiling and press my hands together in front of me like I'm in prayer.

"God?" I whisper up into the air. "Hi. It's me, Ava."

I hope he's listening right now.

"If you want to do me any favors and this whole reincarnation thing is real, I beg of you..."

I take a deep breath and plead with all my heart.

"Can I be one and done?" I implore.

I'm not surprised God doesn't answer, but I still plead again.

"One and done."

CHAPTER 37

"SEX AND TRUTHS"

"A VIRTUOUS WIFE IS A crown to her husband, and a shameful one is like rot in his bones."

I read the Proverb, carefully written onto a plaque, over again and point it out to Lisa as we walk through a shop in Calabasas.

"See this?"

"Truth," Lisa says.

"No doubt," I agree and stare at the quote again.

Huh. Makes me wonder. "You don't think *I* was rot in Darian's bones?"

"Are you insane?" Lisa looks like she thinks I am.

"What?" I shrug. "Maybe I'm the reason he went down the path he did."

"*You're* the reason?"

I think about it for a moment. "I'm trying to be more self-aware."

"Blaming yourself for Darian's failures is not being self-aware, it's making excuses for another individual's mistakes and justifying the pain he caused you."

"I'm not justifying it," I defend myself. "I'm just taking ownership for the hand I played in the failure of our relationship."

"I'm proud of you for that," she says sternly. "But he did what he did on his own, with his own free will—a liberty we all have. If you start blaming yourself, I'll call your sister. We will gang up on you and I promise, you won't like it."

Lisa holds up a cute zip sweater. "This would look so good on you. Try it on."

"I love it," I say taking the hanger from my friend. I look at the price tag and hand it right back.

"Out of my price range right now," I say to her. "I can't emotionally invest in it because it might turn into a financial decision that I will regret later."

Lisa doesn't argue. She nods then says, "Maybe I'll get it for me."

"Perfect. Then I can borrow it."

Lisa and I enjoy another hour of shopping before we meet up with my good friend, Aria, for lunch at a local Italian restaurant. I've known Aria for many years. We met in New York around the time I also met the infamous New York City. We became fast friends. She's a successful actress who happens to be one of the smartest people I know. I don't think I've met anyone more nerdy or brainy than Aria. Sometimes I think she reads encyclopedias just for fun. If she hadn't been discovered at a young age, I'm pretty sure she would have been a neurosurgeon.

"You look so good!" Aria pulls me in for one of her bear hugs. "Seriously, it's like a five-ton weight has been lifted off of you. Whatever you're doing, keep it up!"

"That's because a weight has been lifted," Lisa agrees.

"Glad I'm not looking so *heavy* anymore," I say sarcastically as we sit at the table.

"I'm starving. The burrata appetizer is amazing, along with the fried zucchini." Lisa flags down a waiter. "I'm going to have to order us some appetizers because I can't wait."

"Sounds delicious!" Aria says as we settle in. Her eyes twinkle as she stares at me. I know she's studying me down to every detail. "So...tell me everything! I've missed you so much!"

I give her the short version—mainly focusing on the ayahuasca, which causes her to almost hit the floor laughing, and the guys I've met. I leave out any reference to New York City because I'm not sure I'm ready or know how I want to talk about him.

"Um..." She puts her hand on her chest, sighing rather dramatically. "I'm sorry, you *kissed two different men*?" She looks at me like I'm a stranger she just met.

"And?" My eyes flicker from her to Lisa, who's already been informed of the situation and who, I might add, was very pleased by my behavior.

"I'm impressed." Aria sounds like a proud mom. "I never thought this day would come. I honestly thought you'd die a virgin."

"But I'm *not* a virgin."

"You basically are."

"I'm not following."

"Sex with the same man for all those years...and not much happened before that."

When she puts it this way, I guess she might be kind of right.

"Now, you're a kissing whore," she adds slyly. "I like it."

I know she's joking, but still—"whore" and "Ava Monfared" in the same sentence sounds like a fantasy novel.

"It's only been a couple of months since Darian and I separated," I point out. "I think I'm doing pretty well."

"Semantics. You've been mentally done for a lot longer." She waves me off. "And in our last conversation about men, you said you'd rather eat glass than have a man come anywhere near your nether regions."

I laugh. "I was exaggerating. Obviously, I was in a bad place."

"Doesn't sound like you're there anymore. It sounds like you're moving on."

"I guess I am," I say slowly.

"Have you sat down with Darian yet?"

"No. I'm not ready to see him in person."

"You can't hide forever," Lisa says firmly. "And the sooner you see him, the faster you'll have closure."

"You'll know when you're ready." Aria studies me. "But Lisa is right, facing him is part of letting it all go. It's part of cutting the cords."

Cord cutting *again*. I remember Mark's advice at the breath work session. He was adamant I do this too. I had forgotten about it, and now I think I missed the last full moon.

"We'll see." I look away from them and know I sound like an ostrich again, but I can't help it.

"How's Don?" I change the subject, asking about Aria's on-again, off-again boyfriend for the last seven years.

"He's Don," she says with a laugh.

"What does that mean?" I ask.

"Well, he proposed."

The way she says it...it's like she's asking me what I'm having for lunch.

"I'm sorry, what?!"

"I second that!" Lisa squeals.

"It's Don!" Aria laughs. "He was in a car accident, and he thought he was going to die so he proposed."

"Wait..." I don't know where to begin. "Is he okay?"

"Totally. But he saw his life flash before him, and he says he realized that I'm part of that life and future."

"Holy. Shit."

"Yeah," Aria says as she pulls out a small red box from her purse and flips it open. A beautiful diamond ring shimmers against the velvet, white cushion.

"OhmyGod!" Lisa and I yell out at the same time.

"It's beautiful!" I say to her.

"Why aren't you wearing it?" Lisa wants to know.

Aria flips the box shut. "Because is marriage really a good idea?"

"Yes!" Lisa says.

I stay quiet.

"Ava?" She looks at me, with what I interpret as hope.

"Look," I say, throwing my hands up. "I am the wrong person to ask about this right now. But you love him. And he loves you. And this is beautiful. So, go for it!"

"That's not much support of the institution." Aria laughs at me.

"It's too soon for me to think about marriage," I respond. "I don't know what else you want me to say."

Before I can go on, the waiter comes over to our table, displaying a bottle of rosé.

"Ladies," he tells us, "the kind gentleman at the bar asked me to have this sent over for you to enjoy."

"That's my favorite!" Lisa exclaims.

We all glance over at the bar, and lo and behold, Travis waves at us. He looks at Lisa and gives her a thumbs-up, and she immediately gets up and walks over to him.

"OhmyGod, is this really happening?" Aria whispers.

"Yes," I whisper back.

I watch my friend walk into Travis's arms and kiss him on the lips. He hugs her tightly and whispers something in her ear before giving her another lingering kiss, picking up his takeout bag and waving goodbye to us.

"Enjoy, ladies," he says kindly. "See you at the house, Ava."

"You're the best!" I say to Lisa's husband.

Lisa sits back down and gives us a giddy smile.

"He's so romantic," Aria says. "I can't believe he just did that."

"I love Travis," I say.

"We're sitting at a table with a woman who has the living embodiment of a great marriage," I say to Aria. "He's so in love with her he buys her bottles of wine when she's with her friends. And lord knows what he whispered in her ear."

We stare at Lisa. She has that secret *I get sex all the time* smile on her face. I decide to let Aria in on what I know.

"Lisa and Travis still have sex three to four times a week, and they've been together since they were sixteen."

"What's the magic trick?" Aria's eyes light up in fascination.

CHAPTER 38

"TRICKS"

For once, Lisa looks shy.

"There is no magic trick," Lisa says with an embarrassed shrug. "I just love him... and I'm insanely attracted to him."

"Still?" Aria looks surprised. "After all this time?"

"Yes!" Lisa laughs.

"No, seriously." Aria shakes her head in disbelief. "For real?"

"*Yes*," Lisa says again. I notice how her face is slowly turning a light shade of red. It's nice to turn the tables on her for a change. "Why is that so hard to believe?"

"Because most people say things change after a short period of time," I interject my own opinion here.

"Not when it's right," Lisa replies. "And not everyone needs to have sex four times a week for it to be right."

"I think they should be," Aria takes a sip of her water.

I laugh and have to agree. "It definitely would be nice."

"But I am seriously impressed." Aria puts her hand on her heart. "Respect."

"I second that," I say.

Aria's eyes are round as she takes a sip of her water. I know she's still trying to process this piece of information.

"But how?" Aria can't let it go. "For real? How? I need to know because this doesn't seem normal."

I chuckle. I'm secretly happy that Aria is asking the question I've always wanted to ask, but avoided because I thought it was none of my business.

"What do you mean, how?" Lisa looks at her like she's crazy. "How do we have sex?"

"No." She shakes her head. "How do you still want each other like that after all these years? And kids! And life! And all that stuff in-between?"

"What do you want me to say? He's my man. He turns me on." I smile at her.

"And you clearly turn him on. I'm just in awe," Aria says.

"When it's right," she tells us, "it's right in *every* way. And I think sex is very important. It's a way to connect when all the garbage of life gets in the way. I think it's a real problem when couples stop being intimate."

Sex was one of the areas that kept Darian and I together at the beginning of our relationship, and one that tore us apart at the end. We stopped being intimate. We stopped touching. Cuddling. Any type of physical activity just ended. I don't even know for how long. But it was definitely...years. Wow. What kind of marriage did we have?

"I agree wholeheartedly," Aria states as she take a sip of her wine. "Don and I have a ton of it too."

The two look over at me.

"What?" I ask.

"You need to get in on the whole sex thing as well," Aria says. "Maybe you should consider graduating to third or fourth base with these *kissing friends* of yours. Ryder sounds hot and has a great name."

I can feel myself blush.

"He is hot. And he likes blow jobs."

"Then what are you waiting for? Do you remember how to give a blow job?" Aria encourages. "Just rip the Band-Aid off. Do him, or do some stranger you never have to talk to again."

"I'm not having random sex," I say forcefully.

"Why not?" Lisa wants to know.

"Because it's just not who I am," I admit. "Look, I'd love to be the one-night-stand girl but that is just so not going to happen. I'm not genetically made that way."

"You never know," Aria says. "You could get loaded one night at a bar and go for it. You don't know what you don't know."

"Highly doubtful." I retort. "Highly, *highly* doubtful."

"I agree with Aria, but I know we might as well be talking to a wall right now." Lisa sounds disappointed, and looks over at Aria. "I think we should just be happy she's kissing."

"What about phone sex?" Aria continues relentlessly.

"OhmyGod!" I know I'm bright red. "Can we just get back to Don and why you're walking around town with an engagement ring in your purse and not on your hand?"

Aria shrugs. "You're single now...shouldn't we take this moment to hit the town together? When is this opportunity going to come again?"

"Nice try at deflecting," I say. "Don is a great guy, and we all know you're in love with him."

"I'm scared." It comes out of Aria's mouth like an accident.

Scared and Aria are not synonymous.

"Of?" I ask.

"What if we ruin everything?" she wonders aloud. "I like us. I don't want to get engaged and make it weird and different. What if we stop having sex or we just stop liking each other or wanting to be around each other the way we do now?"

"That's not going to happen." Lisa tries to brush her concern off.

"How do you know?" Aria asks.

I look at Lisa. I'm curious too because I'm feeling Aria's concern. I won't say that out loud, but I silently agree.

"I've seen it happen," Aria says. "I've seen friends go from being the most amazing couples in the world to getting married and something completely changes. I've *seen* it. When you're single together, there is a fear that one of you can always escape so you're always on your best behavior. When you're married, you don't give a damn because you know that to get divorced—no offense, Ava—is going to be a shitstorm and you might as well just stay miserable and suffer through it."

"You make a solid argument," I agree.

"But not all marriages turn out that way," Lisa contests. "Some are like mine—a rollercoaster ride in many ways, but the passion and the love and the need for each other is there. And it's palpable. I *know* we are not the only couple out there who has this going on."

"No," I concur, thinking of Faith and Nick and Gia and Will. "You're not alone, but it's rare. You're part of the one percenters."

"Maybe...but at least you know it's possible," Lisa says, pointing at me.

"I guess," I say.

"All you need to have is hope."

"And good dick," Aria finishes.

CHAPTER 39

"TOPANGA CANYON"

"My name is Magdalena," the hippie with hair down to her butt tells me as I stand in her kitchen at a spiritual commune my friends Cass and Rachel dragged me to.

Since my ayahuasca experience, I'm suddenly the resident psychedelic/shaman/spiritual expert for many of my Persian friends. Cass, short for Mohammad, is a successful restauranteur who's thinking about opening a vegan restaurant in a hippie commune in Topanga Canyon. Rachel, his Latin wife, thought it would be great if I joined them on a visit out to the commune to help them see how legitimate the shaman and the facility are.

What I learned before joining them is that Topanga Canyon is the spiritual mecca of Los Angeles hipsters. This is where you come to trip out, talk to trees and, apparently, find God. I hadn't realized He was so readily available to meet in these canyons. Had I known this, I would have probably made a pilgrimage out here a long time ago.

"Is Magdalena your real name?" The words come out before I can stop them.

"It is my name." She doesn't look too happy with my question, so I feel like I need to try and smooth things over with her.

"What I meant by that is did your guru give you that name?"

"My guru is Mother Nature. So yes, she gave me this name in ceremony."

"She did?" Rachel asks bluntly.

I'm grateful Rachel is wearing glasses, which is her usual style, so I can't make eye contact. I can only imagine what she must be thinking. She and Cass are super conservative. I'm shocked we're even standing here.

"She spoke to me." Magdalena sounds like she's tripping on something. "It was magic."

"What was your name before Magdalena?" Rachel wants to know.

"Sara."

Sara. Plain and simple. Slightly boring. A little bit like toast. I'm thinking Magdalena is definitely more glamorous.

"You do ayahuasca?" Abe looks at me and asks.

Abe owns the place and happens to be a billionaire. He's also of middle-eastern descent. Since his name is Abe, I'm assuming it might be short for Abdullah or something of that nature, but I can't be sure. He's standing in front of us in a long, white tunic and holding onto a vape pen. He takes a puff and watches me.

"I did," I tell him.

"Where?" His accent is thick and indecipherable.

"In Grass Valley."

"So you met the Mother?" He looks intrigued.

Cass and Rachel are watching me like hawks. I'm going to have to answer the question, even if they think I'm as out to lunch as Magdalena.

"I think so," I say honestly.

Abe smiles knowingly and then motions for us to follow him down a tree-lined path. "I want you to come and see the performance."

Abe leads us to a clearing where we come upon a small colosseum filled with people. And I'm not exaggerating—this thing is built *exactly* like an ancient Roman colosseum.

We follow Abe. He points to a group of people carrying in a giant tea kettle and small cups.

"You go," Abe says, tapping me on the arm.

"Go where?" I wonder. "Leave?"

"All of you go drink some tea," he orders.

"Tea?" Rachel asks him. "What kind of tea?"

"The good kind." His smile scares me.

"I don't know what that is," she says candidly. "I don't speak your speak."

"You will commune with Mother Nature when you drink the tea," Abe says.

"It's not ayahuasca, is it?" I narrow my eyes.

"No!" Abe thinks this is funny. "Are you crazy? Trust me. I will take care of you."

I look over at Cass and Rachel, who are staring at me for guidance. Crap. We might be in trouble if I'm in charge, because I'm thinking we drink it. In Idaho, Gia told me to surrender. Isn't this what it's all about? Surrendering to everything?

I stand.

"Let's go!" I nod toward the tea.

"Really?" Cass looks shocked and unsure.

"Totally." I give them a thumbs-up. "We got this."

I mean, I did ayahuasca. How hard can *this* tea be? For all I know, I can have another profound experience.

"*Avalie...*" Cass busts out my full name with a heavy Farsi accent. This is a warning. I know it. He knows it. But I still persist.

"Totally."

I must be convincing because both Cass and Rachel follow me. We sit at the tea circle. There is a lot of sage. Like a lot. It singes my eyes even worse than the load of burning sage Shaman Azria waved over Mark and me. After we cough up our lungs, a woman pours a tea-looking substance into cups and passes them around, one by one.

I stare at the clear liquid, then at the woman who poured me the cup. She gives me a smile of encouragement. It looks safe enough, so I down it. I must say, it doesn't taste so bad. Rachel follows, then Cass, and they both look unimpressed. We leave the circle so others can take their turn. They start to play music as people line up to get more tea.

As usual, these are precisely the moments I always have to use the ladies' room—when they're nowhere to be found and you're in a strange venue. I turn to Rachel and ask if she knows where I can find one.

"Up the stairs and in the small house across from the big house," she says, to my disappointment, because this means a long haul. I hurry off on my journey, making my way up the gladiator stairs. Somehow, I'm able to decipher Rachel's directions.

Later, when I'm walking out of the ladies' room, I happen to come upon Magdalena and another woman in deep conversation. They don't see me, so I'm able to overhear.

"Abe says this peyote is quite strong and laced with kundalini sex magic energy." Magdalena sounds excited about this prospect. "He says it's going to get us going."

"I hope so," the woman with her returns. "All I want to do is have sex with Bo out in the arms of Mother Nature."

"If it's the same stuff we had last week," Magdalena says, "you have nothing to worry about. In fact, Bo isn't going to be enough."

My heart rate speeds up. And not in a good way.

Peyote. Laced with sex magic?

Oh shit.

I'm relieved when I see Cass and Rachel standing outside the house waiting for me. I notice how some of the people, who were at the colosseum, are falling on the plush beanbags and Moroccan style beds that are suspiciously sprinkled around the property.

"Guys..." I start to say in a most grave voice.

"What's wrong?" asks Cass anxiously.

"We drank a sex magic peyote concoction," I tell them.

"What does that mean?" Rachel looks scared.

"It means we're going to start tripping out in about forty-five minutes, and I think everyone is going to have an orgy here."

CHAPTER 40

"THE CALL OF THE WILD"

CASS LOOKS LIKE HE'S BEEN stung by a bee. "Let's get out of here!"

We rush out to the parking lot and find his car.

"We don't have long," I tell him and look at my iPhone. Crap. It's been at least fifteen minutes since we drank the peyote. How long did it take for the ayahuasca to hit? I'm betting we'll be working within the same time frame.

What ensues is probably not the safest moment of my life, but it's one of the more hilarious ones.

We get in his car and make our way to where Cass and Rachel live in Santa Monica.

"I think we should eat something," Rachel says with conviction. "Maybe it'll help us get over whatever tea we just took."

"Good idea," Cass says, and pulls right up to R+D Kitchen.

Food sounds like a good idea. We're seated in the restaurant and so far everything remains fairly normal.

"I'm not feeling anything, are you?" Cass asks as I sit across from them at the table.

"No," I say.

"Me neither," Rachel says.

I pick up my menu and stare down at it. Instead of English, the words resemble ancient, indecipherable scribble. I squint and try to focus. I think the word says appetizer, but I can't be sure. I put the menu down and look at Cass and Rachel.

Their faces are completely electric blue. Rachel even has bright blue eyes. Huh. I think they might be feeling something as well, because suddenly they're busy focusing on the lights in the restaurant.

"They're so pretty." Cass confirms my suspicion a second later.

I wish I could respond but I'm unable to form words. But gosh, does my skin feel good. I run my hands along my arms and am in awe over how good I feel.

The waiter walks over to us. "What can I get you?"

"Bread," Rachel says.

"Creamed corn?" Cass asks.

"A pizza?" I wonder.

I think the waiter realizes what he's dealing with because he smirks at us before leaving with our order.

"That," I say, lifting my finger and pointing at him. I watch how lights shoots off my hand. I wonder if Cass and Rachel can see it too.

"What about that?" Cass's eyes narrow.

"Are you seeing it too?" I wonder aloud as I observe my hand vibrate through space.

"No," Rachel says and shakes her head.

"Great!" Cass says a bit too enthusiastically.

"Is my mouth hanging open?" I ask. "It kind of feels like it is. My jaw is vibrating as well. So are my teeth."

"Me too," Rachel says. "I think we're tripping."

"For sure," I agree. I lean back in my seat and stare up at the lights. I understand why they were riveted before.

"How long does it last?" Cass asks in concern as he sinks back into the booth with Rachel.

"I have no idea," I tell him.

"Oh shit," he says suddenly. "Abe is calling."

"Don't answer," I command.

"I can't," he says.

A purple cartoon mushroom with legs starts to run past me on the table.

"Cass?" I watch the mushroom start to do a dance for me, then he waves.

"Yes?"

"If you decide to open a vegan restaurant in Topanga Canyon…" I wave back at the mushroom man. "I think this tea should definitely be on the menu."

ↅ

Days and countless laughs later, the novelty of the Topanga Canyon experience wears off and I realize that maybe I shouldn't surrender to every opportunity thrown my way.

Lisa pointed out how lucky we were that nothing went wrong. And she's right. Yes, we can laugh about it now, but maybe I was a little foolish with my enthusiasm. There is such a thing as surrendering to life but not to stupidity. And not knowing what I was in for—drinking a foreign substance and encouraging my friends to do the same—was not an example of the *right kind* of surrender. It's an experience I won't soon forget and a lesson that's burned in my psyche forever. I don't even remember how we managed to call an Uber or get to Cass and Rachel's home. Luckily, the tea wore off on Cass fairly quickly and he was able to get us home safe. But still. Lesson learned.

Speaking of learning lessons…I'm leaving tomorrow to stay with my family in Orange County.

I open my diary app and jot down notes about my time with Lisa and her family.

I learned that reincarnation could very well be a thing.

And maybe, just maybe, Darian and I were fulfilling a karmic lesson we each had to learn. Yes, this does feel a bit airy fairy but it also feels real. If I see him as a lesson and myself as a student trying to figure out what it all means, maybe my attitude will change. And that's all I want.

Growth.

I learned that sex is very important.

Without intimacy, you disconnect. And there *can be* that special connection out there that makes me crazy with desire. Maybe I won't be as lucky as Lisa and have it four times a week after more than twenty years together, but I think I need to be having it at least once a week. Or twice. Maybe three times. Or who knows, maybe I'll give Lisa a run for her money? I realize sexual connection is imperative because it keeps you bonded in your relationship. It's a chemistry and magnetism you always want to have. It's more important than we give it credit for.

I learned that fear of the unknown is normal. And Aria's fear that marriage might change her relationship is not only okay, but it's also valid. We're allowed to be afraid of change, but if you're brave enough to take a step toward something new, that's when something really wonderful and life-changing can happen.

Another thing I've learned here with Lisa and Travis, listening to her friends and their stories of divorce and watching my friend with her husband and children, is...

Surrender.

It *is* the answer.

Once you let go, once you realize there is nothing you can do to change what is happening outside of your orbit—once you realize life will play out the way it wants, no matter how hard you try to make it something else—that's when you can find true freedom.

Surrender is allowing the universe to provide—to do its thing.

Come what may.

When we stop trying to manipulate a situation into whatever desired outcome we need to have happen, life becomes a lot easier. You just flow. You *be*. That's what real surrender is.

Divorce happens.

Relationships end.

That's life. My story and Brenda's may be different, but in the end, we're both in the same place. Divorced. Had we surrendered to our situations instead of fighting tooth and nail, maybe it wouldn't have been so hard. I fought against the reality of mine for years. I saw the iceberg full speed ahead but insisted on keeping the same trajectory.

The takeaway?

The Titanic would not have done well under my watch either.

92657
NEWPORT COAST
"ARE YOU PERSIAN?"

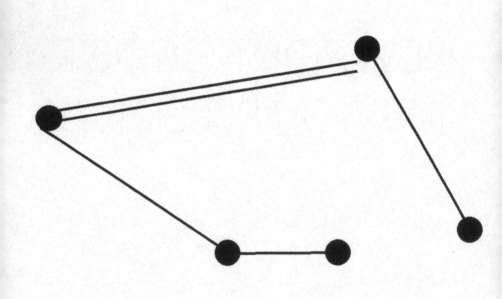

CHAPTER 41

"THEY CALL HER, EL JEFFE"

WE'RE AT MY SISTER'S PLACE, and my mom is cooking up a storm in Layla's recently remodeled gourmet kitchen.

"Your cousin has a khah-seh-gar coming here today," my mother tells me. As usual, she left out this piece of information before I arrived. It's so annoying when she does this.

A suitor and his family are coming over for tea and dessert to see if my cousin could be his potential wife. Khah-seh-gar-(ee) is an age-old Persian tradition of matchmaking. From the moment of conception, a Persian mother is hell-bent on one thing—to see her child, male or female, married off well. Potential prospects are analyzed and dissected from an early age. If you have a childhood friend of the opposite sex, he or she is immediately a potential future partner. Their parents are studied. Their bloodline analyzed, including who their ancestors are. This is where the Persian revolution plays a key role.

Where did the family fall in the hierarchal chain in Iran before they came to America? What did they do for a living? This matters to *all* Iranian expats.

A lot.

I find it mind-boggling that this still exists in modern times, but for some in our culture it works, and they feel safe with this tradition. I guess in the end, you know you'll find *someone* to marry you.

"Vhy you make eh-face like dhat?" My mom narrows her eyes.

She starts pounding the raw cutlets into round patties for Jane, her help, who'll be frying them for her. Mom's gone all-out. There is a giant pot of rice cooking on the stove and various stews are simmering away. It smells delicious.

"I'm not making a face," I lie, because I know I was. "I'm just annoyed we're going to have company."

"Now you don't like people?" My mom's voice is dangerously soft.

"I'd rather be spending time with you guys alone," I say calmly. "Is there something wrong with that?"

"Soraya needs to find eh-husband." There is urgency in my mother's tone that cannot be missed. "She is forty-nine! Never married, not finding *anyvone*. Who vants to be eh-single at fifty? She get too old very soon."

I feel like it's time to point out the obvious to my mom. "That could be your own daughter in the near future."

"But you ver e-married vonce! At least you get married *vone* time."

"And that makes it okay?"

"Yes. Somebody married you."

"And?" I'm trying to follow her logic.

"Nah-ting is wrong vith you."

I burst out laughing.

"Vhat's so funny?"

"All of it." Then I ask, "So, does this mean you don't want to see me get married again?"

"No!" She looks horrified by this prospect. "You have to marry again, ve find you somevone good dhis time."

"Who has to get married?" Layla walks in the kitchen, opens her subzero refrigerator, and pulls out a bottle of water. Her hair and makeup are perfect, as per usual, and she's wearing a cashmere black pajama set—even though it's still summer and about ninety degrees outside. But in rain, hail, snow, or heat, Layla loves her cashmere. And she loves to wear black as most Persians do.

"Avalie has to find eh husband very fast," Mom says as she pounds another patty together. "Longer she vaits, more picky she gets."

"We don't have to wait too long for me to get picky," I admit. "I think I'm already there."

"Don't say dhat!" Mom says, scolding me like I used profanity.

There's no point in arguing with her, so I just focus on my sister. "Where's Ella?" Ella is my thirteen-year-old niece.

"She's in Balboa for a birthday party," Layla tells us. "She'll be back in a few hours. She's so excited you're staying here and can't wait to see you."

"Me too."

"She wants to bake with you tonight," Layla says. "We bought all the stuff yesterday."

"I'm in."

"Layla, did you order kabob?" Mom asks.

"Not yet." Layla sounds exasperated. "I told you, Ben is going to take care of it."

Unfortunately, my brother-in-law, Ben, takes that moment to enter the room. I feel sorry for him. Taking orders from my mom is never an easy task and there's always an issue. It's usually because of her miscommunication in "Far-glish" as we like to call it, but nobody is brave enough to tell her—not even my dad.

"*Salaam, Khanoom Bahzarghan,*" Ben says politely to my mom. "Hey, Ava."

I get up to give him a hug and a kiss on the cheek. He's the best. *The best.* He's been in my life since I was thirteen years old and has always been overprotective, loving, beyond caring, and just wonderful to me. I love him as though he were born my blood brother, and the entire family believes my sister couldn't have gotten luckier with him. Ben is the kind of guy who could be dropped off in a crowd of strangers and come out being everyone's friend.

He grabs a napkin and wipes the sweat beads off his forehead.

One thing about Ben is that he's always hot—the temperature is never right, and he's uncomfortable about this. He's also uncomfortable when someone touches something without washing their hands in the way he deems proper. These are the two major issues Ben seems to always have.

"Did you wash your hands?" he asks as he watches me take a piece of pita bread and dip it into the yogurt dip my mom made with shallots.

"Yes," I mumble, but I get up after he says this and walk over to the kitchen sink. I wash my hands, avoiding eye contact.

"That's what I thought." He claps his hands together. "Can you do me a favor and not dip the bread in the yogurt that everyone is going to eat from?"

"Leave her alone," Layla mutters. "She's going to leave if you keep this up. This is her house too. She's my sister. Don't make her feel uncomfortable."

"I know it's her house." Ben holds up his hands, looking disgruntled. "But we have rules."

"It's all good." I laugh. "And he's right."

"See, Layla?" he says. "Your sister even agrees with me."

"Why do you have to be so annoying?" Layla asks him.

"You just like to argue. Like you do at your job all day." Ben holds his hands up like he's Mike Tyson in a boxing ring. "You wanna fight me, champ?!"

"What is wrong with you?" Layla shakes her head at him like he's lost his mind, then looks over at me. "Do you see what I have to deal with?"

"Ben-joon," Mom says, interrupting what could turn into a mini argument. "Did you order the food?"

"How many people are coming over?" I stare at all the food she's already prepared. There's a lot there, so I'm assuming it's going to be a large group.

"Dhey are four. And dhe rest is our family." I do the math in my head. That can't be more than twelve people, and that's if Ben's parents join. She's made food for at least thirty people. I know I shouldn't be surprised, but I am.

"Don't you think this is enough?" I infuse a healthy dose of sarcasm in my voice in the hopes she'll take note.

"*Nah!*" My mom ignores me and points at Ben. "Four koobideh kabobs, two soltani, two barg, teh-ree joojeh kabobs, four salad shirazi, and five tadighs."

"OhmyGod, Mom," I cry out in horror. "Have you heard of the word gluttony?"

"You vant people to be hungry?"

I hold my hands up in surrender. Persians love food. End of story.

"When is Soraya getting here?" I ask, wondering where the hopeful future bride-to-be is.

"She's here—just upstairs in the guest room getting ready. She had to go into work this morning, so I told her just to get ready here. She's straightening her hair," Layla says,

"See, Avalie?" Mom chimes in and points at my curls. "Your cousin knows men like eh straight hair. Dhis vild look is ceh-razy."

I ignore my mom's comment.

"Who's the guy?"

"He's eh-doctor," Mom interrupts again. "He vorks in San Diego. Divorced. Vone kid. Good family."

"He's a chiropractor," Layla whispers to me.

We lock eyes and both do our best not to giggle.

CHAPTER 42

"ALL BETS ARE OFF"

"Where's Dad?" I ask.

"He's coming," my sister says. "He went to the office."

I'm not surprised. Our father is obsessed with work. He never stops—not on weekends, holidays, or special occasions. In fact, one of his favorite sayings is that you die when you stop doing what you love—in his case, his environmental work.

My mom's cell phone rings and it's my aunt Nedda on FaceTime. I know she wants to see what's going on. We have a word in Farsi—*foo-zool*—that basically means nosy. Persians like to know what's going on at all times. What can I say? We're a curious people. My aunt is no exception.

I pick it up since my mom's hands are full.

Like Mom, Aunt Nedda tends to hold the iPhone in strange positions so you can't see her whole face. I'd say she's a solid B in FaceTime skills and my mom is a D, borderline D-minus.

"Hi Khanoom." My auntie smiles at me.

"Hi Khaleh. We miss you."

"I miss you," she says sweetly. "Vhat you guys doing?"

She knows exactly what we're doing, but I humor her. "We're trying to land Soraya a man."

My aunt giggles. "I hope he's a good vone."

"We hope so too!" Layla calls out.

"Vhat your mom is cooking?" This is the next important question my aunt has.

I turn the phone and hear my aunt ask my mom if she thinks that she's made enough food. Mom gives me an *I told you so* side-eye and tells my aunt about all the meats she ordered.

"Avalie." Mom's gaze brands me. "Get up and help," she commands in Farsi as she hangs up with my aunt.

"Okay!" I throw my hands in the air like I'm under arrest. "What do you want me to do?"

"Help me with the dining table," Layla orders. "Tell me if you think it looks good. I'm not sure."

I walk into the other room and roll my eyes. My sister's dining table looks like it was professionally set by a decorator. It never ceases to amaze me. Her and my mother are the Persian equivalents of Martha Stewart.

Layla has laid moss down the center of the long table and there are wild, purple flowers scattered all over. White candles are intermixed along with two vases filled with an assortment of spring flowers. It looks like a fairytale.

"It looks amazing!" I tell her as soon as she walks in and assesses her creation.

"You think so?" Since she starts to take a series of pictures, I know she's impressed with her creation.

"OhmyGod, Layla!" Our cousin Soraya enters the room. "It is eh...really beautiful."

"You look so pretty." I walk over to give her a hug and a kiss.

Soraya has shoulder-length, black hair, and bright brown eyes. With her infectious laugh and friendly personality, she's extremely likeable. I think she'd be a catch for anyone.

She's one of my favorite cousins. She came over from Iran a few years ago and has been working her butt off since. She's a dental assistant and I admire her drive and tenacity. She hasn't taken handouts from anyone, wanting to forge her own path and make something of herself. She spent her twenties, thirties, and early forties in Iran, in an on-and-off relationship with a man who was never going to marry her. Turns out, he had another family she didn't know about in Dubai. The years in-between were spent mourning his loss and bemoaning the fact that she spent so much time being an idiot. After a long hiatus from the dating scene, she's now ready.

Yes, Soraya's ex was a total douche, and she was heartbroken for so long. But the breakup instigated so many good things for her, and I think she sees that now. I think of Pegah's favorite quote from Steve Jobs—the one about connecting the dots—the dots for my cousin certainly make sense in retrospect.

"Gorgeous, Avalie!" Soraya hugs me hard. "How vare you doing?"

"I'm doing good," I say, smiling at her. "Are you ready to meet him?"

Soraya seems optimistic. "I hear he is a good guy."

"That's what my mom said. Have you seen a picture?"

"No." Soraya doesn't seem too concerned by this. "Dhey never look like dheir picture anyvays. I see him vhen he gets here."

"What's his name?" I ask.

"Joseph."

"What's his real name?" I narrow my eyes.

"Shozaf," Soraya confirms.

"Makes sense."

☙

Shozaf, his mom, dad, and sister—the latter who seems to be afflicted by permanent case of stink eye—are comfortably sitting in my sister's living room a few hours later. Jane is currently offering tea to the group.

From the moment Shozaf and his family arrived, there has been one uncomfortable silent moment after another. My mom and dad are sitting with Soraya acting as chaperones. Ben is just walking in and out of the room because he's *foozool*, and his parents are also sitting down with the entire family, trying to fill in any awkward pauses that they can.

When I got my first glimpse of Shozaf, I knew Soraya might be in trouble. He's about five foot two and dressed in a printed Gucci jogging suit. He's also wearing a Gucci Cuban hat and Ferrari gloves. If he could have strolled in with a cigar, I think he would have.

These are the exact kinds of moments my sister and I cannot be in the same room or proximity of each other for. If I happen to glance her way, all bets are off and nervous laughter will ensue. The kind that would make us run out of the room in a fit of giggles. Yes, we are *that* immature, even though we are grown-ass women.

The two of us happen to be in the family room spying on the events occurring in the room right next door. They can't see us, but we can see them.

"I don't think he's the one," Layla whispers to me.

"No." I vehemently shake my head. "Definitely not feeling *that* vibe."

I watch as Soraya glances down at her tea every time Shozaf asks her a question.

"Ava!" my niece suddenly exclaims in excitement as she body slams me with a hello.

I hug her back tightly and kiss her cheek.

"You're as tall as I am!" I exclaim, smiling into her cute little face.

"Everyone's taller than you, Auntie Ava." She thinks this is hilarious.

"Did your mom tell you to say that?"

"No, it's just kind of obvious," Ella replies.

"What's that in your hand?" Layla asks her.

My niece is holding onto a giant sombrero. It is almost as long as I am.

"I won it at the birthday party! It's funny."

Ella puts it on to show us, and she looks so ridiculous we burst out laughing.

"That thing is amazing," I say, and take hold of it. "I've never seen one so big!"

"Try it on," Ella encourages me.

"You look ridiculous." Layla laughs as I put the giant hat on. Ella takes a picture of me.

"Please don't post this on Instagram or Snap it," I beg her.

"I won't!" Ella says.

"It can be the picture for your dating profile." Layla looks highly amused by this prospect.

"Ha ha," I return sarcastically. "Should we go back to the room and listen to what's going on?"

"I can tell you what's happening." My sister glances over in that direction. "A lot of uncomfortable energy is moving around that room."

"Auntie Ava should go in with the sombrero on." Ella giggles. "That would be hilarious!"

"I'm sure," I reply dryly as I take off the hat. "Can you imagine?"

"Yes, I can." Layla's intrigued by this possibility. "But you're too chickenshit to ever do something like that."

Chickenshit? Ha. I'm all about surrender now, particularly since this decision won't have any hallucinogenic effects.

"Excuse me?"

"I'll bet you—"

"How much?" I interrupt her.

"A hundred dollars." Layla locks eyes with me. "To put the hat on, pretend like there is nothing wrong with how large it is, go sit in the room, drink a full glass of tea, *and* keep a straight face."

"That's a serious bet?" I challenge. "It's worth more money."

Layla sizes me up.

"Five hundred," she finally says.

"*Five hundred dollars!*" Ella squeals in delight, looking beyond excited. "That's so much money!"

"You can't come into the room." I voice my conditions. "You and Ella can't come into the room, because then I'll laugh."

"Fine." Layla and I stare at one another.

"Deal."

CHAPTER 43

"THE MEXICAN HAT DANCE"

THREE MINUTES LATER, I ENTER the room wearing the larger-than-life sombrero and holding onto my cup of tea like it's my lifeline. I sit down in the chair next to my dad. I'm careful not to make eye contact with him or, God forbid, my mother.

Naturally, the conversation comes to a standstill with my arrival. I smile at Shozaf's parents like this—me wearing a sombrero—is the most normal thing in the world. I take a small sip of my tea. Their eyes are bugging out of their face and it's hard not to laugh. My cousin Soraya's gaze is firmly glued to her tea again. Now I understand why she kept staring so intently into her cup of tea. She's using it as a defense mechanism.

Ben immediately gets up and leaves the room. His parents rush to fill the silence and I'm happy when they start to talk among themselves.

"Ava." I hear my dad's low whisper. "What the hell is that on your head?"

"It's a sombrero, Dad."

I can only imagine what he must be thinking. His silence is telling. Finally, he voices his disapproval. "I don't like it."

I can't argue with him so I only nod. I sit there, sipping my tea and smiling like a loon. I wonder how this will play out in the Persian community for me. I forgot to take that aspect into consideration, because this will definitely be a story Shozaf's parents will tell many people. I guess Persian society will already think I've lost my mind because I'm getting a divorce.

"Avalie." My mom's voice sounds threatening. If she could expel fire like a dragon, she would. And she'd make those *Game of Thrones* dragons look tame in comparison.

I'm surprised it took this long for the earth to rumble. I glance over at her.

Oh shit.

She's flaring her nose and placing her forefinger on the tip. When I was younger this meant she was coming for me. As in, you're about to get your ass handed to you, I'm coming for you, and I'm being nice by giving you a head start. But I won't be so nice when I catch you.

At that moment, I swallow the rest of the tea in one gulp, burning my throat. I stand awkwardly. Because the hat is so large it bobbles back and forth on top of my head. I move my head around, hoping to balance the hat correctly again.

"I'll check on the rice," I announce to the room. I walk out with as much dignity as possible.

When I reach the family room, there is no one to be found. I walk into the kitchen and find Layla, Ella, and Ben hysterically laughing.

"Shozaf's face!" he says.

"Did you see the look on your parents' face?" Layla says to him as they laugh uproarously.

"Gaga looked really mad," Ella says.

"And just like that, you get to pay me five hundo." I hold out my hand.

"It was worth every penny!" Layla exclaims.

"Avalie."

I turn around and am surprised to find my dad standing there, staring at me in complete disappointment. He doesn't look like he thinks my little stunt is funny at all.

"Take that damn thing off." He hasn't raised his voice, but for my dad—a man who never gets mad about anything—he looks pretty pissed off.

I take the sombrero off and watch him with wide eyes.

"It's Layla's fault," I say, immediately telling on my sister.

"I am so disappointed." He shakes his head at us.

"Dad!" I defend our joke. "It was funny!"

"It was mean," he says instead. "You were making fun of Shozaf and his honest efforts to find a wife."

"Honest efforts? Come on, Dad," Layla chimes in defensively. "That's a little excessive—"

"No." Dad shakes his head. "We are supposed to make people feel good about themselves. Not bad."

Dad's comment hits me hard in the gut.

"It was just a joke," I say with a sigh.

"But his pursuit of Soraya is not a joke."

"Dad." I hold up my hand. "He's never even seen or talked to her before today. I think you're overreacting."

"He came here to find a wife," Dad says. "You might not agree with the tradition, but for many people it works."

"Where's your sense of humor?" I try to vindicate myself.

"Your mother and I raised kind girls," he says instead. "Please don't disappoint us again."

He starts to walk out of the kitchen, but then stops and picks at the platter of feta cheese, bread, and herbs that my mom put together for lunch.

"There's kabob in the oven," my sister tells him. I know she's hoping he'll like us again if we feed him. "I can make you a small koobideh sandwich with lavash."

"I'm not eating meat anymore," he informs us.

"Since when?" I ask. Dad loves meat more than anyone I know.

"Today," he tells us. "I'm only having lentils for lunch."

Layla and I lock eyes. Neither of us believe him but we'll let him have it. Dad, meanwhile, doesn't notice the controversy he started with this comment. Instead, he looks over at me and looks kind of amused.

"Your mother is pretty pissed off." He smirks and adjusts his glasses. "I know you're an adult, but I would seriously consider hiding."

⁊

After everyone but immediate family leaves, Ella and I start to bake. Or, to be honest, Ella bakes; I'm just sitting and eating a spoon filled with frosting, watching her do her thing. My mom, sister, auntie (via FaceTime), and I are talking over the events that transpired.

Before Soraya left to go home, she let us know that thankfully, Shozaf was not *the one*. I'm happy my instincts were correct, considering my mom let me know rather passionately that I humiliated the family in what we will call from this moment on "The Sombrero Incident." I did corner Soraya before she left to make sure she wasn't mad at me for acting like a crazy relative.

"Vhy vould I be mad?" She smiled good-naturedly. "It vas funny. You should have seen your mom's face."

She covered her mouth with her hand and shook her head. "*She* vas mad."

Oh, I knew that. She had given me a good earful when she finally caught me, and obviously didn't care who was listening. I think Layla's neighbors might have heard.

"Are you okay, though?" I searched her face for any signs of disappointment.

"Vhy not?"

"You were excited to meet him," I admitted. "He wasn't what you were expecting...."

"So vhat?" She seemed surprised by my thoughts.

"You're not disappointed at all? You've been single for so long and I know you want to meet someone...."

"Do you tink I'm scared I'll be alone?"

I shrugged. To be honest, I didn't know if I was asking the question more for her or for me.

"Sometimes, yes," she admitted softly. "But when I meet new people, even like Shozaf, and I get hope—"

"Hope that there are single people out there?" I wondered.

"Hope dhat I'm one step closer to finding *him*." She sounded like an innocent, wide-eyed teenager—not like someone who's seen love become such a disappointment.

"And if you don't?" I couldn't believe I asked her this, but I wanted to know.

"Avalie, you have to be more positive. I don't tink like dhat," she schooled me. "I vill find a good man and until I do, I vill still be happy."

After she left, I thought about our conversation. Maybe I'm putting too much pressure on what I *think* a relationship should feel like. I should just be happy I've even met guys to date, who want to take me out. Who are attracted to me.

It doesn't always have to be magic from the start. Not every story begins that way.

Of course, now my brain goes right to the only man who's gotten under my skin. The one who still hasn't texted with a time, date, and location for our date.

Annoying.

"Will you try this, Auntie Ava?" Ella interrupts my New York state of mind.

I dip a spoon into the dough and taste. "Amazing."

"Thank you!" she tells me, and continues on with her baking.

"Ella khanoom," my aunt calls out from my mom's iPhone. "Sing me some Hayedeh."

My niece has an incredibly soulful voice, and the whole family loves when she sings tunes from their favorite long-deceased musician. Hayedeh was like the Barbra Streisand of Iran—she was a national treasure, and her music is still beloved.

"I don't feel like it," Ella says. "I'm baking now."

"Come on," Layla urges. "Just sing something."

"Beh-khoon," my mom says in Farsi, demanding she sing.

I feel sorry for my niece. Parents love to tell their children to "just do" whatever it is that they want them to do. Like circus creatures, they want them to perform on command, as if it's so easy to perfectly belt out a song from the most beloved Iranian singer of all-time.

"Mom!" Ella gives her a dirty look.

"Ella," my mom says again. "Beh-khoon!"

Sing, she says. Just sing.

And then my niece throws down and does just that. Her voice echoes through the kitchen and permeates the soul. She sings each line with passion, even closing her eyes through some lyrics, the love song moving her too. When she's done, we're all smiling and I want more.

"That was incredible," I tell her.

"Thanks, Auntie Ava."

Ella gets busy on her iPhone and I look over at Layla.

"It makes me happy that she knows so much of our culture."

"Are you kidding me?" my sister says. "Our roots are the foundation of who we are and who we become. It's a part of us that we have to keep alive forever, even if we are living in America. It's how Dad and Mom raised us, and how I hope she'll raise her children one day."

I look over at my niece.

"We can't let our culture die with our generation."

CHAPTER 44

"NOSY"

We are at Darya Restaurant in Orange County.

Darya means *ocean* in Farsi. This place is one of the most famous Persian restaurants in Orange County. It's known for its authentic-tasting kabobs and meats, which draws in all Iranians. It's a favorite and it's always packed. The irony is, when we're not making Persian food at home, we're often eating it at a restaurant. God forbid we try a different cuisine. When my mom asked me what I wanted to eat, I told her something light, maybe a salad.... And she drove us straight here.

"We ate kabob the other day," I remind her as we get out of the car. "I wanted a salad."

"You can have a shirazi salad," Mom says.

"I don't want shirazi. I want a kale salad."

Mom completely ignores my comment.

"Why do you bother?" Layla asks once we're all out of the car.

"I don't want to run into the entire Persian population for lunch," I whisper.

"You won't."

"Nice try. We are *so* running into people we know," I grumble, giving my sister the side-eye. "They're going to stare at me with those sad looks and a ton of judgment...like I have a disease because I'm divorced."

"Who cares?" Layla says.

"It's annoying." I pout.

"Don't vorry," Mom offers. "Nobody is here today. I promise."

"What are you going to do when you go to your first mayh-moo-nee?" Layla is referring to a serious Persian party. "Now *that's* going to be a scene."

We step inside the restaurant, and it's packed. I look over at my mom, who is suspiciously avoiding eye contact with me. I hope we don't run into people we know who are nosy enough to demand a story about what's going on in my life. I know this is wishful thinking on my part—it would be like walking into Disneyland and hoping you don't see any kids.

Still, it happens faster than even I expected.

"Oh no." I look over at Layla with dread. "It's Maryam!"

Layla is equally alarmed.

One of my mom's friends who is especially *foozool* (nosy) rushes us as soon as we enter the restaurant. For Maryam, there are no boundaries and no subject is off the table. She is uncomfortably aggressive. Her dark brown hair is done up, and she's so blinged out, it looks like she's wearing at least twenty-five carats of diamonds.

"Avalie!" She rushes over and pulls me into an embrace before I can try and make a run for it. "Let me look at you," she says in Farsi. No one can dissect quite like a Persian woman. We have this skill down pat.

She checks me out, analyzing every part of me—from the top of my head to the tips of my toes. The silence is uncomfortable. Then, she delivers her diagnosis. "You don't look good."

From the corner of my eye, I can see my sister's shoulders start to shake in laughter.

"No?" I ask.

"Nah. Ah-slan (not at all). Your face is too small. You look much older. Your mahh-dher needs to take you for a facial."

"I'll look into that." I look over at Mom, who takes the opportunity to embrace her friend and give the proper hellos.

"Darian vas alvays a bad guy," Maryam says. "Choose better next time."

"That's a good idea." There's so much sarcasm in my voice, I'm surprised she can't hear it.

"Ve find you khah-seh-gar." Maryam offers to find me a suitor.

"No," I say quickly, thinking of Shozaf. "No, thank you. I'm good."

"Speak to your daughter," she tells my mom in Farsi. "Tell her the longer she's single, the worse off she'll be."

My mom shrugs her shoulders, like I'm some hopeless case.

"When she's ready," Layla says, jumping to my defense. "She's not there yet."

"She is not getting younger," Maryam declares. "But I have to go. I'm so happy I saw you."

She gives me another pitiful smile then takes off.

"That was painful," I say to Layla as I exhale.

"She's harmless," my sister says.

"She's rude," I return.

"Khak beh-sahr-am!" Mom curses in Farsi, which basically means, *let me throw dirt on my own head.* We look over at her in surprise.

"Chi?" Layla asks. *What?*

"Your fadher is here."

My eyes skim over the tables, and sure enough, there he is.

Our father, the newly declared no meat eating human, is sitting at a table with a few work friends. He's eating a plate filled with beef—a soltani to be exact, which is a substantial piece of filet and a long skewer of koobideh or ground beef. Dad didn't just race back to being a meat eater in less than two days...he did a long jump.

I look over at my mom. She is taking in every part of the situation.

Her nose flares.

Uh oh.

"You two eh-stay here," she commands. "I vill be right back."

We watch as she makes her way to my father's table. With every step, the force of her anger propels her forward, like Maleficent bidding the forest to do her will.

Poor Dad.

Layla and I watch our mom give him the nose flare and finger tap. Even from this distance, I can see his eyes widen. He knows what's coming. She points over to Layla and me, and we wave at him. He gives us a *what can I say, I like meat too much* smile.

"He doesn't even look embarrassed," Layla says.

"Nope," I return in amusement. "He's back to being a proud, kabob-eating member of society."

"It's a good look for him," my sister suggests.

"It is."

CHAPTER 45

"DALAI AVA"

"SHELLY HAS A GUY SHE wants you to meet," Faith tells me, as we dine together with our girlfriend Christina at the Pelican Hill Resort.

Faith and Christina drove down from Beverly Hills for a night so we could catch up.

"Shelly has good taste," I admit. She's a great friend of Faith's who I happen to trust.

"I asked her to join us for a drink." Faith is jazzed. "She sounded excited when she brought this guy up. She can't wait to tell you all about him."

"OhmyGod, *I* am so excited for you!" Christina's got that big, infectious grin of hers plastered on her face. "This chapter in your life is going to be so liberating! You have so much to look forward to."

Christina is the friend who is always happy. Always positive. Always looks at life as a glass-half-full kind of situation. You know that person who is maddeningly optimistic?

That's Christina. But she *is* the one who coined the phrase all her friends have borrowed at one time or another over the years... *I'm addicted to peace.*

That is one addiction I would like to ask the universe to give me.

"I know I do," I agree, even though I do have moments of uncertainty.

"I have to tell you, Ava," Christina says, studying my face in amazement, "happiness looks good on you."

"I'm learning to surrender," I explain, then start to spew out my newfound spiritual mantras.

"You're like the Buddha of divorce," Christina says.

I burst out laughing. "Hardly."

"You kind of are," Christina goes on.

"How so?"

"You're not sitting under a tree contemplating the meaning of life, but you're staying with amazing girlfriends and learning by example and *living* life. That's the best kind of spiritual growth you could ask for," she explains. "Think about all you've learned."

"When you put it that way, I guess you're right," I say. "But I feel like calling me 'the Buddha of divorce' is going a bit too far."

"I think the title fits you perfectly."

Before I can answer, two things happen. First, the waiter brings out our crab cake appetizer and it immediately occupies my thoughts. Second, Shelly arrives in a whirlwind. Even here on her staycation, she looks super busy and in a hurry. She never stops. She's an attractive woman in her late fifties with an energy and work ethic I extremely admire.

"Ava." She leans over and kisses me on the cheek. "You look great. Did Faith tell you I have a man for you?"

She cuts right to the chase, and sits down.

"She did."

"What can we get you?" Christina asks Shelly.

"Nothing," she says. "I can't stay long, but I had to come and tell Ava about Tom."

"We're intrigued," Christina says eagerly.

Shelly smiles widely before giving us the mystery man's résumé.

"Tom owns over fifty-five plastic surgery clinics across the country. He does *very* well."

Instantly, I can't help but wonder if this piece of information is the first thing out of her mouth because the rest of the package might not be that great....

"How old is he?" Christina asks.

"Sixty-seven." Shelly meets my gaze and my heart sinks to the center of the earth. "He has two kids."

"What does he look like?" Faith asks the next obvious question.

Shelly sighs and admits, "You'll have to fix him."

"Fix him?" My voice sounds small, even to me.

"He has a very long mustache."

"How long?" I probe.

"It runs past his chin," she says with a straight face.

No one says a word.

"And..." Shelly begins.

There's an *and*? God help me.

"He has a combover." She uses her hand to show us, in case none of us know what that is. "But I promise, you can fix all of this. He has good bones, like a house," she rushes out, hoping to reassure me.

I still don't know how to process any of what she's just told me.

"I fixed my husband." Shelly gives me an optimistic smile. "You can fix *any* man."

I can't find the words.

"You can't be as picky as you were when you were younger." Shelly is now the *tell it like it is* dream crusher of what's available to Ava Monfared.

I pick up my martini and take a *really* long sip.

"Sixty-seven is too old for Ava," Christina offers, thankfully.

"Yes," Faith agrees. "I think we need a little younger. And no long mustache?"

"He's a great catch," Shelly pleads, and looks at me. "Forget about the mustache. You might like it. You never know."

"I'm pretty sure I know." I try my best to smile.

"Give him a chance," she cajoles. "Go on a date. He's very generous."

"I don't know if I want to broaden my horizons to sixty-seven quite yet," I say, and I don't think Shelly likes my answer because she looks rather disappointed in me.

Does she think this is the only prospect I have? A man in an age group almost thirty years older than me... Is this *it*?

Shelly looks at her watch and stands. "Okay, then. I'll see you guys later. But I think you should consider a date, Ava."

She leaves just as she came—in a whirlwind. There's an unusual quiet at the table, and given the circumstances, I feel like I should be the one to break it.

"I have a question," I say, my voice even and calm.

"Yes?" Faith looks nervous.

"What is it about me that says I'm okay to be set up with a man who has a mustache down to the floor and a combover?"

Christina and Faith burst out laughing.

"No. I'm not laughing," I insist. "I *really* want to know. I feel like it's your duty as friends to tell me. Because I need to know what kind of energy I'm giving off here."

They continue laughing. Faith dabs her eyes with her napkin; she's in actual tears. "I honestly don't know what Shelly was thinking."

"She was trying to be nice," Christina sputters out, lips twitching.

"Yes," I reply, before taking another sip and finishing my drink. "I'm going to need another one of these—pronto."

"At least we laughed," Faith says as she giggles to herself.

"I should be crying!"

"Where's the joy in that?" Christina says with that peaceful way of hers.

"I don't know if I can find joy in Shelly's suggestion for my future man," I admit.

"See this moment, right now?" Christina motions to us. "You'll remember this forever. And so will Faith and I. Not only will we remember it, we'll laugh when we think about how ridiculous Shelly's suggestion was. And whenever this memory comes to us in the future, it'll bring us happiness. *That's* all there is to life."

Faith and I smile at Christina.

"We should thank Shelly. She just gave us the perfect moment to remember forever." Christina says.

It's in this second I realize Lisa's whole theory on past lives must be a real thing. Christina makes me believe in them because I'm pretty sure, in a previous life, she must have been a saint.

CHAPTER 46

"GUILTY PLEASURE"

LAYLA AND I ARE LYING on her bed watching *Sleepless in Seattle*.

Ben took Ella out for a tennis lesson before going to have a father-daughter dinner together, so Layla and I have the house to ourselves. We ordered pizza and are now watching one of our all-time favorite movies.

It never gets old.

"You should see the smile on your face," Layla says, interrupting my fangirl moment. "You look so dorky, I should take a picture."

"I can't help it! This movie makes you hope for something magical."

"I thought it only exists for the few 'lucky ones'." Layla throws my own words back at me.

"Maybe I'd like to be lucky too," I whisper in longing.

"You are *extremely* lucky, Ava. You just keep forgetting."

I know there is so much more behind my sister's words. It's not about finding a man. It's about how fortunate I am, during this circumstance in my life, to have all that I do. Most do not. I know this. But when you're knee-deep in your own crap, it's very easy to lose sight of that.

Reminders are always good.

We watch as Meg Ryan's character gets out of the elevator at the top of the Empire State Building. My hand automatically covers my heart. I hear Layla sigh. Then we watch Tom Hanks exit the elevator a second later, seeing her character for the first time. He has that look on his face—like he knows she's the one. It's like magic. My heart fills with longing—what would it be like to have a man look at you like that? I guess if I never find out, at least I'll have *Sleepless in Seattle* to watch.

"Why is this movie *always* so good?" I wonder out loud.

"Because there's an innocence that's enchanting about it, and it shows that true love always finds a way."

"I'd like to think so."

Snuggling into the pillow, I replay the end of the movie in my head.

"What's going on with New York City?" Layla asks, pulling me out of my daydream. "You haven't talked about him."

"No," I say.

"Why not?"

I quickly fill her in on everything, and she's more than a little mad I waited so long to tell her. She's excited that I'm going to see him and doesn't seem to care as much as I do that he hasn't reached out yet.

"I haven't heard from him in a while now. I don't want to read into anything."

"You're not."

"And I don't even know if I like him."

"*You don't know if you like him?*" Layla laughs in my face. "Are you joking?"

"What?" I say shiftily.

"Just pull up your messages with him and let me judge if you're reading into anything," she commands.

"Why?"

"Tone," she tells me. "I feel like I can decipher his tone better than you. I think you're emotionally connected already, and you haven't even seen him in forever."

"I am not emotionally connected. I am *curious*."

"Right," my sister says doubtfully, elongating every syllable. She takes the phone out of my hands and, being the excellent detective that she is, scrolls through the messages in record time.

She is quiet for too long.

"Huh." Her eyes widen and flicker in surprise.

"Huh? What does 'huh' mean?" I demand.

Layla locks eyes with me. "He just texted you."

"What?!" I screech, grabbing the phone from her hand.

"I thought you don't know if you like him?" my sister says smugly, relishing in my hyperventilating reaction.

"Honestly, how can I know when I haven't seen him in all these years?" I grumble back, but immediately look for his message. The butterflies in my stomach flutter into my throat and are about to come out of my mouth, I'm so nauseous.

> **New York City:** Are you free for dinner next Wednesday night?

I look over at my sister since I know she read the message. "That's in eight days."

"You can add...impressive." She says sarcastically.

I feel my face and body start to flush. The thought of seeing him makes me faint. A feeling of uncertainty overwhelms me, and I'm flooded with a myriad of emotions. Why do I feel so differently about New York City versus the other guys? Why does he throw me so much? Is this kind of feeling too much, too soon?

"I don't know if I'm ready."

"I just listened to you bitch for over twenty minutes about his lack of messages and your different theories about why he's gone silent," Layla says in disbelief. "And you're *not* ready?"

"Then why am I so nervous?" I put my hands to my cheeks, trying to lower my rising temperature.

"It doesn't take much to do the math.... You had a connection to New York City before and you want to know if you'll feel the same way."

"Hopefully I won't have a connection."

"Why would you even say that?" Layla says, astonished.

"It scares me."

"Why?"

"It's like opening Pandora's box."

"Just have fun with it," she says. "Don't put any pressure on yourself. You've been letting go of so many of your old hang-ups— let this one be whatever it's going to be as well."

"I just don't want to get hurt again. It's too soon for another wound."

"You don't even know what this is yet," Layla says gently. "Maybe he's just a bridge to make you feel again...or maybe he's something more. You just don't know. If you don't see him, you'll *never* know. And if you don't pursue it, you could regret it."

The regret part is what gets me. Because I think I would.

"You're right." I open up his message again. I can't let this man throw me off-balance so much. I'm made of stronger stuff.

"Don't write back just yet," Layla orders. "Make him wait, like he's made you."

"I will."

"Although," she adds with a chuckle, "you *have* made him wait for thirteen years."

❦

I message New York City back that night in bed.

I feel like it's safe because I know he's on the East Coast and is probably asleep, which makes it not as nerve-racking for me.

> **Me:** I'm free.

Just as I put my phone down on the nightstand, it pings back. My heart stops.

> **New York City:** How have you been?

I'm again filled with the crazy kind of nerves. I write back immediately because my brain is lacking oxygen since I'm currently floating in space.

Me: I've been good. I can't complain. And you?

He writes back quickly.

New York City: It's been a stressful few weeks but it's calming down now.

Me: Work stuff?

New York City: Comme Ci, Comme Ca

I laugh.

Me: Do you want to talk about it?

New York City: I want to talk about you.

My heart slams in my chest. I watch the text bubbles come up and I know he's typing again.

New York City: Tell me about Ava.

I can feel myself blush.

Me: What do you want to know?

New York City: Everything.

He makes me forget how to breathe.

Me: Everything?

New York City: Yes.

I wonder...and then I let go of my hang-ups and just go for it.

Me: I'm a Pisces.

He responds by hitting the heart emoji on my sentence.

Me: My favorite color is blue. I love too many shades of it, so I can't pick just one. And purple, sometimes. But mostly, blue.

He hits the heart emoji again and I keep going.

Me: I love the ocean. I have a secret fantasy of sailing away and living like a vagabond out on the sea, going from port to port. Just seeing the world in a different way and being free. I think it would be the ultimate adventure.

He takes a second to write back, and for a moment, I wonder if I overplayed my hand. But then—

New York City: Let's go.

A dumb, goofy smile creeps up on my face before I can stop it. If Layla were here, I'd never live it down.

Me: Shouldn't you get to know me some more before committing to an indefinite amount of time at sea together? I could be crazy.

New York City: I'll take my chances.

I smile.

Me: Brave.

New York City: I know you enough.

Me: Enough?

New York City: I know a lot about you from when we first met years ago. I have a sense you're the same with a twist.

He continues typing and I hold my breath in anticipation.

New York City: And all the other ways I want to get to know you—those have to be done alone and in person.

Oh. My. God. He's flirting with me!

New York City: Just the two of us out at sea is the perfect backdrop.

This is *definitely* flirting. And I am definitely a loser who can only manage to put her palms to her cheeks and whisper, "OMG!" to the air. He must sense what's happening across the country, because he writes—

New York City: Don't be scared.

Me: I'm not.

Lie. Okay, "scared" isn't the right word—nervous is more apropos. And anxious.
Definitely anxious.

New York City: Liar.

Me: I don't scare easily.

I don't know if this is necessarily true either, but it seems like the right thing to say.

New York City: I wish I could see you right now.

My heart slams in my chest.

Me: Aren't you in bed already?

New York City: If you told me you were in the city, I'd meet you anywhere you wanted right now.

An emoji is all I can manage at first, because he just stole my ability to function on any human level.

Me: That's very sweet of you.

New York City: It's the truth. Needless to say, I look forward to seeing you again.

Me: Me too.

New York City: You put a smile on my face right before bedtime.

Me too.

Me: I'm glad.

New York City: Good night, Ava. Sweet dreams.

CHAPTER 47

"LAST OF THE MOHICANS"

"AVALIE," MY MOM SAYS AS we sit with my grandmother around the dining table, plucking and cleaning mint and other herbs she purchased from the Persian market. "Bring your grandmother some melon."

My grandmother, the matriarch of our family, is the most precious thing ever. She's in her mid-nineties and has always been a pillar of strength and knowledge for all of us, especially the female grandchildren.

Despite growing up in Iran, and living her entire adult life there with its conservative social customs, my grandmother was always the one to scold her children for being too strict and rigid. She was the most open-minded Persian grandmother I could have asked for. She would even yell at her children for not letting their kids date or go out to school events, like football games or dances. She was this knowledgeable woman who defied her culture and was educated in the ways of the world. She knew that the key to our comfort and ease in America was to assimilate and adapt. She was the best of the best in every way.

I say "was" because my grandmother now suffers from dementia.

We find it both a blessing and a curse. The blessing is that she doesn't remember the grief of losing my grandfather—considering they were married when she was fourteen years old and were together for over seventy-five years. If she was fully cognizant, we know his loss would be unbearable.

The curse is watching her deterioration, which is especially difficult for my mother, who is the eldest and has always been the closest to her. My mom is good at hiding her sensitivity and pain—in that way, she's a lot like my grandfather was. He was a mayor and governor for many different cities in Iran and had a no-nonsense, take-no-prisoners, military attitude. He was tough and strong, and he passed these attributes on to his eldest.

There are times when I've seen Mom break when she's with my grandmother—moments when I see her pain radiate like a beacon of despair from her eyes. This is her precious mother, and though death comes for us all, it's still a heartbreaking process to watch.

Before the dementia, Mamanjoon would periodically play little pranks. They were quite often hilarious. My favorite one is when she pulled one over on my cousin's American girlfriend, Mary. Mary is very sweet and truly a people pleaser. She had many encounters with my grandmother over the years where she would speak to her in English and, after someone translated, my grandmother would respond in Farsi. After two years of dating my cousin, Mary had finally been proven worthy, so my grandmother let her guard down. Mary asked a question and was expecting my aunt to translate it, but my grandma answered her back in perfect English.

I'll never forget the look on Mary's face when she walked over to me and said, "Your grandma has understood everything I've said for over two years. That's interesting." The only appropriate response was to tell her she was being tested. My grandmother had to be sure Mary loved my cousin. Oh, how we all laughed over *that* moment. Not Mary, of course...but the rest of us.

When I bring back the plate of melon for my grandmother and place it next to her, I'm awarded with a big smile and sweet words of adoration.

"Merci, Mamanjoon," I say as I kiss her on the cheek.

I'm at my parents' house for the day to visit with my grand-mother and go through some of my mom's old jewelry. Layla is joining us after she drops Ella off at Russian math.

"Ahs-leh-kar cheh-toh-reh?" My grandmother asks me how Darian is for the tenth time. She can't fully grasp that we are no longer together, even though my mom keeps reminding her over and over. I guess my marriage to my ex is another life event that's ingrained in her memory a specific way and will never be altered.

Before I can answer, my mom does. God, is she quick. She asks her mother to please not mention his name again.

Mamanjoon gives me an innocent smile.

"I forgot," she says with a thick accent in English.

I have to laugh.

"It's okay," I repeat back. "I love you."

"Me too," she says and laughs joyously. "I love you, honey."

I'm overcome by my feelings for her. She is so precious, and we are all so lucky that she's ours. I have to hug her again and just breathe her in. She whispers praise to me, telling me how much she loves me and would do anything for me or any of her grand-children. I pull away and kiss her on the cheek.

"I love you more," I say.

She gives me another angelic smile.

"Avalie." Her voice sounds like sugar. "Men are shit."

I'm so happy I don't have anything in my mouth. I burst out laughing while she proceeds to tell me how most men are essen-tially garbage and that Darian was no exception to the rule and that I should just forget about men in general because they aren't worth the trouble.

There she is—my old grandmother.

My mom tells my grandmother that I *must* marry again.

"You really want to plan another wedding, don't you?" I shake my head at my mom.

My grandmother grabs hold of my hand and squeezes.

"Avalie," she says with urgency.

"Yes?" I say in Farsi.

"Zen-deh-gee hah-meen-eh." She tells me that this is life. "Bah-lah oh pah-yeen dah-reh."

It has ups and downs.

"Ah-dahm me-yahd oh-mee-reh."

People come and go.

"Famil-eh keh hah me-sheh poh-sht-eht oh dah-rahn. Bah doost-eh-yeh- khoob."

It's your family that always has your back. And good friends.

"Toh khay-lee jah-voon-ee."

You are so young.

"Hah-me sheh dohm-bahl eh yehck-chi-zee boo-dee."

You have always been in search of something.

"Hah-tah, bah-reh-yeh, Khoh-dah."

You've even been looking for God.

"Rooh-eht...joon-eht, too-yeh ghalb-eht-eh."

Your spirit is there in your heart.

"Hah-me-sheh oon-jah-bood."

It's always been there.

"Rooh-eht khah-steh me-sheh. Moh-ghe-yaht-eh ah-rah-mesh-eh."

Your soul will get too tired. It's time for peace.

"Dohm-bahl-eh he-chi nah-bahsh. Fagh-at beh rooh-eht rah-at-ee- bee-are."

Stop searching. Just settle your soul.

She reaches out and takes my hand. She is so wise.

If your soul is happy everything else will fall into place. I promise you.

"Yehk rooze vahkh-tee man-neest-am toh me-geeh, maman-joon, harf-ash doh-rohst bood."

One day, when I'm not here you will say, my grandmother was right.

The last bit makes my eyes water and I start to cry. I can't help myself. I reach out, pull her back into my arms, kiss her, and tell her again how much I love her.

Meanwhile, my mom makes a joke about how my soul will be better off with a husband.

"Nah." My grandmother looks offended, and then proceeds to tell my mom that I should *not* get married and should just go find a boyfriend and have fun sex.

I have to cover my mouth.

She. Did. Not.

My mom doesn't look as horrified as I would think. She looks over at me and gives me a long, hard stare.

"All I want is for you to be happy," she tells me in Farsi. "That's all I ever wanted for you and your sister."

I get up from the table and walk over to my mom and hug her tightly.

"I know," I whisper to her.

"My heart vas broken for you," my mom admits, and I watch in shock as tears start to form in her eyes. "Dhis is not dhe life I vanted you to have. It makes me sick vhen I see you so sad."

"It's not your fault," I tell her, and we both start to cry.

And then in Farsi she proceeds to tell me.

"You are our little girl. Your father and I would do anything for you. We just want to see you happy. I don't want anytihng to ever happen to you, and this sadness only brings sickness and disease. There is nothing else that comes from it."

"I know. I love you so much, Mommy."

"I love you more."

We hold on to each other for a moment longer, and then I pull away and go back to my seat. My mom and I share a sweet smile. I feel good, and somehow, more put together—like the pieces of the puzzle keep fitting into place.

And I feel strong.

The strongest I've ever felt.

"Avalie?" Mom smiles.

"Yes?"

"Peh-lease go see Jonathan and color your hair." She stares at my tresses. "You need eh-highlights. It's too dark. You look like eh-ghost."

∽

A while later, I'm sitting out on my parents' balcony staring out at the view. I have my diary app open and I'm thinking about my family. The smell of Persian food, the feeling of warmth and famili- arity that it somehow brings, and the sound of laughter coming from the house is everything and reminds me of all the good mem- ories I had growing up. My mom is talking on the phone with one of her friends, and my sister is joking with my grandmother. The sounds are familiar, are ones I grew up with, but somehow—at this moment—the nostalgia hits me in a different way.

I've learned so much from my family...my whole life with them has been a lesson. But this time, receiving their wisdom feels different.

I learned that a relationship can come in the most unconven- tional way.

Not everyone gets to meet their soulmate on a date or run into them at a bar or restaurant. Sometimes, we have to actively search for and seek out love.

And there's nothing wrong with that.

I learned to see beauty in the present. Even if I'm offered some- thing I wouldn't typically go for, I know that one day even these memories will make me smile and feel that damn nostalgia again.

I learned that taking chances can lead to something magical. Look at Meg Ryan in *Sleepless in Seattle!* There was a good chance that Tom Hanks wouldn't be there waiting for her—and yet, there he was. There was a good chance I'd never hear from New York City again...and yet, I did.

Because I took the chance.

Finally, I learned something that I've always known, but maybe needed a little reminder about....

The wisdom of your family is a thing of beauty. It is to be cher- ished. There is so much you can learn from your foundation.

They are your roots.

And if you settle into your roots, they will never grow in the wrong direction.

90272
PACIFIC PALISADES
"TAKE ME HOME, COUNTRY ROADS"

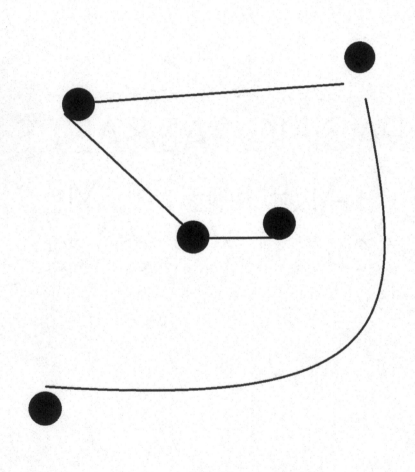

CHAPTER 48

"UP CLOSE AND PERSONAL"

FOR THE FIRST TIME IN over two months, I drive past my old home.

Or should I say, my previous life.

It's like watching an old movie and remembering all the scenes that took place. It's surreal. I don't know how it's possible for me to feel this way, because I lived here for over seven years. I would walk these streets and see the same people, the same dogs, and the same cars on a regular basis. Now it's like visiting a foreign land, or being in the twilight zone.

I don't even recognize it.

And shockingly, I don't feel any extreme emotions.

Not sadness. Not relief. Not anything. It's like I had a lobotomy.

While I was driving here from Orange County to begin my last summer stay with my neighbors, the Graysons, I wondered if I had made a colossal mistake. Was going back to my old 'hood a good idea for me right now, considering how far I feel like I've grown in accepting everything that's come my way? Scratch that—I don't *feel* like I've grown.

I have grown.

But I love the Graysons and they were so kind to me during the last year of my old life. I don't know what I would have done without their support.

Ironically, I only met them after five years of living in our home. The couple is notorious in the neighborhood for being extremely private. They live across the street from my old house in a magnificent estate that makes you feel as though you're in Provence, France. The home and the land are an enigma, just like the couple.

Tom Grayson is what I like to call a man of mystery. He's in his late seventies, English, wicked smart, quite debonair, a true gentleman, and extraordinarily kind. After knowing him for all these years, I still don't quite know what he did for a living before he retired. But I do know he had a good time traveling the world. He was even in Iran at one point in his life—and he's got the carpets to prove it.

His wife, Laura, is who I met first when I went out for one of my daily "feeling sorry for myself" walks. I happened to be crying myself to death next to a bed of her roses—I might have even drowned a few. I had stopped next to her spectacularly manicured, private, front gate and was having a moment. This had become a pattern for me. I would walk, stop at someone's front lawn or gate, and suddenly burst into uncontrollable tears. At the time, I didn't know what I was crying about. I just knew I was immensely unhappy.

"You're too young to be so sad," Laura had said to me in a kind voice.

I had jumped in surprise. I'd never seen her before that moment. Not even a glimpse.

Not in five years.

Laura is elegant and classy in a way that makes you just want to stare. She wears no makeup, has never had any *work* done, and is one of the most attractive women I've ever seen. And she doesn't even color her hair. True story.

So there she was, having just popped out of a hidden, secret side gate to cut some flowers, and she happened to stumble upon me sobbing all over her roses.

"I'm so sorry!" I had said to her, and then proceeded to lift my t-shirt and use it to wipe the snot and tears away.

Clearly, I had no shame.

"Don't be sorry," Laura had said, holding a basket filled with some of the flowers she had already cut. She picked out a perfect pink rose for me and extended her hand. "Smell this. I promise it'll make you feel a lot better."

I took the rose and inhaled deeply. She was right—it *did* make me feel better.

"What on earth happened that's making you cry like this?" she had asked me.

"I don't know," I admitted in a whisper. "It's just something inside me that hurts. And it won't let go."

Laura gave me the kindest smile.

"I've been there before," she said. "If you listen to your heart, I promise you will find your way out."

And that was it. From that moment on, the Graysons became Ava Monfared tribe members.

I hit the call button at their security gate and am immediately buzzed in. Once I'm through and up the private drive, I feel like I can breathe again—even the air around their place feels better. I pull into their carport and park near the guest house. I take a moment to look around. The home is extremely serene and spa-like—the greenery, the flowers...the wide-open space that is so rare to find in Los Angeles. It feels like I'm on some European estate.

I'm not surprised that Laura and Tom come out to greet me, and I'm so happy to see them. It's been too long. We exchange pleasantries and I'm invited up to the veranda for a glass of wine and cheese.

"How have you been?" Laura asks after we settle in.

"All the couch surfing has been good for me," I tell her. "It's been so nice to visit everyone and catch up."

"We've missed you around here," Tom says.

"I've missed you too," I say.

"How did it feel driving into the neighborhood?" Laura wants to know.

"A bit surreal," I admit, "but it doesn't surprise me. I sort of expected it."

"Yes," she agrees. "I guess it was. And how are things with Darian? Have you seen or talked to him?"

"I've been avoiding him."

Laura gives me a look.

"I know, I know. I can't hide from him forever. I just want us to have some space and time before we face each other again."

"It will be difficult no matter what," Laura offers. "I've been through it and it's never easy."

"Me too," Tom adds, then looks over at his wife with a big grin. "But the second time was a charm."

"Obviously," I say, and laugh.

I watch the two of them for a second, and I'm in awe. Laura gazes at her husband like they just started dating. I swear, *that's* the energy emanating from her eyes. After over forty years of marriage she still has that look. That look that says—*he's the one.*

I can't help but wonder if I'll ever have the same kind of love, or if it's like winning the lottery—something only for the lucky few.

"I'm glad you think so, honey," says Laura, laughing. "I don't believe we've done too bad."

"No, we haven't."

"There's hope for you, Ava," Laura proposes.

"But take it easy with all of that." Tom waves her comment off. "Don't be in any hurry. You're just getting out there again. You're finishing off a chapter of your life—you don't have to rush! Unless, of course, it falls in your lap."

"I'm not planning on it," I promise them. "I'm just taking it a day at a time. I've adopted a new phrase."

"What's that?" Tony asks.

"*I surrender.*"

"Oh." Laura is intrigued. "What's brought on this new age way of thinking?"

"I don't know…. I've just been letting myself experience everything around me. I'm letting myself be free."

"Give me an example," Laura presses.

"Well, I drank ayahuasca with a shaman in Grass Valley when I was visiting my cousin, Pegah." As the words come out of my mouth, I almost regret them.

Tom surprises me a second later. "I did that, too—in my thirties. I drank yagé and lived and traveled through the Amazon with the indigenous people. I even took Laura back to meet everyone."

"I'm sorry if I seem shocked." I'm reeling, knowing my mouth is half open in surprise. "I'm still stuck on the part where you said you lived in the Amazon."

"You don't believe me?" Tom teases.

"I believe you," I say. "I'm just amazed."

"Laura, go get the albums for her to see," Tom requests, and Laura leaves us.

"Why are you so surprised?" he asks curiously.

"It just doesn't seem like something you'd ever do." But then, Tom *is* a man of mystery.

"Why not?"

I shrug. "It's pretty full-on."

"It is." Tom agrees with a wicked smile. "But I'm a firm believer in experiences. And psychedelics fit into that niche."

Laura returns a minute later with their albums, and I flip through the books. I'm treated to pictures from their travels around the world. It's amazing to see their lives evolve with every turn of a page. They started off so young together, bright-eyed—ready for anything the world would send their way. As I move through the pages, lines begin to form around their eyes and their countenance seems wiser. When I reach the end of their album, they begin to look more and more like the Laura and Tom I have come to know, their youthful avatars a distant memory of the past.

A photo album is a funny thing. In a small picture book with only thirty or so pages, you can see the highlights of someone's entire existence. And you can move through it in less than ten minutes.

It's a strange way to see a life.

"These pictures are incredible," I say.

"We also took a few years off and sailed around the world," Tom tells me. "The goal was to stop and experience different ways of life. We went wherever the wind took us."

I think about my text exchange with New York City, about telling him my desire to sail the world and experience life in a different way. I never knew Tom and Laura did just that.

"I'm completely shocked," I admit. "I can't believe you guys have literally lived my secret dream."

"You want to sail around the world and take a few years off of regular life?" Tom asks in surprise.

"Yes, I do." I can hear the passion in my response. "It sounds so perfect."

"It is," Tom agrees. "Some of the best memories we have."

"It looks that way," I say, still flipping through the album.

"Maybe a trip around the world will be your next big adventure," Laura predicts.

"That would be a dream come true."

"When you have enough faith and work toward a goal, the dreams that seem far off tend to come true," Laura says.

CHAPTER 49

"BELIEVE IT OR NOT"

"THE EYEBROW PERM IS THE new thing," Bobbi, my brow lady, tells me as I recline in her chair under the magnifying light she has directed at my face.

"Eyebrow perm?" The picture in my head is *not* a good one.

"Yes. It will knock ten years off you. You'll feel like a whole new woman."

Well, now I'm curious.

"But what does an eyebrow perm do exactly?"

"It makes them look fuller, fluffier, and your face more youthful," Bobbi says with conviction. "You will look gorgeous. I promise, you'll love it. Every woman in LA has surrendered to this new beauty regiment."

Huh. They're *surrendering* to it?

I think about my upcoming date with New York City—"gorgeous" is exactly the look I'm going for.

"What the heck. Let's do it!"

"You won't regret it." Bobbi gets to work.

Exactly one hour later as I stare at my face in the car mirror, I would beg to differ. I do most definitely regret the eyebrow perm. In fact, I regret it so much I want to cry. It's remarkable how much eyebrows matter on a face and what a bad brow job can do to the configuration. My eyebrows are a cross between Frida Kahlo's eyebrows and Groucho Marx's mustache. I immediately FaceTime my sister.

"Why can't I see you?" Layla asks when she picks up. The camera angle is flipped around for now.

"Because you have to promise me something." I know I sound devastated.

"Oh no. What did he do again?"

"Darian has nothing to do with this," I say. "It's all me."

"What do you mean?"

"I did this to myself." And with that rather dramatic introduction, I flip the phone around and let my sister have a look. I'm praying she'll tell me it doesn't look as bad as I think. That I look younger. That the now thicker brows have done wonders for me.

Something, *anything* positive.

"When are you seeing New York City?"

Uh oh.

"In two days." I try to read her face.

She's giving nothing away. She only nods. "Can you stand by for a second?"

"Sure." I wait patiently.

She puts me on hold, and then, before I know it, my sister's back on FaceTime. Except now, she's added my cousins—Pegah and Nina. I wave at them.

They stare back at me in disbelief, like I'm something from Ripley's Believe It or Not.

Pegah covers her mouth and starts to giggle.

"It looks like a pack of rabid gerbils have been electrocuted and have taken refuge on the top part of her eyes." Layla speaks as though she's a commentator at a Best in Show dog competition. "We can no longer refer to them as eyebrows."

"No," Nina agrees. "I don't think we can."

"Ava!" Pegah can't stop laughing. "What did you do?!"

"She told me I'd look ten years younger!" I howl.

"And you fell for it?" Pegah shakes her head at me in disappointment.

"This really scares me," Layla says. "It seems like you're gullible enough to turn yourself into a cat lady."

"Rude!" Even though I'm annoyed, I'm still laughing uncontrollably because it *is* funny. "How am I going to fix this?"

"Go shower," Nina, the doctor in the family, commands. "Take some hair color remover and wipes and just go at them."

"You can't go meet New York City like that!" Pegah bellows. I phoned her days ago and she knows I'm seeing my crush soon. "If your eyebrows are still standing up that way in two days, you need to cancel."

"You look like you're in shock," Nina adds.

"Why did the universe do this to me?!"

"The universe?" Layla snorts. "This is all your own handiwork. I would leave the poor universe out of it."

"I agree," Pegah says.

"Me too," Nina admits.

"Don't tell Mom. *Please*," I say to Layla.

"I'll try not to."

Layla doesn't last five minutes. My mom and auntie call me a little while after I hang up with my cousins. They both take turns trying to figure out what farm animal my brows most resemble before yelling out different natural remedies to fix them. My mom is worried they'll fall out; she thinks I should really take it easy and just throw some olive oil and saffron on them and hope for the best. After I assure them I won't make any more dramatic changes, they let me off the phone.

When I get back to the Graysons' guest house, I grab a bottle of wine and head up to the main house for dinner. The glass doors are open to the kitchen, and I'm surprised to find both Tom and Laura cooking together. Tom has an apron on and is chopping onions while Laura is reading the recipe out loud. They're both nursing a glass of red wine and look so at ease I could watch them forever.

"Hello!" Laura smiles over at me when I walk in.

I notice her stare at my eyebrows for a second longer than necessary.

"I permed them." I feel the need to mention what's going on.

"Ahh." Laura looks confused. "You can perm brows too?"

"I guess. I know I look ridiculous."

"Not ridiculous." Tom scrutinizes them. "Different."

"You're being way too kind." I smile self-consciously and try to cover them with my hands. "I know it looks like I've been electrocuted."

"A bit," Laura agrees, and we all laugh.

"You need wine. This will help."

"I hope so." I say, and take what's being offered and what's already open. "What are you two making?"

"I hope you're hungry," Laura says. "We're trying a new recipe for mushroom risotto tonight."

"Smells delicious!" I say, and take it all in. Laura moves around Tom and places her hand on the small of his back. "I love that you two are cooking together."

"We do this at least three or four times a week," Laura informs me as she places a kiss on her husband's cheek.

"She uses it as an excuse to boss me around."

I laugh.

"Really?" Laura puts her hands on her hips and narrows her eyes in jest.

"You're right," he says, like he's been defeated. "You're *always* bossing me around."

"You guys are funny." *And perfect together*, I think.

Laura smiles at her husband, who continues being the sous-chef. I watch them move around each other so comfortably. You can tell they're enjoying this simple act of cooking together, and I can see why. There's a reverence for the meal they're going to have with one another. They're putting genuine love into their food. It's a ritual. And it works for them.

"I'm not sure if you have a question, or if it's just the permed eyebrows." Laura winks at me.

"Ha! No question, I'm just enjoying watching you two."

"I promise it will be a good meal," Tom says, as he starts to fry the onions and mushrooms. "Don't worry."

"I believe you."

When we sit down twenty minutes later, it's just as delicious as he promised. I enjoy the meal tremendously and even take leftovers back to the cottage.

Then I get to the business of my brows. After a thorough scrub with sea salt, water and make-up remover, I send pictures to Layla. Looking at the before and after shots, I think I did a good enough job.

It's way past ten when my phone pings. I get excited, thinking it might be New York City.

My stomach drops.

It's not New York City.

It's Darian.

Or *The Ex* as he's now known in my phone. I haven't heard from him in over a month. The last message was about our furniture storage and it was very matter-of-fact and unemotional—he wanted me to go and pick out all the items I wanted and said he'd keep the rest. I was surprised he was making it so easy for me.

The Ex: How are you, Ava?

I'm so taken aback by his text that I just stare at it for a long while, as if I'm not seeing it. Is this the question he should be asking me after all this time? Like what's gone on is no big deal? But then, what else is he supposed to say?

I decide I can no longer be an ostrich, and that it's time to put my big girl pants on. I write back.

Me: I'm good. How are you?

The Ex: Oh, you know, *living the dream.*

That's one of his favorite sarcastic sayings. I hated when he said it before, but this time it makes me smile.

Me: What's up?

The Ex: I think we should talk.

Me: About?

The Ex: Us.

I feel sick.

Me: There is no *us* anymore.

The Ex: There was an us for over twenty years. Ava, a lot of time has gone by, and I want to talk to you. In person. I have things I need to say.

I stop breathing.

The Ex: Call it closure. Call it whatever you want, but I think we both deserve this. There is too much history between us. It can't all have been for nothing.

I close my eyes and try not to let my emotions get the best of me. I am suddenly feeling the need to cry my heart out. I'm transported back in time—I'm in the house, suffocating from all the emotions he invokes in me. It's like a tsunami hitting me at once.

But I know I can no longer hide.

Me: Okay.

He takes a second to respond.

The Ex: Okay. When do you have time?

Me: Next weekend? Sunday?

The Ex: Perfect. Tell me where you'll be, and we'll find someplace around you.

Me: Sounds good.

I can't believe I just agreed to see him.

The Ex: Good night, Ava.

Me: Night.

When I put my phone down, I have a major moment. My heart *hurts*. The reality of us not being together hits me hard. Maybe it's because Darian and I have not texted each other civilly in a long time—not since our separation—and hearing from him like this puts things in perspective.

We are no longer together.

After twenty-plus years, Ava and Darian Monfared are no longer a couple.

They no longer share the same bed.

They no longer check in with each other.

Say good night when they're traveling.

Plan a dinner.

Watch a movie.

Cuddle.

They no longer say I love you.

Ava and Darian Monfared.

They once were...

CHAPTER 50

"BED OF ROSES"

"IF YOU CUT THE STEM here it doesn't hurt the rose," Laura tells me, putting another flower in her woven basket. She wants me to have a bouquet for the guest house.

I'm with her outside, watching her work in her magical garden. I'm taking in the general tranquility of it all. It's so peaceful to be surrounded by nature. I could sit out here for hours.

"You have the most beautiful flowers," I say as I admire the splendor of her garden. A moment later, I feel compelled to smell the roses.

"They're chosen for their fragrance."

"Well, they're each their own slice of heaven." I move around and inhale the essence of each flower. It's sensory overload. I take my time, enjoying the moment, before I take a seat on the wooden bench and watch Laura move around the area, tending to her passion.

Everything she does is with ease and grace. She's a combination of whip smart and calm, to a point that I don't believe she ever loses her shit or has her feathers ruffled. She has an air about her that makes me think nothing ever bothers her, even though I know that would be an impossibility.

Laura is someone I admire and love to talk to. I always feel like I walk away having learned something about life and about myself. She's a rare person to find and I'm lucky to call her a friend.

"You're thinking so hard that I can feel you," she says as she continues moving through her garden.

"I guess I kind of am."

"Why is that?"

"I was admiring your calm. It's a thing of beauty."

Laura smiles at me. "I'm not always so calm."

"I can't imagine another state of being for you," I return. "You exude it."

"Tom might disagree with you, but thank you for the compliment."

I watch her clip another flower.

"I heard from Darian," I announce. I haven't even told my sister that he texted, or that I agreed to meet him. A part of me doesn't want my family to know, because I feel like I need to have this first and maybe final interaction with him on my own terms, without pressure or commentary.

Laura stops what she's doing and looks over at me. I can't tell what she's thinking. "And?"

"He wants to meet. And talk about everything...and I agreed."

"How are you feeling about it?"

"I'm spinning."

"That might be unavoidable," she says. "Be kind to yourself. Everything you're feeling is normal."

"Normal, yes," I say, "but the idea of seeing him still makes me queasy, even though I'm in a better place now."

"Maybe it won't be as bad as you think."

"It feels strange to see him now after all this time apart. When I think about it and our life, it's just all so surreal."

"Why surreal?"

"I guess it comes down to the simple fact that we were together for so long and now we're not." I try my best to explain what's happening inside my head. "I don't know how to be around Darian anymore."

"You'll get used to it," she assures me.

"But how will I feel?"

"You'll know when you're there; don't worry about it so much."

"It's hard not to."

"Adopt a different attitude," she advises. "Start to see him from a different perspective."

"How do you mean?"

"Maybe you should see him as a friend," she says. "As someone who shared so much of your life with you in many different ways—just like a friend. And now you've drifted apart. You've become two different people."

"Is that how you made it work when you got a divorce?"

"Mine was different. I was younger. We weren't together for as long as you and Darian."

"And how do you see it now?"

"I see it as a lesson," she explains. "I wonder why I worked myself up so much. I wonder why I ever cried over him. Why we fought so much over *nothing*. Why all the little minutia mattered so much—because Ava, it doesn't. When you get to be my age, you'll see life so differently. That part with my ex is just a distant memory now."

"Isn't that sad?"

"It doesn't have to be sad. Good or bad, I always see memories as a thing of beauty."

I think about my own relationship and quietly disagree with Laura. But she's got experience on me, so who am I to argue with her?

"Even the ones that fill you with grief?" I ask, thinking of my grandfather.

"Those are the best." She smiles. "Those are the ones that remind you that you're human. That life is fragile and poignant, and it's all about the moments—like this one right now."

"Sometimes I feel like I'm surrounded by people who are made so differently than me.... All my friends and family, even you, make it sound so easy."

"That's because it is easy," she says. "It's perspective. It's changing the way you look at things."

"I feel like I have been," I admit.

"You definitely have," she agrees. "And the second you do that, your life will shift. Now you just have to change the way you see Darian."

"So, I should stop seeing him as a giant asteroid about to breach the earth's atmosphere?" I say with a hint of sarcasm.

"Yes!" Laura laughs. "Maybe start to see him as a boat that just dropped you off at a new, exciting and exotic port, filled with all sorts of adventures awaiting you."

CHAPTER 51

"NEW YORK CITY"

I AM SURPRISED I'M SO calm when I exit the elevator onto the Waldorf Astoria rooftop for my dinner with New York City.

For two whole days I've done nothing but obsess over what this dinner will be like.

Will I be attracted to him?

Will he be attracted to me?

Will it be awkward?

Natural?

My poor sister and Pegah were subjected to all of my crazy thoughts and put up with a million texts about what to wear, what to say, and how to behave.

"You can't predict anything," Pegah had said to me on FaceTime. "Really. You know nothing and can guess nothing. So, what are you doing to yourself right now?"

"Obsessing?" I returned in annoyance. "Wouldn't you?"

"No." She sounded like she thought I was nuts.

Zelda took that moment to take a seat on top of her head and screech at me.

"Ah," I said. "I've missed her shrieks."

"Even she agrees with me," Pegah had said, ignoring my comment. "Just go with it. No pressure. Have fun."

No pressure, except this is the man I've been thinking about all summer. No, even longer than summer. For years. This is the man I've *always* wondered about. The man I fantasized about. The man who somehow, in one night, was able to take up residence in my bloodstream and turn it to fire.

And there's a part of me that believes this man is what's kept me from being into the other men I've met this summer.

My phone rings just as I walk over to the crowded bar.

It's New York City.

"You're beautiful." His voice is exactly as I remember it—strong, raspy, and with a hint of that New York accent that I find hot.

I immediately look around the bar.

"Where are you?"

"Admiring you from afar," he says. As usual with this man, my heart picks up its pace.

"This isn't fair." I try and act as composed as I can, considering he's watching me. "I can't see you."

"Would you like to?"

"Yes."

A second later, I feel a touch on the small of my back. I know it's him. It's like a thousand bolts of electricity surge through my body. It's definitely him.

Finally.

I slowly turn around and come face-to-face with my New York City.

He is exactly as I remember him.

More handsome in age. His smile, still irresistible. And the energy emanating from his eyes is as intense as before.

"Hi," I whisper.

"Hi back." His voice is husky and he pulls me in.

He wraps his arms around my waist and envelopes me in his embrace. For a brief second, my body is a little stiff, but then I melt into him. He buries his face in my hair and I hear him breathe me in. He holds onto me for longer than what's probably appropriate, but I don't care.

"Ava," he whispers in my ear, before moving back and staring down at me.

I feel shy. It's hard to keep his gaze, but the intensity I see blazing back at me doesn't give me any other choice.

"It's been a long time," I say.

"Too long," he returns, before kissing me on the cheek and taking hold of my hand. He leads me over to a table that has a small couch on one side and two chairs on the other.

He has me sit in the more comfortable spot—the couch—and takes the seat across from me.

"I'd sit next to you, but I want to stare at you," he says with a smile.

I can feel myself blush.

"Don't be shy," he says sturdily. "I don't want you to be shy with me."

"That's a big demand." But I meet his gaze head on. "I'm a bit shy by nature."

"We don't have time for that. And I don't want to waste a moment with you."

My heart stops. The look in his eyes is so fiery that it takes my breath away.

"I want to hear everything about you," he says.

"You first," I deflect. I'm still too nervous to lead the conversation. I'd rather hear about him. "How's work? How's your family? How's your world? Tell me everything."

"I'm not going to let you off the hook," he says as he cocks his head to the side.

"I know." I laugh. "But you first."

"Where would you like me to begin?" His smile is roguish.

"I'll leave that up to you."

"I can't complain. My life has definitely been filled with a lot of adventure over the years. I guess I can give you the highlights."

"I'd love that."

As we go through a bottle of wine, he proceeds to tell me about his life these last thirteen years. I learn he lost his aunt and uncle in a tragic plane crash about five years ago. That incident, he says, changed his entire family dynamic and profoundly changed him. He tells me about his ex, how she fulfilled a need he had and that he loved her but wasn't *in love* with her. I hear about his close bond with his brother and their yearly trips together. He opens up to me like a book, and I take it all in. There's nothing he shies away from.

He's funny, self-deprecating, and kind—all of which comes through with every story he tells. New York City is a good man.

"Can I ask you something?" I say.

"You can ask me anything."

"Are you at the place where you're wondering what it all means?"

"Are you asking me if I'm having an existential crisis?"

"No. Maybe... Kind of?" I hope I sound sane. "I don't know. Sometimes I think I was handed pieces to a jigsaw puzzle and I was tasked with putting it all together...but I feel like pieces are missing, or they're somehow still not fitting right."

"Maybe they're not supposed to."

"But it's a picture that should look a certain way."

"Says who?" He cocks a brow. "It's life. It's never going to be perfect."

"Says who?" I smile back.

"It can be *almost* perfect."

"I like that." I lean forward and rest my chin on my hand, staring at him for a long beat. "You seem so grounded now, and it's not just an age thing—it's a you thing."

His grin is contagious. "I'd like to think so."

"Can I catch whatever you have?" I tease.

"I'd love to infect you." The look in his eyes tells me he might want to do a bit more than *infect* me.

"There's that blush again," he says.

"I can't help it."

"I don't want you to."

He watches me for a moment longer, then changes the topic.

"My aunt and uncle's death made me realize how precious time is," he starts, and locks eyes with me. "And how much I was taking for granted. I lived like nothing would ever end."

His comment about time speaks to me.

"In what way?"

"In every way," he explains. "Even in the relationships I chose for myself. I wasn't fulfilled, but I stayed. I knew things were missing but I stayed because I thought I had all the time in the world."

I think about my own relationship with Darian.

"I can relate to that," I agree.

"I'm sure you can," he says knowingly.

We're both quiet for a moment.

"Do you want to talk about him?"

"Not really. There's nothing to say except we didn't make it."

"What's your one regret?" he asks.

"Three months ago, I would have said that I had wasted so much time." My eyes flicker to his. "But now, my attitude has slowly shifted. Maybe I didn't waste any time. Maybe he was exactly what I needed at that point in my life."

He contemplates my words. "Well said."

"Maybe I was searching for answers that don't exist."

"I can get on board with that. And now?"

"Now what?" I ask.

"What are you searching for now?"

"Me," I whisper.

CHAPTER 52

"THE KISS"

"Do you want to know what I see when I look at you?" New York City smiles tenderly.

"What do you see?" I challenge.

"Someone smart, wiser than her years, innocent yet intoxicating, beautiful with a touch of sadness in her soul that tells me there is depth there, layers that I'd like to uncover...and a splash of magic that I find irresistible."

My breath comes out in a flutter. His words are more seductive than anything I've ever experienced.

"I'm not wasting my life anymore, Ava." His voice is passionate, his gaze direct. "I follow my heart instead of my mind now, and it's a strange way to live for someone who's always been guided by logic. But everything about it feels right."

"It sounds right."

He looks down at his glass of wine before his gaze flickers right back over to me.

"If you'll excuse me," he says. "I'll be right back."

"Of course."

When he's safely away, I pull out my phone. My sister and cousins have blown it up. There's a nonstop text chain between them discussing my evening and waiting for a sign from me. I smile and send a quick text.

Me: He's so cute.

I add the emoji that has hearts for eyes, just for good measure. Layla is the first response.

> **Layla:** Tell me everything!

> **Me:** I'll call you after dinner.

> **Layla:** It's nine-thirty. I'll be dead asleep. Give me something.

> **Pegah:** Yes! Something!

I think about the evening so far.

> **Me:** I think I'm in some seriously deep shit.

I leave it at that and put my phone away. I don't want to elaborate on the fact that I'm completely enamored with the guy after spending only a couple of hours in his company. I watch him make his way back. He doesn't sit down right away, but instead, stands on my side of the table. I look up at him and we share a smile.

"Can I sit next to you?" he asks politely.

Butterflies immediately flutter in my stomach.

"Yes." I think I sound breathless—the kind of breathless that happens when you're so into someone and realize it's probably super obvious.

He sits next to me.

My entire body reacts to his proximity, and it takes everything I have not scoot myself into the corner and as far from him as possible. I'm that frightened of my reaction to him.

His leg touches mine and I think I'm going to break out in a full sweat. His gaze moves over my face before settling on my lips, then back up to my eyes.

New York City has invaded my space in every which way.

"You're so beautiful," he says again.

"And you're super sexy."

The words come out before I can stop them. My filter is gone, and I've spoken my secret thoughts out loud for him to hear. I put my hand over my mouth in horror.

Way to be cool, Ava.

Luckily, the smile he gives me tells me he likes what he hears.

"So are you," he whispers, reaching out and brushing my hair away from my face. "I've thought about you a lot over the years."

"Me too."

Argh! *What is wrong with me?!*

"Oh yeah?" His tone is cocky but flirty, and I like every part of it.

"Yeah," I whisper.

He gives me a look that tells me he wants to kiss me.

"We have to get out of here," he says urgently.

He flags our waiter down a second later and pays the bill. He grabs my hand, leading me away from the crowded rooftop, down around a bend close to the pool, and to an area that's secluded. Moments later, he has me pressed up against a wall with his hands tenderly holding my face.

His gaze burns into my soul.

"Hi."

"Hi," I whisper back.

"I'm going to kiss you now," he tells me, in a way that I can't— nor would want to—argue with.

"Kay."

There are kisses. And then there are *kisses* that take something from you, stealing a piece of you that can't be replaced; you know you'll never be the same again. Kisses that people measure each other up against...

The kiss you've been searching for all your life.

This is that kiss.

Maybe it's destiny. Maybe this moment was always meant to be. Whatever it is, I am eternally grateful to him. He just changed something in me *forever*.

In one sweeping moment, New York City sets me on fire.

⁓

"Tom and I want to offer you a solution for the next phase of your life," Laura says to me

as we sip a glass of wine on her veranda.

I look over at her.

"We love having you here," she says. "We want you to know our guest house is yours to move into, if you'd like. It's not a permanent solution for you. It's a temporary one. But I think it will alleviate some of the stress you have."

"I don't even know what to say," I murmur.

Laura smiles at me. "It's been empty since our son stayed there with his wife years ago. We'd love to help out in this way while you get back on your feet."

I can feel tears brimming in my eyes. The way my family and friends have embraced me during this time is something I'll never be able to repay. My heart tightens when I think about the love that's been showered on me.

"You guys are too kind."

"We want to see you succeed," she says in a gentle voice. "This area is familiar to you. It's safe."

I immediately want to say yes, but I know how much they like their privacy.

"You're sure?" I ask.

"We wouldn't offer if we weren't."

"Then...yes." It's the perfect solution for me at this stage of my life. I know she can hear the gratitude in my voice. "I would love that more than anything."

"Then it's settled. The place is yours whenever you'd like to move in."

⁓

New York City: I can't stop thinking about you.

I smile when I read his text. He writes me again before I can respond.

> **New York City:** I'm staying in town another week and I'd like to see you tomorrow night.

I feel relieved he's not leaving too soon. I don't want him to. I want him to stay as long as he can.

> **Me:** I would love that.

> **New York City:** I'll pick a spot.

> **Me:** I trust you.

He sends me a devil emoji face back. I laugh and send him the angel emoji back.

> **New York City:** I might have to corrupt you, Ava.

My heart slams in my chest.

> **Me:** I'd like that.

I put my phone down and place my hands on my cheeks, trying to calm my nerves even though it's impossible. No matter what happens with New York City, he's made me feel alive in a way that I never dreamed possible. I don't even know who this person is or where this giddy feeling is coming from....

He's made me feel again. The same kind of way I did in high school—in fact, it's like I'm a teen again. All I want to do is get together with him and make out.

Who knew?

I think about Laura and Tom and their life together. What they have, what all the couples I've stayed with have...it appeals to me in a way I used to think I was closed off from. But now, I want that too.

I want to love fiercely and to have it be returned.

I want passion.

I want to be lusted after.

I want to be adored.

Cherished.

Loved.

I want a man to want me in every way, even when I'm grey haired and old. Even on a bad Ava day. I want to fight and then make up. To know that I'm not one fight away from the end of a relationship.

I grew up with Darian.

For my next chapter, I want to grow old with someone.

That's my wish.

PLANET EARTH
SOMEWHERE
"POOH, OWL,
TIGGER,
PIGLET & AVA"

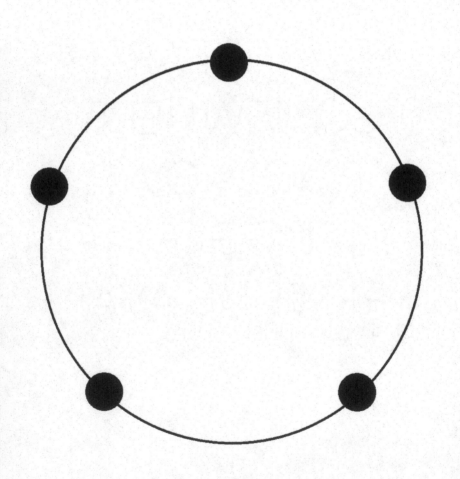

CHAPTER 53

"TEACHER"

As in every type of relationship, there is a potential for things to fall apart—but only after a series of irreversible incidents.

Maybe that's what this is. A culmination of all those incidents that both Darian and I are responsible for. Maybe he was trying to push me out. Or maybe it's as he says: he thought he couldn't make me happy.

Or maybe it's as simple as—it was just never meant to be.

Whatever it is, we're here now. In this moment.

Together.

This is the chapter you read before you write *The End*.

I'm hit with a tsunami of emotions when I see him sitting at the table at Islands Restaurant. He looks different to me. Somehow older, in just a few short months. He could be a complete stranger sitting in the booth—that's how surreal it is to see him.

After spending so many years together, and being in tune with each other in so many ways, it's not a surprise to see him feel my energy when I walk in. His body tenses and he cocks his head to the side, like he knows I'm here. When his eyes find mine, they look as sad as I feel.

The tears come because they must.

This *is* sad.

When I reach the table, he stands and pulls me into his embrace. We hold each other like this for a long while as I silently sob into his arms. This was never what I thought would happen to us—this fateful tale that seems to befall so many couples who start out so in love. This ugly end.

This was *never* supposed to be us.

He pulls away and stares down at my face. His smile is bittersweet; he's as emotional as I am.

"Why are you crying, Ava?" His voice is filled with pain. "Don't cry. It's not your fault I couldn't make you happy."

His words are like a knife in my heart.

Because he's right. But it's not his fault, either. The real tragedy is that, in all the years we spent together, I could never love Darian the way he wanted because I never loved myself.

I see that now. So clearly.

"I'm so sorry," I say to him. "I'm so sorry if I ever hurt you."

Darian's eyes widen in surprise. He looks down, then right back into my gaze. I see the pain there. I know I caused some of it. And for that I am *truly* sorry.

"We hurt each other." His voice is choked up.

"We did," I agree. "And I think it's time we start being kind to one another. And I guess it starts by letting go."

I cry as I watch the tears stream down his face.

"We had a lot of good times," he says as his voice quivers with emotion. "So many years together. No one can ever take that away from us."

"No, they can't."

"I just want to be happy." He says the words I whisper like a mantra to the universe every night in bed. "And I just don't think we made each other happy."

"We didn't," I murmur.

"We tried to," he says, before smiling bitterly. "But I guess we failed at that."

"We didn't fail...we lived the only way we knew how to with each other. And we both made mistakes."

He nods his head and tells me, "I promise I'll make it right by you."

"I know you will." I say it because I believe him.

"Did you ever think we'd end up here?" he asks.

"No."

"Neither did I," he says softly, then gives me a sad smile. "You know, I fell in love with you the second I saw you...all those years ago."

He never told me that. This is the first time. And it hurts in the way that it must.

"Me too...you were my world."

"I never thought I was."

"And I'm sorry for that."

He reaches out and cups my cheeks in his hands, placing a soft kiss on the top of my head.

"I'm sorry for hurting you so badly, Ava. Please forgive me."

"I do," I assure him.

Once upon a time, a young, wide-eyed, innocent girl married her high school sweetheart. They had high hopes for their life together. They thought they would have it all: money, success, happiness, health, romance, and an immense love for each other.

And then something went wrong.

It wasn't her fault.

Or his.

It was just life.

It was a culmination of choices that led to where they find themselves now. They each had a hand in their demise. They each took turns tearing down the foundation that was perhaps too fragile to begin with.

So that boy and that girl decided they couldn't make it together anymore. They had to go out and find their own way. It didn't mean what they had wasn't good enough. It didn't mean they were failures.

They didn't fail.

They won.

They won because they were strong enough to know that they each needed to find their happiness within themselves, and it was okay if their lives could no longer be together.

As I close my eyes and hold onto Darian like there's no tomorrow—in an intimate embrace that I know will be the last between us—it dawns on me.

For my entire life, I've wanted to please people. To make everyone else happy. To make sure they were okay; that they had enough to eat and drink; that they were emotionally all right; that they were satisfied. That *they* were happy. In all those years I never thought about me. And then Darian became the one person I focused all my attention on. What I wanted didn't matter because it was all about him—even down to the food I would buy for the house. It was about him and my quest to somehow try and make him happy while still retaining a piece of myself. And then one day, I woke up and realized that the piece of myself that I was still trying to keep was slowly flittering away.

I was losing my sparkle.

And what happened as a result was that my unhappiness began to consume me—to consume us. It was an energy that filled our entire six-thousand-square-foot house and it began to plague our marriage. Like an ominous shadow covering the sun, my restlessness never allowed us a chance to try for happiness.

It wouldn't allow it.

Because somehow—I think somewhere deep inside—I knew we were never meant to be. As heartbreaking as it was to admit. We were a puzzle that was never meant to come together. Pieces would always be missing.

There was a lot I had to blame myself for in the failure of our marriage.

And despite it all, despite the immense fear and sadness he caused me, Darian would be a piece of my heart for eternity.

At the end of the day, I believe we are souls here on this earth that come together to try and learn and evolve. Some of us rise to the challenge and others ignore the call, but there *is* always a shift. An irrevocable elevation of the soul. A graduation of sorts.

And my break-up with Darian shifted me.

It woke me up.

It made me see the world fully for the first time. All the people I've spent my nomadic summer with have been my teachers. They helped restore my self-confidence and have guided me.

Finding closure with Darian has become the ultimate lesson in rediscovering myself.

CHAPTER 54

"REINCARNATION"

I STARE OUT AT THE Harvest Moon from my bedroom at the Graysons' cottage. The moon is massive in the sky tonight—a thing of true beauty.

I think about my conversation with Darian. I think about seeing him after so long, and about all the emotions he evoked in me. Then, like a flashing neon sign, Mark's words about cutting the cords with him come to mind. He told me that to truly let go I'd have to cut the cords that held us together.

I look up at the moon, and even she seems to be daring me to do it.

I don't waste any time.

I take my yoga mat outside, sit down on the green grass, and stare up at the sky. I start to replay my life with Darian. My husband...to my ex-husband.

From the moment we met in high school.

To our wedding.

To the demise of our relationship.

I replay so many moments, especially the poignant ones that I can remember. I think about our life together and smile. We had so many beautiful times. He helped me with so many things, just as I hope I did for him.

And I love him.

I will always love him.

But it's time for me to release him.

I close my eyes and picture us in the vast expanse of the universe. We're both floating in the sky staring at one another, connected by cords. And then I slowly start to see the cords fall away. Even in this vision, we both try to hold on a second longer than necessary...but I shake my head.

"It's time, Darian," I whisper. "It's time for us to let go."

Like magic, the last cord falls away and I picture us floating off in opposite directions in space. I can feel tears streaming down my face because it's a sad, bittersweet moment.

But it's also one filled with hope.

"I will always love you," I say.

I will always love you too, Ava, I can hear him say back to me.

"If you ever need anything from me, I'll be here for you," I whisper.

And I will be there for you, he says back to me.

"It's strange to think of my life without you in it."

It is for me too. But you know you'll be fine. You always were.

"I guess I was," I say through my tears. "And now it's time to let go."

I know it is.

"Goodbye, Darian." I'm sobbing now.

Goodbye, Ava.

Much later in the night, after all the tears and prayers, I open my diary app.

I realize once you get over the whys and just accept whatever it is you have to accept, life gets a lot easier. The moment I let go and surrendered was the second everything just stopped. That noise. The chatter that pollutes your brain and makes you think you're mad...it stops because it has nowhere to go.

That's the truth.

We are the architects of every single emotion and event in our lives. We paint the picture. We write the scene. We live the moment.

There is no one you can point the finger at but yourself.

I realize that now.

I see my life as this great, big novel—where each chapter is a different lesson—and sometimes it's a great chapter. And sometimes, it's a shitty one.

But it's a story. And it's mine.

It has meaning and purpose. And it's brought me one step ahead in my evolution.

I've realized that life *is* a book.

And we're each the stars of our own bestseller. There is an imprint we each leave on this world.

What I've learned is this—

In the end, it is about who you are in your life and how you make people feel.

So, as I think about my life until now, I can say...

I've made people happy.

I've made some sad.

I've brought joy.

I've broken hearts.

I've brought sunshine.

I've brought anger...

And I've brought love.

But with every emotion, every action, every little thing I did right or wrong, I know that I tried. I know that I am spectacularly flawed. And yet I know I am still beautiful.

That's what I know.

And I know something else as well...

Whether big or small, there is a footprint I've left in the lives I've walked through. In the relationships I was allowed to see. In the homes where I lived. In the lives I intermingled with.

I am there.

And they are with me.

Forever.

~ The End ~

ACKNOWLEDGMENTS

WHEN YOUR LIFE FALLS APART and you think you've got nowhere to go but into a cave of grief and darkness, God has a funny way of putting all the right angels into your life.

This book exists because of them.

First, I'd like to thank my family. Mom, Jasmine, Bahman, Ella, Nedda, Mina, Mojee, Nina...thank you for giving me unconditional love, support, and reassurance during the darkest, yet most awakening time of my life. I could not ask for a better family. There is so much I'm grateful for, and you guys top the list. I am so happy I chose you. Thank you. Thank you. Thank you. Sorry for all the tears, but I love you so much! You're the family people dream of having.

And now, in no particular order...

Fran, Rick, Matthew, Lianna, Alex, Teddy, Lucky, Puff, and Bentley...thank you for adopting me into your family and opening your outrageously incredible home to me. From the moment I wheeled my suitcase into your driveway I felt nothing but your love and desire to see my success. Fran, you were my biggest cheerleader during this time and you never let me lose hope; even during the moments I could see no light, you lifted the veil for me and helped me heal. I am forever grateful to have you and your family as part of my tribe. I love you guys.

Giuliana, Bill, and Duke. I have known you through it all. You've seen everything. You know everything. And you've lived it with me. You've always been nothing but filled with love and loyalty for me, pushing me to be the best I can and I can't tell you how much I appreciate it all...or what you mean to me. Giuliana, you are the best friend a girl can only wish to have. I will never forget everything you have done for me... how many times you've lifted me up. How many laughs we've shared. You're my family and I love you. Forever and ever.

Liat, Trevor, Austin, and Hannah. Thank you for opening your home and life to me. You took care of me and made sure I had everything I needed. I can't tell you how grateful I am for your friendship and love. Liat, we became friends fast—a soul connection as you would say ☺ and I am so grateful for you in my life. Colet call forever!

AnnaLynne, Christina, Larry, Jorge, Jake, David, Carlton, Genevieve and Liz...my beautiful friends. I may have intermittently done some couch surfing with you guys, but your advice, love, and unwavering belief in the beauty of my future pushed me into the light. I am so very grateful to have such loyal friends— friends who always show up. Thank you for loving me. Thank you for teaching me to be better.

Zelda...you have a special place in my heart forever.

Linda and Tony. I don't know how to thank you both for opening your home and life to me in the way that you did. I know you don't believe in destiny, but I do. And I know my angels put me in the perfect place where I could feel secure and find myself again. Your cottage is a safe haven. And your love is everything. Thank you from the bottom of my heart for it all. I don't know how I can ever repay you and your kindness.

To my team...Nicole, Lesley, Georgana, and Theresa. Thank you for believing in this book. For pushing this book and for making this girl's dreams come true. I appreciate you so much!

Finally, thank you Adriana for loving *Uncaged Summer* as much as me. I'm so happy this book landed in your lap. Thank you for everything you've done!

And one more thing...

I believe in love.

In true love.

I believe there's a time and place for everyone. That sometimes certain people exist in just a few chapters in your life, but their memory and the love you shared will always live forever.

And I believe there's someone out there for everyone.

Sometimes the journey takes longer because we have to find ourselves...

Or maybe we have to reconnect with who we've always been.

ABOUT THE AUTHOR

COLET ABEDI IS AN AMERICAN Iranian bestselling author, and a television and film producer. She was born in Virginia and currently lives in Los Angeles. When she's not writing, she's either off on an adventure in a far-off land or planning her next getaway. She writes contemporary romance, and young adult and women's fiction.